I0778124

Where Loyalty Lies

Where Loyalty Lies

ELLE CHRISTOPHER

"The people and things you are loyal to say multitudes about your character."

— UNKNOWN

Published by Stonegate Press

www.ellechristopher.com

Designed by Elle Christopher

Identifiers: LCCN 2025912045 | ISBN 9781966386063 (hardcover)

ISBN 9781966386049 (paperback) | ISBN 9781966386056 (ebook)

For the love I'll never stop aching for—
Our story didn't end.
It just found a new way to be told.
In these pages, we are still us.
Still loving. Still holding on.
Still finding each other in the quiet.

And for my kids—
The reason I keep breathing.
The reason I believe tomorrow can still hold beauty.
This life—messy, mended, miraculous—is for you.
Everything I have left, I give to you.
May you always know that you were my why.

CHAPTER 1

Breaking Free

I wore the life they gave me like a diamond collar. Beautiful. Restrictive. Designed to impress, tight enough to silence.

Because expectations are the heaviest cages. You don't see the bars until you try to leave.

The walls felt tighter tonight. The silence sharper, heavier somehow. I moved to the closet, my fingers brushing over clothes picked more for image than comfort. Carefully, methodically, I began to pack. This wasn't a breakdown. It wasn't a rebellion. It was the quiet start of something I should have done years ago.

My hand hovered over the rows of designer blouses, the glittering gowns Brad loved for me to wear. I skipped them all. I wanted nothing that reminded me of the woman I had been trained to be, the perfect wife standing silently by his side.

I shoved jeans, sweaters, and simple T-shirts into the suitcase, pieces that felt like me, or at least, the girl I hoped I could become.

The black dress caught my eye from the back of the closet. The one from last week's gala. The one Brad had chosen.

"This is the one you need to be seen in, Emerson," he had said, smoothing the fabric over my hip like he was adjusting a mannequin. It wasn't a suggestion, it was a decision already made.

I had smiled for the cameras, posed by his side, and played the role everyone expected me to play. Like the life we built was real.

It wasn't.

That night, after our photo op and his usual lap around the room, we ended up at a table full of his colleagues, people who talked in dollar signs and name-dropped like it paid a commission. Someone had asked what I did, and before I could answer, Brad cut in.

"She's an editor," he said with a tight smile. "You know, fixes typos and grammar. It's cute."

A few people laughed. Not kindly.

I had tried to smile, tried to shrug it off, but the heat behind my eyes said everything. It wasn't the first time he'd done it, shrinking me down so he could feel bigger. I was never important unless I was part of his image. And even then, it was only because my father owned the law firm.

Everything else about me, my thoughts, my work, my voice, had always been something he tolerated, not valued.

It had been unraveling for months—years, really. The gnawing emptiness, the conversations that circled and went nowhere, the loneliness that lived even when Brad was standing right beside me. I had tried. I went to therapy, sat through sermons, devoured every self-help book that promised to save a marriage. Everything they said would work—if I was willing to work hard enough. I thought I was the problem. That if I just tried harder, prayed harder, and smiled harder, it would finally feel like home.

But the harder I fought, the clearer it became. I wasn't broken. The life I had been shoved into was.

"Brad, I can't keep living like this," I had said one night, standing across from him at the long marble island. "I want to be in love. I want real happiness. You deserve that, too."

He didn't even look up from his phone.

"You're being dramatic, Emerson," he said flatly, as if I were a child throwing a tantrum. "Anyone would kill for what we have.

A good life, security, status. Stop making problems that aren't there."

It wasn't the first time I had said it. It wasn't even the fifth.

Every time I tried to reach for more, Brad made it clear there was nothing wrong with our marriage. As long as I stayed quiet, wore the right dress, and smiled at the parties. As long as I kept pretending.

"You don't need to be in love to be successful," he had told me once. "You need to be smart."

He didn't want a wife. He wanted a reflection of his own ambition. And I had been foolish enough to stand there and wonder why I felt invisible.

I zipped the suitcase halfway and sat on the edge of the bed, staring out across the room. The penthouse gleamed around me, cold and spotless, every surface shining with emptiness. It had never been a home. Just a stage.

My phone sat on the nightstand, face-down. I picked it up, scrolling through my recent calls. The last one blinked up at me: Mom and Dad. I hovered over it, remembering how that conversation had gone.

"I'm not happy," I had said, struggling to keep my voice steady. "I'm not asking you to fix it. I'm just telling you. I can't do this anymore."

There had been a pause. The kind that says everything louder than words. Then my mother's clipped voice. "Emerson, you have everything a woman could want. Why can't you just be grateful?"

To them, this life wasn't supposed to make me happy. It was supposed to make me enviable.

I dropped the phone onto the bed and stood up. There was more to pack. More to leave behind.

Brad hadn't taken everything from me. But he had chipped away at the parts that mattered most—my independence, my confidence, my belief that I deserved more than curated perfection.

A month ago, I'd been laid off from the publishing house where I worked as an editorial director—the one place that had still felt like mine. When I came home and told Brad, he had barely blinked.

"Good," he said, setting down his wine glass. "You don't need to waste time working. Focus on us."

By "us," he meant himself. His career. His needs. His image.

And when I had mentioned applying for a new job, anything that would let me keep a piece of myself, his face had hardened.

"You don't need to work, Emerson," he said. "It makes me look bad. Like I can't take care of my own wife."

He hadn't asked how I felt about losing the thing that kept me breathing. He hadn't even pretended to care.

"You'll regret this," Brad had said the last time I brought up divorce. "Don't be stupid, Emerson. You're nothing without me. You're going to end up broke and alone."

But I didn't care. Broke and alone sounded better than this. At least I'd have a chance to be happy —even if it meant starting over with nothing.

I wanted something real.

Something he would never be able to give me—because he didn't even understand what it meant. I wasn't broken. I just didn't belong in the life they built for me.

Brad had always been there. Not by my choice, but by design.

Our families had been friends long before we were born—the Sinclairs and the Caldwells. Money. Power. Appearances. We grew up in the same circles, attending the same charity galas, the same family vacations, the same country club brunches. From the outside, it must have looked inevitable. And maybe, to them, it was.

When we were young, I didn't think much of it. Brad was just another boy in a suit, another polished product of the world our parents built. But as we got older, the plan started to reveal itself. Not because I wanted it to. Because they did.

When I was seventeen, my father gave Brad an internship at his firm. It wasn't a favor. It was positioning. They weren't helping his career—they were setting the foundation. And I was part of it whether I knew it or not.

Dad brought him to dinner that summer, smiling in approval as Brad slid into our world with ease. "He's great," Dad said, grinning. "Ambitious, smart. Exactly the kind of man you need, Emerson."

I hadn't connected the dots yet. Brad was just... there. At every holiday. Every event. Always included. Always assumed. And when he started showing interest in me, it wasn't a surprise. It was an expectation.

Mom had wasted no time planting the seeds. "You and Brad would make the perfect couple," she said one morning over coffee. "Imagine your life. If you married him, the wedding would be the talk of the town."

She didn't ask how I felt. I had told her anyway.

"Mom, stop. I don't love him," I said, frustration cracking through my voice. "He feels like a brother." She only smiled, as if it didn't matter. "Passion is for the movies, Emerson. Real life is about partnership. Stability. You'll grow to love him."

Dad had agreed. "Trust me, sweetheart," he said, resting a hand on my shoulder. "Brad will take care of you. He's the kind of man you need."

And I trusted them. Because I didn't know any better. Because I had been raised to believe they knew what was best.

The night before the wedding, I sat them down, trembling, trying to find the courage to make them hear me. "Mom, Dad, I can't do this. I don't love Brad. I don't even like him that way."

My mother's face had hardened immediately. "Do you have any idea how much money has been spent? How much planning has gone into this? You're not calling it off, Emerson. Think about how bad that would look."

Dad had been calmer, but his words cut deeper. "You're just nervous. Every bride feels that way. Trust me, you'll be fine. Brad is the best thing that's ever happened to you."

The next day, I walked down the aisle, numb inside, the whole world blurring as I moved through the motions. The wedding was everything my mother had dreamed of. Grand. Impeccable. A spectacle designed to be envied.

Everything, that is, except me.

Maybe that's why I never changed my name. Deep down, I had always known I wasn't really Mrs. Bradley Caldwell. Not in any way that mattered.

Tears burned my eyes as I yanked the suitcase closed. I had trusted them. I had smiled for the pictures and allowed everyone to believe I was content. I even let myself believe that maybe, if I tried hard enough, I could be. But I wasn't. And deep down, I knew I never would be—not here, not with him.

I reached for the nightstand and picked up my grandmother's journal, the worn leather soft under my fingers. She had been the only person who ever truly believed in me. The only one who saw the girl underneath the polished packaging.

"Follow your instincts, Emmy," she used to say. "You know what's right for you. Don't let anyone else decide your life."

Gram never fit the Sinclair mold. She was wild in a way that scared my parents. Unapologetic. Authentic. When I was younger, her words had been a lifeline. A whisper that maybe, just maybe, I was allowed to want more than the life my parents carved out for me.

I tucked her journal carefully into my purse, pressing it close to my heart for a moment. The room around me felt colder now —the walls, the furniture, even the air. It had never been a home. It had only ever been a mirage.

. . .

Two days ago, I gave my parents one last chance to see me. To hear me. To believe me. I had gone to their house, heart pounding, words tumbling out—how lost I felt, how much I needed something real, how I couldn't stay in the marriage any longer.

My mother had barely let me finish. "For heaven's sake, Emerson," she said with a sigh. "Not this again."

She didn't ask why. She didn't ask what I needed. She asked what it would look like. "You have no idea how lucky you are," she said.

When I tried to explain—when I tried to tell them how hollow it all felt—it was met with the same polished, practiced dismissals.

"You're overwhelmed," my mother said, her voice cool and composed. "You just need a few days away. Clear your head. You'll see things differently."

Dad, ever the strategist, had only nodded in agreement. "Brad is a good man," he said. "The son I never had."

Their loyalty wasn't to me—it was to the life they'd built, the story they clung to, the image they needed to protect.

There were good memories, too—before everything became about image and control. Back when I was still small enough to be loved without conditions. I remembered sitting on Dad's shoulders at the Fourth of July parade, clutching a sparkler in one hand and a dripping snow cone in the other, certain I was the luckiest girl alive. Or the way Mom used to braid my hair while singing along to old records, calling me her little star. That love had been real. But it didn't survive who I grew up to be.

The tears had burned, but I had refused to let them fall. I had spent my whole life trying to fit into the flawless image they expected.

But I wasn't doing it anymore. I wasn't staying where I didn't belong. This time, I wasn't asking for permission. This time, I was choosing myself.

With a sharp crack, the door flew open, cutting through the silence like a gunshot.

I went still. His footsteps were heavy as he entered, each one deliberate. The air shifted, colder, thicker. Brad stopped in the doorway, his tie hanging loose, his face flushed. His eyes landed on the suitcase by my side, narrowing.

"What the fuck is this?" His voice was low, cutting.

Adrenaline surged through me, but I didn't turn. I couldn't.

"I'm leaving, Brad." I forced the words out. They felt shaky, like a bridge about to collapse.

Brad laughed, sharp and bitter. "Leaving? That's cute." I flinched at the sound of his keys hitting the floor. "And where the hell do you think you're going?" he demanded.

My pulse roared, but I forced myself still. Chin up, eyes locked. My voice came quieter this time, but I made sure it didn't waver. "Anywhere but here."

His expression darkened. "You're not serious."

"I am."

His laugh died, replaced by a dangerous calm. He stepped closer. "You're pulling this shit again?"

I held my ground. "I'm done, Brad. I've been done for years."

His fists clenched. "After everything I've given you. Everything I've done for you."

"You didn't *give* me anything. I worked for this, too. And everything you've done has been for you and your image. Never for me."

His eyes darkened further. "You're insane. Do you even hear yourself? You'd be nothing without me, Emerson. *Nothing*."

The words landed like a slap. But they didn't break me.

I took a step back. "Maybe. But I'd rather be nothing than stay here with you."

His smirk vanished. Something darker replaced it. The air between us felt tense, like static before a storm.

Brad moved in a blur, his steps deliberate and heavy, until he was towering over me. Brad's fists clenched. Without warning, he turned and punched the wall, the crack of drywall splitting sharp through the air. Dust rained down as a jagged dent bloomed beside the doorway. He'd always had a temper.

"Do you think the world owes you something?" he hissed, his face inches from mine. "Spoiled, useless little brat."

My heart pounded so loudly that it drowned out the silence.

"I'll figure it out," I said, my voice unsteady but firm. "I'm done living for you. And for them."

His laughter was cold. Harsh.

"You won't last a month. When you're broke, alone, and begging for help, don't even think about crawling back."

My fingers locked around the suitcase handle. "I'm not coming back."

Brad's bitter laugh followed me as I moved toward the door—sharp, ugly, full of everything he didn't have the words to say. Not love. Not regret. Just anger. Just failure.

I moved past him, keeping my steps steady even as my pulse raced. At the threshold, I paused for half a breath. Not because I doubted myself. But because this was the last time I'd ever stand inside a life I never chose.

The door shut behind me with a final, hollow click. Louder than his threats. Louder than any argument.

It wasn't only a door closing. It was everything ending.

The hallway was quiet, my footsteps the only sound. My chest was tight, my steps unsteady, but each one felt lighter. My hands shook, but my resolve held.

The elevator chimed. I stepped in, gripping my suitcase. As the doors closed, I exhaled slowly, releasing the weight I hadn't realized I was carrying.

The penthouse, Brad, my parents... they all felt farther away. Their expectations and control had been a second skin, but it was finally starting to fade.

As the elevator descended, it felt like layers of it were peeling away. Piece by piece.

. . .

The crisp night air hit me, as I walked through the parking garage. I inhaled deeply, letting it fill me.

I slid into my car, my hands gripping the steering wheel like it was the only thing anchoring me. My eyes drifted to the passenger seat, where my grandmother's journal rested. I ran my fingers over the creased leather as I picked it up, holding it close for a moment.

I started the engine. The hum calmed my nerves.

As I drove away, I didn't bother looking back.

Atlanta shrank in the rearview mirror, mile after mile pulling me further from everything I had known. The further I got, the more the world outside shifted. The sharp edges of glass and concrete softened into rolling hills and stretches of open land. The trees lining the highway stood half-bare, clinging to the last chill of winter while reaching for the warmth of spring. A season between seasons. A life between lives.

My phone buzzed on the seat beside me. Brad's name lit up the screen.

I didn't answer.

I knew what would come next. He would call my parents. He would spin his story and paint himself as the victim. And they would believe him.

Their voices rose in my mind, sharp and disparaging.

Brad's a good man, Emerson. You're being emotional.

But their words didn't have the same weight they used to. I wasn't that girl anymore.

I was free.

CHAPTER 2

A Fragile Refuge

Each mile carried me further from my old life, but the chains of it still clung to me. I clenched the wheel. Had I made a mistake?

No. Going back wasn't an option.

The drive had taken just under two hours, but it felt like I'd crossed a lifetime.

The road ahead was empty, silent. I didn't know what the future held, but I knew where I was going. My grandmother Bernice's cabin on Emerald Ridge Lake. It had been mine since she passed away seven years ago, but I hadn't been able to set foot there since the funeral.

The lake emerged through the trees, silver and still. The cabin stood there waiting—older, worn, but familiar. I had spent every summer here growing up, dropped off while my parents traveled, entertained clients, or simply needed a break from pretending to be a family. I cut the engine and took a deep breath as I took it in. The porch sagged. The once cheerful blue paint had peeled. A pair of weathered rocking chairs still sat side by side, their slats brittle and faded to a soft gray. One held an old cushion flattened by time and rain. A wind chime Gram made from silver spoons and driftwood swayed lazily near the door, its soft clinks oddly soothing. Beneath the porch, a stack of firewood sat mostly dry, tucked behind a lattice skirt missing several panels. A crack ran through one window like a scar.

It wasn't the storybook sanctuary I remembered. It looked broken. Like me.

Exhaustion settled into my bones—heavy from the argument with Brad, the weight of my decision, and the long drive. A million thoughts ran through my head, but I pushed them aside. Despite its appearance, the cabin's familiarity gave me something I hadn't felt in years. Comfort.

I stepped out, the cool spring breeze brushing against my sweater. Gravel crunched beneath my boots, the scent of damp earth and new growth in the air. The steps creaked under my weight, and the rusty lock resisted before finally turning.

The door groaned open and stale air rushed past me. Inside, a dusty lamp flickered on. Its glow was weak but familiar. On the wall hung photographs in mismatched frames—snapshots of summers long gone. Me in pigtails, holding a mason jar of lightning bugs. Gram in her garden hat, mid-laugh. A younger version of her and my grandfather by the dock, him holding a fishing pole, her barefoot and beaming. The hallway floor creaked familiarly beneath my steps, each groan of the wood like a whisper of welcome.

I hesitated. I hadn't expected the wave of relief that came over me. It looked like a time capsule from my childhood—the threadbare rug, the wooden furniture, the walls lined with shelves of Gram's antique books. A smile tugged at the corner of my mouth. Layers of dust coated every surface and cobwebs hung in the corners like ghosts, but somehow, it still felt special.

The cabin was cold. I cranked the old thermostat, waiting for the heater to hum to life. The warmth came slowly, but it dulled the chill just enough to settle in.

I moved through the house slowly, my hand grazing the

familiar surfaces. The burn mark on the kitchen counter where Gram and I had baked apple pies together. The green velvet armchair where she read to me for hours, her voice weaving worlds into the walls of this little cabin. The narrow hallway that led to the back bedroom, where I used to curl up beside her and fall asleep to the smell of lavender and cedar.

I could still hear her laugh. Loud and joyful. Like music only I could hear. The memories pressed close, each one vivid and alive. Summer afternoons spent painting wildflowers out by the dock, Gram's hands steady as she showed me how to blend the colors just right. Mornings spent in the garden, learning how to coax life from the dirt.

Lazy evenings sprawled across the old quilt, our makeshift book club stacked between us, reading and arguing over which characters we loved and which deserved a better ending. It had always been the same rhythm here. Books, paint, dirt under our fingernails, laughter in our lungs. Real life.

I remembered one summer afternoon on the front porch, my head resting in Gram's lap, my face hot with angry tears. I had been thirteen, crushed after another fight with my mother about the proper way to dress, to smile, to be.

"I don't fit, Gram," I had choked out, the words catching in my throat. "No matter what I do, it's never enough."

She didn't shush me. She didn't tell me to behave. She just smoothed my hair back from my forehead and said, "That's because you're not meant to fit their little boxes, baby. You're not meant to be small." Her voice was so calm, so sure, like she had no doubt in the world about me. "You're made for wild places and big dreams. Don't ever let them shrink you to fit." Even then, even when I didn't fully understand, something in me cracked open at her words—and something stronger took root.

It was Gram who taught me to keep a journal. She showed me that writing wasn't just about putting words on a page—it was about expressing yourself in a meaningful way. We used to write poems for each other, trading them like little gifts. Some were serious. Some were silly. One of our favorite things was writing haikus together—about the sun, a frog, a boat, or whatever caught our eye. I owed my passion for writing to her. She saw it early and nurtured it in a way no one else ever had. She never told me to be quieter or less emotional. She told me to write more. To say it all. And to never apologize for it. I didn't know it then, but those quiet summers here had planted the seed for everything I would one day need to survive.

I stepped into her bedroom, half-expecting to find her still there—curled up in the chair by the window, a novel resting in her lap, her glasses slipping down the bridge of her nose. The room smelled ever so faintly of lavender and old paper, a scent so familiar it almost broke me. I crossed to the nightstand and picked up a small framed photo.

Gram's smile beamed back at me—soft, timeless, full of a light that hadn't dimmed with age. She had been the picture of effortless elegance, even in the simplest moments—her short brown curls always perfectly tousled, her eyes sincere and sparkling. Her skin held a beauty you couldn't fake or buy— glowing with kindness, with a life fully lived.

Something sharp and bittersweet tightened in my chest.

God, I missed her.

I brushed my thumb across the glass, smiling faintly at the memory. I had always loved how our eyes looked together in photos—hers green, mine blue—like two shades of the same story.

The bed sagged slightly as I sat down. The pink quilt was still there, faded but soft. I pulled it around me, and for the first time in what felt like years, I let myself cry. Not just for what I was leaving behind. But for everything I had lost long before tonight.

I used to crave comfort like this. Even when Brad was in the same room, I always felt... alone. There were nights I'd walk into a room and he wouldn't even look up from his phone.

"Brad, can we talk?"

"Can it wait? I'm dealing with real work here."

I stopped asking after a while. He'd only call me emotional, accuse me of sabotaging his mood, or worse—say nothing at all.

We were strangers in a penthouse built for pretending. I lived with a man who saw me as furniture. Quiet, decorative, and convenient.

After a long while, when the tears had dried and the weight in my chest loosened just enough to breathe again, I pulled myself from the bed. The cabin wasn't just cold—it felt frozen in time, every surface draped in a layer of dust, every corner a snapshot of the life Gram and I had once shared.

I moved slowly, finding old cleaning supplies under the sink, and set to work. It wasn't about making the place sparkle. It was about clearing space, shaking the dust off the memories, making room for something that still lived beneath the grief.

As I scrubbed the worn wooden counters and wiped down the shelves, I found myself smiling at small things—a chipped teacup left on the windowsill, a painting of the lake we had made together, the old rusty watering can by the back door. Every beautifully imperfect object was a breadcrumb leading me back to myself.

Back in Gram's bedroom, I pulled open the cedar chest at the foot of the bed. The familiar scent of mothballs and old paper wrapped around me. I pushed aside sweaters folded with her careful hands, antique linens she could never part with, until my fingers brushed something crisp and thin.

A yellowed envelope, tucked between the folds, marked simply: *Emmy.* My heart stuttered. I sat down on the floor, the envelope trembling in my hands. I recognized her handwriting instantly—looping and steady, like the woman herself. Slowly, I unfolded the letter.

The ink was faded, but her voice leapt from the page as clearly as if she were sitting beside me.

Emmy,

If you're reading this, then something has led you back to the cabin. I hope you feel safe here—I always did. Everything you need is already within you, sweet girl. I want you to be happy. Not the happiness your parents always tried to shape, but the kind you create for yourself. I always knew that one day, you'd find the strength to stand up for what you truly want and deserve. Keep going. You're stronger than you think.

With love, always,

Gram

The words blurred through the tears that filled my eyes. It wasn't just a letter. It was a hand reaching through time. It was permission I hadn't even known I was still waiting for.

Maybe the cabin had been waiting too. Maybe Gram had known all along that I would need a place where the noise of everyone else's expectations couldn't reach me.

A place where I could finally hear my own voice.

It wasn't the walls or the furniture that made it home. It was the invisible thread she left stitched through every memory.

This was never about running away. This was about coming home.

I pressed the paper to my chest, closed my eyes, and breathed her in—the unconditional love, the endless encouragement, the quiet belief that I was meant for more than playing a part in someone else's story.

When I finally folded the letter carefully and tucked it into the journal on the nightstand, a strange calm settled over me. Maybe it was the way the cabin still held her energy, stitched into every wall and floorboard. Maybe it was just exhaustion.

But for once, I didn't feel completely lost.

The wind rattled softly against the windows, and somewhere outside, the lake lapped against the dock. I moved to the window and stared out at the dark water. The trees framed the shoreline, their bare branches reaching like skeletal arms toward the sky. In the moonlight, the whole world looked raw and stripped bare. Like it had nothing left to hide.

Neither did I.

CHAPTER 3

Weathering the Unknown

I ignored my mother's first voicemail.

By the second, she was already calling me selfish and irresponsible. I didn't need to hear the rest. I knew exactly what she'd say. And I was not going back.

I turned my focus to something I could control: errands.

The drive into town steadied my nerves. The familiar curves of the road and the trees blurring past the window, gave me something solid to hold onto.

The bell above the door jingled as I stepped inside Drucker's General Store. It was just as I remembered it. The air smelled like old wood and fresh bread. Shelves were packed with everything from canned goods to fishing tackle, creating a sense of controlled chaos.

I grabbed a cart and moved through the aisles, mentally checking off my list—coffee, tea, milk, bread, peanut butter, shampoo, batteries.

At the register, an older man with glasses resting on the bridge of his nose gave me a polite nod. His name tag read Arnold.

"You stocking up for the storm?" he asked.

"Storm?" I blinked. Outside, the sky was still calm.

"Yep. Local news says it's moving in fast. If I were you, I'd get home before it hits."

I paid, mumbling a thanks as I grabbed my bags. The thought of getting caught in a storm alone made me nervous.

By the time I reached my car, dark clouds had swallowed the sky. Thunder rumbled in the distance. I threw my bags in the trunk and jumped into the driver's seat just as fat drops of rain began smacking against the car.

As I turned onto the winding road to the cabin, the rain started coming down hard.

Sheets of water blurred the road, my wipers struggling to keep up. Every twist and turn made my chest tighten.

Before I could react, the branch appeared.

I hit the brakes hard.

The tires skidded, and the car lurched to a stop just feet from the fallen tree limb. "Crap," I muttered, smacking the wheel.

The rain pounded against the windshield while the wind howled through the trees, sending smaller branches across the pavement. I scanned the road. No way around it. The shoulders were too narrow, the mud too soft. There was no chance I was moving that thing.

I grabbed my phone. No signal. Of course.

I let out a slow breath, trying to think. But before I could come up with a plan, headlights flashed in my rearview mirror. It was a truck.

Relief flooded through me as the engine idled, tires crunching over wet gravel. The door opened, and through the rain, a man stepped out. His white T-shirt was soaked, clinging to his body. He was tall, broad-shouldered, and muscular. Rain dripped from his dark hair, trailing down his arms. He moved toward my car like the downpour didn't exist—slow and completely unshaken.

He stopped at my window, eyes flicking from me to the fallen branch. "Trouble?"

His voice was calm, as if this were just an ordinary day.

"You could say that." I rolled the window down slightly. "There's no way around it."

He nodded once, assessing the situation with a single glance. "It's big, but I can move it."

Before I could respond, he was already at the branch. He crouched by the thickest part, testing its weight. His muscles flexed beneath the soaked fabric of his shirt. Rain dripped from his jaw. He braced himself, his boots planted firm against the pavement.

I watched for a moment, then hopped out of the car. "Let me help." I grabbed the smaller end. The wet bark was slick under my fingers, the weight heavier than I expected. But I dug in, pulling against it anyway.

The rain pounded, the wind was lashing against us. The man moved with quiet strength, like he had done this before.

Together, inch by inch, we dragged it toward the shoulder. Finally, the road was clear.

He straightened, rain dripping from his face as he looked at our work. "That should do it."

I should've been relieved. Instead, I stood there, heartbeat thundering, watching him in the storm. I flexed my fingers, barely noticing the sting at first. But as the adrenaline faded, a slow burn crept up my palm. I glanced down. Blood, smeared with rain and dirt, trailed from a small gash near the base of my thumb. "Damn it," I muttered, shaking my hand out.

The man caught the motion. His gaze flicked down, brows pulling together. "You're bleeding."

"It's nothing," I said automatically.

He exhaled through his nose. Unimpressed. "Come on."

I hesitated, but he was already walking toward his truck. Too tired to argue, I followed.

The cab smelled like leather and rain as he pulled open the

passenger door. A sharp chill clung to the air, and I realized I was starting to shiver.

He reached behind the seat and grabbed a small first aid kit, flipping it open. "Let me see."

I held out my hand. His fingers wrapped around mine, warm against my cold skin.

"You must've caught it on that damn branch," he mumbled, running a gauze pad over the cut.

"It's not that bad."

He gave me a look. The kind that saw right through me. "Do you always brush things off like this?"

I opened my mouth, then shut it.

He didn't push. He simply shook his head, a flicker of amusement in his eyes.

"Hold still."

I did. I watched as he worked. He wiped away the blood, his touch sure and precise.

When he pressed an antiseptic wipe to the cut, I sucked in a sharp breath.

"Sorry," he murmured. He wrapped my hand, snug, but not too tight. When he was done, he sat back, studying it like he wanted to make sure it was just right. "There. All set."

I flexed my fingers, comfort settling in my chest. Not from the bandage. From the careful way he did it.

"Thank you," I said, my voice softer than I meant it to be.

"It's what I do." His lips quirked. "You okay?"

I nodded. "I am now."

We stepped back into the rain and he walked me back to my car.

He opened my door and turned back to me. "I'm Sam, by the way."

"Emerson," I said, sliding into the seat.

"Drive safe, Emerson." He closed my door and then walked back to his truck.

I should've started the engine. Should've pulled away. But

instead, I sat there, watching him in the rearview mirror. The way the rain darkened his shirt, the way he moved like the storm didn't faze him.

My fingers still tingled where he had touched them.

I wasn't sure what it was exactly—the kindness, the calm— but something about him stayed with me.

CHAPTER 4

Wisdom Beneath the Pines

Days passed in a quiet, strange rhythm. I cleaned. I unpacked. I tried to make the cabin feel like home. I stocked the kitchen with basics, found an old quilt for the swing outside, and I even hung one of Gram's wind chimes near the porch. It should've felt like progress.

But even as the days stretched into a second week, something inside me stayed restless—like I was moving through someone else's life, wearing shoes that didn't quite fit. The silence wasn't empty, but it wasn't comforting yet either. Just... unfamiliar.

I tried to shake the chaos I'd left behind in the city, but despite my efforts, Brad's words clung to me. I needed something else. Someone else.

I threw on my hoodie and stepped outside. The cool morning air hit my skin—crisp with that unmistakable bite of early April. The lake was calm and beautiful, like something out of a painting. I thought about sitting on the dock all day, letting the quiet settle into me. But something else was pulling at me.

Gram had a close friend. A neighbor. I wondered if she still lived here. "Ute," I whispered.

The path to her house wound through the woods—the kind of trail you wouldn't find unless you knew to look for it. A few minutes later, the trees opened up, revealing a small cottage. It looked like something out of a fairy tale. The roof was covered in moss, and smoke swirled up from the stone chimney.

I stepped through a wooden arbor draped with dried herbs and flowers. It felt like stepping into another world. It felt magical.

I remembered golden summer afternoons when Gram and Ute would sit on this porch, sipping tea and laughing in a language I wasn't old enough to understand. Ute used to sneak me cookies when she thought Gram wasn't watching, while I twirled around in her pretty clothes, pretending to be a princess. They would laugh and clap, never once telling me I was too much or too silly. Here, I was always enough.

"Come in, dear," a voice called out.

I hesitated, then pushed the gate open and followed the stone path to the front door. A woman stood there, waiting—as if she had known I was coming. She was impossible to ignore—platinum-blonde hair cut into a sharp, daring bob, framing a face that was both elegant and intense. Her hazel eyes seemed to pierce right through me, unwavering and unreadable. She exuded effortless confidence, as if beauty was simply second nature. She looked like she had stepped straight out of a magazine. Every detail—her hair, her jewelry, her outfit, even her shoes—was striking and unexpected.

"Emerson," she said, her voice warm but firm. "I've been expecting you."

I hesitated. There was something familiar about her, a memory out of reach.

"Expecting me?" I asked, startled.

"I saw lights on when I drove by Bernice's cabin. I just assumed it was you." She studied my face for a minute. "Oh my, you're the image of Bernice. A younger version, of course." She giggled, the sound light but knowing.

My throat tightened at the mention of my grandmother.

"She was one of my best friends." Her smile deepened.

Ute was always around when I was little, having coffee and chatting with Gram. But I hadn't seen her in years, and the details were fuzzy, blurred by time.

"I remember seeing you," I admitted slowly. "It's been a long time."

She nodded as if she understood. "You were the apple of Bernice's eye. She spoke of you often." She motioned for me to follow her inside.

The scent of freshly baked cookies filled the air, sweet and warm. A huge grand piano sat front and center in the main room. Books were stacked in elegant towers across the back wall—everything from poetry to philosophy, spines worn soft from use. A delicate chandelier hung from the ceiling, its crystals catching the light.

Everything looked as if it had been in place for years.

Ute gestured for me to sit in a chair near the fire and poured two cups of tea. The scent of mint and something floral wrapped around me like a memory. She handed me a cup and then took a seat across from me.

"She told me so much about you, dear," Ute said, looking at me with an intensity that made me squirm. "She said you were like her in many ways. And that you carried more potential than you ever realized."

I blinked, caught off guard. "She never said that to me."

"She wouldn't," Ute said with a knowing smile. "Bernice believed in letting people discover their own strength. But she saw yours, even when you didn't."

Her words settled over me like a blanket—warm, but heavy with implication.

"She was always encouraging," I sighed, staring into my cup. "She wanted me to be... myself."

"Because she knew you could be," Ute said gently. "But you can't step into who you're meant to be if you let others dictate your life."

The idea scared me, but deep down, I knew she was right. She must have seen it on my face because she leaned in and said softly, "Change isn't easy, my dear. Letting go of what you know, even if it hurts... takes guts. But holding on to something that's breaking you? That's no way to live."

The words settled deep, stirring something raw inside me. She really did know about me.

Ute passed me a plate of cookies, and for a moment, we simply sat, the crackling fire filling the silence. I took a bite, the sweetness lingering on my tongue longer than I expected. Maybe it was the cabin, maybe it was the memories of Gram, or maybe it was just the way Ute looked at me—like she already knew—but something in me loosened.

"I never really had friends," I said quietly, surprising myself. "Not real ones, anyway."

Ute said nothing, just watched me patiently, letting the words find their way.

"My life back there..." I trailed off, searching for the right shape of it. "It was all about appearances. My friends, if you could even call them that, they were obsessed with the illusion of perfection. Everyone always trying to one-up each other. The perfect marriage. The perfect house. The perfect vacation. It didn't matter if they weren't really happy, as long as they looked happy enough for the Christmas card."

My voice cracked, and I looked down at my hands.

"I tried to fit into that world," I whispered. "I thought if I smiled enough, if I wore the right dress, said the right things, I could be happy too. But it was never real. None of it."

Ute leaned forward, her expression so soft it nearly undid me. "And you knew it," she said. "That kind of knowing... it never leaves you."

I nodded, a lump tightening my throat.

"You don't have to be who they taught you to be," Ute said, her voice warm. "You're allowed to want more. Real love. Real peace. Real friends. People who see you and love you as you are."

Her words were a comfort I didn't realize I needed.

I let out a shaky breath. "It's just... it's scary. Walking away. Starting over with nothing, no one."

Ute set her teacup down with a soft clink. "It might be the hardest thing you'll ever do," she said simply. "But it's also very brave."

The fire crackled between us, the silence heavy but not uncomfortable. I didn't feel judged. I didn't feel small. I just felt... heard.

"You've already taken the first step," she said, cradling my face with her hand. "It'll all work out."

Ute let out a quiet hum. "Perfection is exhausting. That's why I quit trying and took up vodka instead."

She winked.

We both let out a little laugh.

"You know," she said, her voice thoughtful, "I almost married the wrong man, too."

I blinked, surprised.

"I was young. Naive. He was perfect on paper—charming, successful, came from the right family." She smiled, but there was something bittersweet behind it. "I thought it was what I was supposed to want."

I stayed silent, afraid that if I said anything, she would stop.

"But something in me knew. Deep down, I knew." She picked up her tea again, swirling it slowly. "So I walked away. Right before the wedding. Scandalous back then, of course." She gave a soft, almost mischievous laugh. "My parents were horrified. My friends whispered. They said I'd be alone forever."

Her eyes warmed as they met mine.

"I didn't marry until my thirties—ancient, in those days. Had my children in my mid-thirties, which was unheard of back then. But I didn't care." She smiled, a slow, certain thing. "It was *my* happiness. Not theirs."

The fire popped softly between us, filling the room with a low, golden light.

"You listen to me, Emerson," she said, her voice quieter but even more certain. "Forget what everyone else thinks. Forget the timelines and the rules. It's your life. Follow your heart. You will figure it all out."

I swallowed hard, something raw lodging itself in my chest.

"Give it time," she added, reaching over to squeeze my hand. "Trust yourself. You're stronger than you think."

I squeezed her hand back, holding on a second longer than necessary. It had been so long since anyone simply believed in me. As I stepped off her porch and headed into the trees, something felt new.

The walk back to the cabin felt different somehow. Lighter. Like I had set something down without even realizing it. Ute's words followed me through the woods, soft and sure, like a thread stitching something broken back together.

As I stepped onto the porch, the sharp, clean scent of pine hit me, and for once, I didn't feel completely lost.

CHAPTER 5

The Courage to Begin

Time passed in a strange, muted stretch. I stayed busy—washing all of Gram's linens and towels, wiping down every shelf, rearranging the kitchen, trying to stitch comfort into the corners of a house that didn't feel like mine yet.

I woke up restless, so I did the only thing that made sense—I started scrubbing away the past, deep cleaning and organizing the cabin. I was halfway through rearranging the books on Gram's old shelves when the crunch of tires on gravel startled me. Peeking out the window, my heart sank. Brad's sleek black car was parked crooked across the driveway, like he owned the place—of course he thought he did.

I set down the book in my hand, one of Gram's dog-eared paperbacks, and forced myself to take a few deep breaths. The last thing I needed was to let him see me rattled. By the time I reached the door, Brad was already there. His knock was sharp, impatient.

I opened it, keeping the screen door between us.

Brad looked the same as always—slick black hair combed to unnatural perfection, sharp, pointy features carved into a permanent sneer. His slim frame somehow made him seem smaller, weaker, even though he tried so hard to project the opposite. The sight of him made my stomach twist.

"What are you doing here, Brad? How did you even know I was here?" I asked, keeping my voice calm even though my heart hammered against my ribs.

"You think I'm stupid? I tracked your phone." He smiled, but it didn't reach his eyes. "We need to talk."

I didn't move. "There's nothing left to say."

"Come on, Emerson." His voice dropped, coaxing. "This is ridiculous. You've made your point. Let's just go home."

"This is my home now."

He laughed under his breath, bitter. "This shack? You're better than this."

The words stung, but I didn't let it show. I stayed right where I was, arms crossed, guarding the threshold. Brad's jaw tightened. "Do you have any idea what people are saying? You're making a fool of yourself. And me."

"I'm not responsible for your image, Brad. I never was."

His eyes flickered, something sharper bleeding into his stare. "Don't do this," he snapped. "You're throwing away everything we built—because you're what? Sad? Lonely?"

Brad kept talking, but I barely heard him.

My mind drifted to the time he found the page I thought I'd hidden.

I'd written down my feelings. A page full of confusion, grief, and the quiet ache of being invisible. Brad found it, held it up like a joke, and smirked.

"This is what you do when I'm not home? Write sad little diary entries like a teenager?"

That night, I ripped the page out, burned it in the sink, and didn't write another word for almost a year.

But that was then.

Now, I held his stare.

"I'm not lonely," I said quietly. "I'm free."

Brad stared at me, breathing hard through his nose. "You're making a huge mistake."

"No," I said, with certainty. "I made the mistake of thinking I could be happy pretending. I'm done pretending, Brad."

For a long moment, he just stood there, the anger and disbelief warring across his face. Something ugly flashed in his expression—wounded pride more than heartbreak.

"Fine," he said, spitting the word like a curse. "You want to throw your life away? Go ahead. But don't expect me to be there when you come crawling back."

"I'm not coming back," I said, and I meant it.

The truth was, I had left long before I packed that suitcase. We lived under the same roof, but our lives never touched.

Separate schedules.

Separate friends.

Separate everything.

It was a marriage built on optics, not love.

There was no passion, no warmth—just a carefully curated image of success. When we were intimate, which was rare, I felt hollow afterward. Like I'd betrayed myself. I never wanted him. Not once. I used to cry quietly in the shower afterward, trying to understand what was wrong with me. But the real problem was simple. I wasn't broken. I just didn't love him. And I never would.

We stared at each other across the room—two people who had once shared a life and now had nothing left to give each other. Brad shook his head, disgusted. Without another word, he turned and walked out.

As he crossed the porch, his hand shot out—and he grabbed one of Gram's old planters, hurling it against the steps.

The ceramic exploded into jagged shards, the soil scattering like dust.

He didn't even glance back. Just yanked open the car door and slammed it shut. The tires spat gravel as he peeled out of the driveway.

For a moment, I just stood there, breathing in the cold air, letting the silence wrap around me like armor. When I finally stepped back inside, the cabin felt different. Safer. Stronger. So did I.

I pulled out my laptop and hesitated for only a second before opening a blank document. I had loved editing books, but deep down, I had always dreamed of writing one of my own. A silly dream, everyone said. Impractical. Unnecessary.

But as I stared at the blinking cursor, I realized I didn't care anymore. For once, I wasn't doing something to be perfect or to impress people. I was doing it because I needed to. Because I had something to say.

I set my fingers on the keys. And I began. The words came slowly at first, but once they started, I couldn't stop.

After a few hours, I needed a change of scenery. I grabbed a warm sweater, packed up my laptop, and drove into town. The Rusty Skillet—an old diner Gram used to take me to for Sunday breakfasts—felt like the right place to land. I hadn't been back in years, but something about it felt like home.

I pushed open the heavy glass door and was hit by a wave of memories. The battered linoleum floors, the jukebox humming faintly in the corner, the worn red booths—it all looked exactly the same.

The place was packed. Every table was full, the low hum of conversation and the clatter of silverware filling the air.

I spotted our favorite booth instantly, tucked by the window, the sun pouring in just the way it used to. The sight of it hit me harder than I expected. My throat tightened, and I blinked quickly, swallowing down the rush of emotion. It was like stepping back into a memory that still hurt, but in the sweetest way.

I stood there for a moment, torn between walking back out and waiting for a table to clear. That's when I caught a familiar pair of eyes across the room.

The guy from the storm the other day.

Sam.

He was sitting alone at a small table near the window, a half-eaten omelette and a coffee cup in front of him. Our eyes met, and for a beat, neither of us looked away. Then he gave a small tilt of his head, an unspoken offer.

I hesitated only a second before making my way over.

Sam pushed his coffee aside and offered a small, easy smile. "Didn't mean to steal your seat," he said. His voice was the same as I remembered—low, steady, a little rough around the edges.

"You didn't," I said, sliding into the chair across from him. "You might've saved me from standing around looking awkward for an hour."

He chuckled under his breath, and for a second, I felt oddly comfortable. "First the storm, now seating rescues," he said. "You're racking up favors fast."

I smiled, feeling some of the tension slip from my shoulders. "Guess I owe you one. Again."

We both laughed, and the sound was warm... easy. The awkwardness lingered a little longer, like static in the air, but it wasn't uncomfortable.

A waitress passed by and I quickly ordered a coffee.

"So..." he leaned back in his chair, studying me with casual interest. "What brings you to Tunbridge? Besides, you know, almost getting flattened by falling trees."

I hesitated, then shrugged. "It's a long story."

"I like long stories," he said simply.

Something about the way he said it made me believe him. I found myself telling him more than I planned. About Gram. About my life. About needing to start over without really knowing how. He didn't interrupt. He didn't offer cheap advice. He just listened—really listened. Like every word mattered.

In between sips of coffee, he told me about himself, too. About growing up around here. About how sometimes, life hands you a different plan than the one you thought you wanted —and it's not always a bad thing.

One cup of coffee turned into two. Then three.

The hours slipped by without either of us noticing. It wasn't like talking to anyone else I'd ever met. There were no masks. No performances. No trying to impress, outshine, or pretend. Just genuine conversation.

Sam leaned back slightly, sipping his coffee. "So where are you staying now?" he asked, his voice casual but curious.

"Stonegate Drive," I said, wrapping my hands around my cup. "Down by the lake."

His eyebrows lifted in surprise. "No kidding. I live on Stonegate, too. Which house?"

I smiled. "The blue cabin at the very end of the road."

He set his cup down. "Bernice's place?"

My heart squeezed a little at the sound of her name. "You knew my grandmother?"

He nodded, a fond smile tugging at the corner of his mouth. "Yeah. I moved back here a few years before she passed. Used to keep an eye on her when I could. She was the sweetest woman. Always sitting out on the porch with a book in her lap. If she needed something fixed, I'd swing by... she'd pay me in freshly baked pies."

I laughed softly, the memory tugging at my chest. "That sounds like her."

He leaned in a little. "Funny... I never saw you around."

I swallowed, the guilt bubbling up sharper than I expected. "Yeah. I used to spend every summer here growing up. But... then life happened. Wrong choices, wrong priorities. I lost myself for a long time." I hesitated. "I married the wrong person. Stayed too long. Forgot who I was."

His expression didn't change, but there was understanding in his eyes.

"I wish I'd visited more, I only lived a few hours away," I added quietly. "I wish I hadn't let so much time pass."

Sam nodded as if he understood without needing all the messy details. He gave me the space to move past it without pushing.

"What about you?" I asked, grateful for the shift. "Have you only ever lived in Tunbridge?"

He smiled faintly. "I was born and raised here. Then life pulled me in different directions for a while. Out of state, mostly. Eventually, I found my way back."

I tilted my head slightly. "Started over?"

He nodded once. "Yeah. Something like that."

There was a weight behind those words, but I didn't press. Somehow, it felt like we both knew the importance of letting some stories stay tucked away until they were ready.

"So what do you do now?" I asked.

"I own the marina."

I blinked. "Really? I remember the old marina. It was pretty rundown back then."

He chuckled. "Yeah. It needed a lot of work. It's changed."

Sam glanced at my laptop and smirked. "What's that for?" he asked, nodding toward it.

"Careful bringing that thing in here. Half the people in Tunbridge still have flip phones. You show up with a laptop, they might think you're a spy or something."

I laughed, surprised by how natural it felt to smile around him. "I'm... trying to write a book," I said, the words tasting strange on my tongue. I waited for the usual reaction—the slight smirk, the polite nod, the quick dismissal.

Instead, Sam set his cup down and looked at me—really looked at me.

"Good," he said simply. "The world needs more people who have something real to say."

I blinked, thrown off balance.

"And even if it didn't," he added, leaning forward just a little, "you should do it anyway. Because it's in you. And that's reason enough."

Something in my chest cracked open at his words. For a moment, I couldn't breathe.

He meant it. There wasn't an ounce of doubt in his voice.

I swallowed hard. "You're the first person who's ever said that to me."

Sam shrugged. "Then you've been listening to the wrong people."

He sat back, studying me like he was weighing something.

"I get it," he said after a moment. "I watched a lot of good people abandon their dreams because of it." His voice dropped lower, thoughtful. "A buddy of mine, back when I lived out west —hell of an artist. Brilliant. But his family wanted him to take over the family business. Told him painting was a waste of time, not a real career. So he gave it up. Took the safe road."

He shook his head in a slow, regretful motion. "I saw what it did to him. Saw the light go out."

Sam lifted his gaze back to mine, steady and sure. "Don't ever let anyone talk you out of your fire, Emerson. Not for them. Not for anything."

The diner's hum faded into a low buzz in my ears. I curled my fingers tighter around the warm coffee cup, grounding myself against the sudden swell of emotion. The lump in my throat was so tight I couldn't speak for a second. All I could do was nod.

He smiled, easing the heaviness between us. "Hey, by the way," he said casually, "we're having a little thing down at the marina this weekend. Nothing fancy. Just some local music, a bonfire, and food. You should come."

I hesitated, caught off guard by how much I wanted to say yes.

He shrugged, like it didn't matter either way. "No pressure. It's a good way to meet some of the town without it feeling like a parade. Figured I'd mention it."

I smiled and tucked a loose strand of hair behind my ear. "Thanks," I said lightly, even though my chest tightened at the thought.

It wasn't him. It wasn't the town. It was me. The old Emerson

—the polished, agreeable version—would have said yes without thinking, without feeling, just to please someone else.

This Emerson? She wasn't ready yet.

I told myself that Sam was just being polite. That I wouldn't fit in. That staying invisible was safer than finding out I was right.

I watched him gather his things and stand up, giving me a simple nod. Like everything didn't rattle him the way it rattled me.

Sam smiled as he lifted his coffee cup and took the last sip. "By the way, I don't think I ever caught your last name."

I shifted slightly. "Sinclair. Emerson Sinclair."

His eyebrows lifted a little. "Same as Bernice. I thought maybe it would be different, you know, since you were married."

I hesitated, feeling the old shame creep in. "I never took his name," I said simply, wrapping my hands tighter around my cup.

A brief silence stretched between us—not uncomfortable, exactly, but heavy enough that we both seemed to feel it. Sam gave a small nod, like he understood.

"Sam Sterling," he said, offering his hand like we hadn't already met. His smile was soft, a little crooked. "In case you were wondering."

I couldn't help but smile back as I shook it. "Good to officially meet you, Sam Sterling."

"See you around, Emerson Sinclair."

The door swung shut behind him with a low thud, leaving a strange emptiness in the air that hadn't been there before.

I drove home with the windows cracked, the wind cooling my overheated thoughts. Sam's presence still lingered, but so did something heavier. Something old and raw.

By the time I pulled into the driveway, reality had started to creep back in—reminding me that the past didn't stay gone just because I wanted it to.

I had just set my keys on the kitchen counter when my phone rang. I didn't have to look at the screen to know who it was. The tight knot in my stomach gave it away.

I answered anyway. "Hi, Mom."

Her voice cut through the line, sharp and already exasperated. "Where *are* you?"

I closed my eyes for a second. "I'm fine, don't worry. I'm at Gram's cabin."

"Brad told us you ran off," she snapped. "I'd hoped you were on your way back home by now. Emerson, do you have any idea what people are saying about us?"

I gripped the counter edge. "I'm not really concerned with what people are saying."

"Well, you should be." Her voice rose, shrill. "This is utterly *humiliating*. You could have had your little crisis quietly, but no —you had to drag the whole family name through the mud."

I swallowed hard. "I'm not having a crisis. I'm finally living my life. And honestly?" I let out a slow breath. "It feels really good."

There was a pause, long and cold.

"And what exactly do you plan to do?" she asked, her tone dripping with disdain. "Be a spinster in the woods? Waste your life playing pioneer woman in that... cabin?"

I pressed my lips together, my heart thudding.

"I'm figuring it out," I said quietly.

She let out a dramatic sigh. "You are throwing everything away."

"No, Mom. I'm finally choosing something. *Myself*."

Another long, heavy silence.

Then, curt and final, "Come to your senses, Emerson. For God's sake."

The call ended before I could say another word.

I stared at the phone, the emptiness on the other end pressing in harder than her words.

But this time?

I didn't crumble.

I set the phone down and turned toward the window, where the late afternoon light poured in warm and golden.

She had her silence.

I was still learning what to do with mine.

CHAPTER 6

Where the Lake Comes Alive

The morning was warm and tranquil as I walked along the pier. The quiet settled over me, calming my restless thoughts. *This* was why I came here. I closed my eyes, savoring the cool wind in my hair and the rhythmic lap of the water.

I headed toward the marina. I'd never had much reason to visit before, but after talking to Sam about it the other day, curiosity pulled me in.

After a twenty-minute hike around the lake, I finally turned the bend—and stopped short.

It wasn't just a marina.

It was a kingdom.

And it was breathtaking.

It stretched across the cliffs above me, a masterpiece carved into the landscape. Cascading terraces, reminiscent of Greece or Italy, seemed to defy gravity, bathed in the soft blush of morning light. At its peak, the cliffside restaurant stood like a crown, shimmering against the sky. Its reflection danced across the rippling lake, music and laughter drifting down like whispers on the breeze —an untouchable world, hovering above the water, wild and breathtaking.

A long, winding stairway connected the crown of the cliffs to the marina below, seamlessly linking two worlds. My eyes followed its path, tracing it down to where life buzzed at the water's edge.

The marina was alive. Boats bobbed, conversations wove through the air, and the scent of fresh water and sun-warmed wood lingered. Wisteria spilled over planters, but it was the peonies—soft pinks and deep reds—that stole the scene, brightening the landscape.

It was beautiful. Welcoming. A place that already felt like it had a story.

A slow warmth bloomed in my chest. Of all the flowers they could've chosen ... they'd chosen these.

It felt enchanted, like I'd stepped into a fantasy. A place where the sunset would stretch across the water in golden, endless waves.

I stood frozen, drinking it all in. Drinking in the way this place—Sam's place—felt like it already knew me.

For a moment, the grandeur of it all felt surreal. But then the sounds of life pulled me back—the hum of conversation, the soft clatter of dishes from the lakeside restaurant, the gentle lapping of water against boats.

I blinked, adjusting to the shift from breathtaking to familiar. This was The Oasis in its entirety—a world of its own, buzzing with movement and purpose. Row upon row of boats lined the piers. Kayaks and paddle boards were stacked neatly under shaded wooden overhangs. There was motion everywhere. Locals loading coolers, couples sipping coffee, employees weaving through the chaos with the kind of ease that only came from experience.

At the marina's heart sat Sundancer, a casual lakeside spot where boaters could pull up, grab a meal, and linger before heading back onto the water. The scent of grilled fish and freshly baked bread drifted from its open-air kitchen, blending with the morning breeze. It felt different from town—warmer and more inviting. A place where people didn't just pass through, but belonged.

And right in the middle of it all, commanding the space like he was born to, was Sam.

I forced my gaze away from the man whose presence seemed to anchor this entire place.

I glanced back at the cascading terraces, still in awe. When Sam said he owned the marina, I'd pictured the old marina I'd seen many years ago. A small, rundown pier with a few boats.

I had no idea he had built something so… grand.

I walked closer, drawn to the energy of the place.

Sam was everywhere. One moment, he was helping unload a shipment from a truck. The next, he was showing a couple to their boat, his voice calm and easy. Employees stopped him with questions, and he answered without hesitation. He was beaming.

I stood off to the side, half-hidden near a row of stacked kayaks, watching him from a distance. He hadn't noticed me, and I was glad for it. This was his world, and I was mesmerized.

He moved like the center of a perfectly balanced machine, every gear spinning in sync because of him. He didn't shout or bark orders. He didn't need to. His presence alone kept everything running smoothly. People smiled when they spoke to him. Their faces lit with genuine appreciation.

He stopped to help a little boy untangle his fishing line. Kneeling down to the boy's level, he shook his hand before sending him off with a grin.

My heart fluttered.

He had this effortless way of connecting with people.

I already knew Sam was a good man, but watching him now, I couldn't help but feel more drawn to him. There was something incredibly captivating about the way he belonged here. This wasn't just a marina. It was a community. And he was its heart.

He looked up suddenly, scanning the marina. His eyes moved past me—then snapped back. A pause. Long enough to make me forget how to breathe.

And then he smiled.

The kind of genuine smile that makes the world disappear for a moment. He stood up, wiped his hands, and walked toward me.

"You found my secret hideout," he said, smiling playfully.

"I had no idea it was... this," I said, gesturing at the marina. "It's incredible."

I shook my head, still trying to take it all in. "I thought the marina was just a little bait shop and a few boat slips. I can't believe how different it is now."

My gaze drifted back up to the cliffside terraces, where soft pink and ivory petals swayed gently in the breeze.

More peonies.

I hesitated, then glanced at Sam. "Did you... choose all the flowers yourself?"

He looked at one of the large planters. "Mostly. Worked with a landscaper, but I picked out what I liked. Why?"

I chewed my lip. "The peonies..."

Sam's brow lifted slightly. "What about them?"

I exhaled a small, almost embarrassed laugh. "They're my favorite."

He tilted his head, studying me for a moment before his lips curved. "Then I guess I have good taste."

"How long have you been running this?" I asked.

"A while now," he said, resting a hand on the back of his neck. "Got the marina up and running first, expanded with Sundancer a few years later, and The Oasis"—he pointed to the cliffs—"was built two years ago." He exhaled, glancing around like he was taking it all in. "I guess you could say I've been at it long enough to know what I'm doing. Turned forty-one this year, so that helps."

I blinked. *Forty-one?*

My eyes did a slow, involuntary sweep over him—tall, built, thick chest and strong arms that stretched the hell out of that T-shirt.

Forty-one looked perfect on him. His dark brown hair was messy in a way that didn't look styled, just naturally good—like he was too busy for vanity but somehow still landed squarely in the casually devastating category.

He caught me staring and gave a small, crooked smile—the kind that seemed to know exactly what it was doing to my pulse.

"You don't look forty-one," I blurted, clearing my throat and trying to sound casual. I did not succeed.

He smirked a little. "No?"

"No," I said, shaking my head. "I mean, I figured you were older than me, but I was thinking mid-thirties, tops."

He leaned in slightly, and it wasn't until we were standing this close that the height difference really hit me. I was five foot nothing. Maybe five-one if I was feeling generous. And he was...

"Six one," he said, catching the way I tipped my head back to look at him. His eyes twinkled with amusement.

I laughed under my breath. "I feel like I need a ladder just to have this conversation."

Sam chuckled, the sound low and easy.

Up close, it was impossible not to notice everything about him. The rugged jawline, the faint stubble, the tan olive skin stretched over sharp, masculine features. His nose wasn't perfectly straight—a subtle, adorable crook like it had been broken once and set imperfectly, gave his handsome face just a little more character.

And then there were his eyes. Warm brown. Deep and beautiful in a way that didn't hit you all at once, but crept up on you slowly.

Every inch of him radiated strength.

I shrugged, feigning indifference, though my face was definitely warm. "Well, forty-one doesn't look bad on you."

His grin sharpened. "Careful, you're starting to flirt with me."

I felt the warmth in my cheeks.

"Alright, since we're throwing numbers around—how old are you?" he asked, eyes narrowing playfully.

"Twenty-eight."

Sam gave me an assessing look. "Old enough to know better, young enough to still make bad decisions."

I squinted at him. "And what does that make you?"

His lips quirked, a slow, knowing curve while a spark of something wicked danced in his eyes. "Better than guys your age."

My stomach tightened.

I forced myself to roll my eyes, but my voice came out softer than I meant. "Confident, aren't you?"

He leaned in slightly, voice dropping to something low. Smooth, dangerous.

"*Experienced.*"

My pulse tripped over itself.

I cleared my throat and glanced toward the water. "So, you gonna show me around or what?"

Sam studied me for half a second longer, like he was considering something. Then he let out a slow breath and motioned for me to follow him down the dock.

I walked beside him, feeling the boards creak gently under our steps, the sun warm on my skin. The sounds of the marina wrapped around us—boats coming and going, distant laughter, the occasional call of a seagull overhead. It was alive with movement, yet somehow it felt peaceful.

He stopped near the end of the dock and turned to face the marina, hands on his hips, looking out at everything he had built —the people, the boats, the life that pulsed through this place.

"You ever build something from nothing?" he asked, his voice thoughtful.

I glanced at him, surprised by the question. "No," I admitted. "I've followed paths that were already paved. Safe ones."

He gave a slow nod. "Yeah. I get that." He exhaled, staring out at the water. "This place... it wasn't safe. It wasn't certain. I put everything I had into it, knowing it was a risk."

"You've built something wonderful here. People respect you. And they clearly love you," I said softly.

His eyes met mine, something softening in his expression.

"Thank you, that means a lot. It's the people who make it wonderful." His voice was warm with gratitude, but there was something else there too.

I wasn't sure what it was—but I felt it.

For a moment, neither of us spoke. The sounds of the marina held our attention. The space between us felt charged with something unspoken. Then he turned to me and smiled.

"You should come up to The Oasis sometime," he said as our fingers brushed. "The view's even better from the top."

"Sometime... yeah," I said, trying to sound calm.

"Alright, back to work. I'll see ya." And he walked back.

I watched him for a few more minutes. Sam wasn't just part of this community—he was the magnet, drawing people in and caring for them effortlessly. And right then, I was beginning to understand what it meant to belong somewhere.

I headed back to the cabin to freshen up before going into town. The warmth of Sam's presence was lingering in my thoughts.

When I stepped into Hometown Grounds, the familiar scent of fresh coffee and cinnamon pastries wrapped around me like a hug. The place was cozy, with worn leather armchairs, creaky wood floors, and a wall of old black-and-white photos of Tunbridge's earliest days.

This was my second time meeting Ute for coffee. Well—the second time we planned to just have coffee. Last week, we somehow ended up spending half the day together, hopping from the diner to the library and talking about life like old friends.

She was waving me over with a smile. Her bright green scarf caught the light, and her emerald earrings sparkled against her crisp white blouse. She looked like she could take on the whole world with a smile and a smart remark.

"Hey," I said, sliding into the seat across from her.

"Right on time." She grinned. "I thought I might have to

finish this whole pot of coffee alone. What a tragedy that would've been."

I laughed, signaling to the waitress for a cup. "No chance. I needed this today."

Conversation with Ute was effortless. We slipped into the same rhythm as before—talking about books, about the town, about life. She shared stories from when she first moved to Tunbridge decades ago, full of grit, humor, and a stubborn kind of hope that made me want to lean closer and listen harder.

I told her about the cabin. About trying to make it feel like mine again.

"You're finding yourself here," Ute said. Her voice, both gentle and wise. "I can see it."

I smiled, though it wobbled. "I think you're right. At least... I'm starting to."

She sipped her coffee, looking at me thoughtfully. "Sometimes it's not about building a whole new life," she said. "It's about remembering who you were before the world convinced you to be someone else."

We talked for hours, laughter curling between us like smoke from the kitchen. By the time I finished my fourth cup, my chest felt a little lighter. The heavy, clenching fear that had followed me since the day I left Brad—it wasn't gone. But it didn't feel so suffocating anymore.

Ute wasn't just a friendly face now. She was something closer to family. Someone who didn't expect anything from me except honesty. And maybe coffee refills.

When I finally rose to leave, the fresh spring air rushing in felt like a clean slate I hadn't realized I needed. I turned back and caught Ute's gaze one last time.

"You're doing fine, Emerson," she said with a knowing smile. "You're braver than you think."

But as I stepped outside, that old voice in my head stirred—whispering that belonging was never meant for someone like me.

CHAPTER 7

Beneath the Surface

Sometimes the hardest part isn't what you leave behind. It's what you're left alone to feel.

The next week slipped by in a quiet blur.

Sam had invited me to an event at the marina last weekend, but I hadn't gone. I hadn't felt up to it. Not because I was hiding. But because, lately, a heaviness had settled over me, a restlessness I couldn't quite explain.

I stayed close to the cabin, only venturing out to meet Ute for coffee. Most days, I read. I wrote. I thought too much. I spent hours circling the same questions, questions I wasn't sure I even wanted to answer. Why hadn't I stood up for myself sooner? Why had I spent years shrinking to keep everyone else happy—until there was almost nothing left of me?

Somewhere along the way, I had started to believe that if people really knew me, they'd disapprove. And maybe I was right. I left Brad. I asked my parents to support me, to simply love me through it. Instead, they made it clear that their image mattered more than my happiness ever would.

I didn't miss Brad. Not even a little. But it still twisted something inside me that it had taken twenty-eight years to finally choose myself. What took me so long?

Gram had seen it coming. She'd tried to plant the seeds early, her quiet words a warning I had been too blind—or too obedient —to hear. She told me that real love, real loyalty, wasn't flashy or loud. It was steady. Unshakeable.

But I hadn't listened. I hadn't even thought to question the life they handed me. I just accepted it—apologizing for the parts of me that didn't fit.

Maybe that was my fault. Maybe it was naïve. But still, the question gnawed at me every time the house grew too quiet: Why didn't they love me enough to want me to be happy?

I was putting dishes away when I heard a noise outside. Peeking out the window, I saw Sam's black truck pulling up. He stepped out, carrying a white paper bag and two drinks. His sleeves were rolled up, revealing strong forearms, and his hair was a little windswept.

For a moment, I forgot about the dishes. I opened the door as he reached the porch. "What's all this?" I asked, nodding toward the bag.

"Lunch," he said with a grin, holding it up like a prize. "Figured you could use it. Especially after being a no-show at the bonfire."

I lifted an eyebrow. "You noticed?"

He gave a casual shrug, but there was a teasing glint in his eye. "Hard not to. Pretty sure you were the only one in town who didn't make an appearance."

I rolled my eyes, feeling a flush creep up my neck. "I wasn't in the mood for crowds."

"Well, lucky for you," he said, pushing the bag into my hands, "this is a two-person party. No crowds. Just a neighbor who doesn't take no for an answer."

I smiled despite myself. "You didn't have to."

"I know," he said easily, stepping inside without hesitation.

I rolled my eyes, but the truth was, just seeing him was already lifting my mood.

"You're just making excuses to check on me," I teased.

"I don't need an excuse," he said, setting the bag and cups on the table. "Wait until you taste this."

He unpacked the food while I grabbed plates and napkins. The smell was incredible, and my stomach growled in response. I sat across from him at the kitchen table, feeling better than I had in days.

"To good food and new neighbors," he said, raising his cup with a playful grin.

I tapped mine against his. The tea was perfectly sweet, a touch of liquid honey balancing the sugar, with just enough lemon to brighten it.

"Wow. This is amazing."

"I told you," he said, unwrapping his sandwich. "Now dig in before it gets cold."

"This tuna melt might ruin every other sandwich for me," I said, taking another bite. "And these fries? I'm not sure I deserve fries this good."

He reached for the salt at the same time I did, and our fingers brushed—just a flicker of contact, but enough to startle me. His hand was warm, rough in a way that made me too aware of mine. I pulled back first, pretending not to notice, but my pulse told another story.

It was easy to forget everything else when Sam was around. His laugh, his smile, the way he made everything feel simple and safe.

But the crunch of gravel under tires shattered the moment.

I froze, my stomach sinking, and turned toward the window. A neon yellow sedan rolled into view, its garish color clashing against the earthy tones of the woods. My chest tightened.

Sam followed my gaze, his brow furrowing. "Friend of yours?"

"No," I muttered, pushing back from the table. "That's Bethany."

Only one person would drive a car like that. The kind of person who lived her entire life screaming *Look at me.*

Anxiety kicked hard in my chest.

She strutted toward the cabin, bleach-blonde hair teased high, a thick mask of concealer smoothed over her face. Honestly, it was a toned-down version of her usual attempt to look beautiful.

I opened the door before she could get close enough to knock.

"Well, don't just stand there, Emerson. Aren't you going to say hello?" Her voice was as grating as I remembered.

"Bethany," I said flatly. "Why are you here?"

"I came to check on you, Sister," she said, drawing out the word like it was a joke. She tilted her head, flashing one of her phony smiles. "Well, look at you. All rustic and… earthy." Her gaze swept over my jeans and sweatshirt with sharp-edged disdain. "It's almost cute, in a tragic sort of way."

I bit the inside of my cheek hard enough to taste blood.

She leaned lazily against the doorframe, tapping the wood with long, fake nails.

"Oh, Emerson. Don't act like you don't know. I couldn't resist coming to watch the show. The golden child, the perfect daughter, finally falling flat on your face." She let out a brittle laugh. "And guess what? I decided to rent a lake house for a while. Just to be close, you know. In case you need *support*." She grinned, syrupy sweet. "Isn't that thoughtful of me?"

My hands tightened into fists at my sides.

"What's wrong with you?" I asked quietly. "You're really going to rent a house just to spy on me?"

She shrugged, unfazed. "Well, someone has to keep an eye on you."

I leaned in slightly, my voice low. "I'm flattered you're this obsessed with me. Really."

Her smile sharpened.

And in that moment, it was crystal clear—Bethany hadn't come to check on me. She had come to enjoy the wreckage she thought she would find.

She smirked, locking eyes with me. "I've been waiting my *whole life* for this."

Bethany had always fed off my pain like it was something she deserved.

I stepped closer, refusing to look away. "If this is what you've been waiting for, you're even more pathetic than I thought."

She laughed bitterly. "You've been the favorite since the day you were born. Daddy's princess. He always loved you more. And I've been stuck in your shadow for years. It's *finally* over."

Her bitterness wasn't new. It was the reason we never had a real relationship. I'd learned to live with it. But now, standing here, I couldn't understand why she still needed this so badly.

"Well, congratulations," I said. "You can be the favorite now. I don't need their approval anymore."

"This place is pathetic. I feel gross just being here," she sneered, her face twisted like she'd swallowed something rotten. "But someone had to come make sure you don't ruin what's left of the family name."

I didn't respond. I didn't trust myself to.

She paused, turning around with a theatrical pivot. "Don't get too comfortable in this shithole. Brad wanted me to give you a message—he expects you to be home tonight. Or else." Her smirk was smug and mean.

I clenched my fists and took a breath. "Or else? Who the hell do you think you are? You have nothing to do with my marriage, Bethany."

She folded her arms, smugness tightening the corners of her mouth. "Look, I'd love to take Brad off your hands. But you owe him. You owe all of us. Go back to him and fix it. Or you'll be sorry."

"I'm not going anywhere," I said, gesturing around the cabin. "And the only messenger between Brad and me will be my attorney." My voice dropped, firm and even. "Leave, Bethany. And get a life."

She stepped closer, eyes flashing. "Make me."

The floor creaked behind us. We both turned.

Sam stood there.

Bethany rolled her eyes. "And who is that? Your knight in shining flannel?"

"Someone who doesn't think family should be treated this way," Sam said, his expression hard.

Bethany glanced between us. "Oh, I see what's happening. Poor little Emerson found herself a handyman to play house with. How quaint."

Sam didn't respond, but the silence around him spoke for itself.

"Enjoy your little rebellion, Emerson. I can't wait to watch this unfold." Her voice curled with disdain as she strutted off the porch.

"You weren't kidding," Sam said, exhaling as he rubbed my shoulder. "She really *is* a piece of work."

I nodded. "I should've punched her."

He laughed. "I'm sure you'll get your chance."

Bethany had always been a bully. But this was different. This wasn't her usual cruelty.

This was a full-scale assault on my existence.

She hadn't come to break me. She came because she thought I already was—and she wanted to make sure I stayed that way.

She was wrong.

Her car disappeared down the gravel road, but her words stayed behind, clawing at my ribs.

I sank onto the porch steps, palms pressed to my thighs, trying to slow my breath. Sam sat down beside me. Quiet. Letting me process without pressure.

After a while, he stood and stretched.

"I've got to head back to the marina for a meeting," he said, giving my arm a soft, reassuring squeeze. "You going to be okay?"

I nodded, even though I wasn't sure I meant it.

"If you ever want to talk, just text me. I can always make time. Here—take my number." He rattled it off, and I punched it into my phone. We exchanged a few more words, simple and reassuring, and then he was gone.

I told myself I wasn't watching him leave. But I was. And when the door closed, I still heard him in my head.

I sat in the silence he left behind, staring out at the woods, my chest tight. Anger simmered just under the surface—not only at Bethany for barging into my peace, but at myself for letting her. Her showing up in Tunbridge wasn't just invasive. It was alarming. Bethany hated it here when we were kids—she'd do anything to avoid staying at Gram's cabin.

For her to show up now, on her own?

Something was off. The thought made my stomach churn.

The silence felt heavier without Sam.

I wished he didn't have to leave. He had a way of steadying the air around me—of making it easier to breathe.

I needed to get out of the house. I grabbed my purse and headed into town, hoping a few errands might clear my head. It was unseasonably warm today, like spring leaning into summer—if only for a day.

The parking lot at Drucker's was nearly empty, just a few trucks and a mud-splattered sedan.

The bell over the door gave its usual ring as I stepped inside, but the sound didn't feel comforting the way it used to. Something in the air had shifted. Hank, the manager who usually greeted me with a big smile, barely looked up from his newspaper as I grabbed a basket.

I tried to focus on my list—fruit, oatmeal, toothpaste—but I could feel it, the way some people's eyes lingered too long, while others turned away like they didn't see me at all.

Not everyone stared. Some glanced quickly and moved on. Others whispered behind cupped hands, their voices slipping through the aisles like smoke. I caught a few words as I passed.

"Such a shame... Bernice was such a kind woman."

"Didn't think her granddaughter would just up and leave her husband like that."

This reeked of Bethany's work.

My grip tightened on the basket as I rounded the corner, nearly running into an older woman studying a jar of jam. It took her a second to register me. Her hazel eyes flickered with something between surprise and uncertainty.

It was Margaret—one of Gram's old friends.

She blinked a few times before a cautious smile touched her lips. "Emerson...?"

"Hi, Margaret," I said softly. "It's been a while."

"You've grown up," she said after a pause, her voice carrying a strange mix of warmth and hesitation. "I hardly recognized you."

I smiled the best I could. "It's good to see you."

Her face softened, just for a moment. "Your grandmother adored you, you know."

"I know," I said, feeling the words lodge thickly in my throat.

Margaret adjusted her basket higher in her arms. She looked like she might say more but thought better of it, giving a small, uncertain nod before turning away. Not cruel. Not cold. Just unsure.

I let out a slow breath and moved on, weaving through the aisles, feeling the careful glances some people gave me. Not everyone looked at me like I was some walking scandal. Some looked sad. Some looked curious. But others—the louder ones— left no room for doubt about what they thought.

Near the front of the store, Bethany had planted herself at the checkout counter, soaking up attention like a stage light had been fixed on her. Her voice was just loud enough to make sure every word reached the people pretending not to listen.

"You wouldn't believe how much she's fallen apart," she said, shaking her head with a mock sigh. "Hiding out in the woods like some tragic midlife crisis. Poor Brad's devastated."

A few people chuckled awkwardly. Some shifted uncomfortably, not quite sure whether to laugh or walk away.

Bethany caught my eye and smiled—a phony smile that practically dared me to react.

"Of course, she's trying to play the victim," she added in a lowered voice that still carried. "Poor thing never could handle real life."

Her words slithered into the air like poison, and for a split second, my vision tunneled. I could have said something. I could have cut her down in two sentences, humiliated her, made her choke on every lie.

But I didn't.

Bethany wanted a spectacle. She needed me to play the villain in her little story. And I wasn't giving her that power.

Without a word, I turned away, walked past her and her little audience, and placed my basket on the counter. Arnold, the cashier, gave me a tight, uncomfortable smile as he rang up my things. He didn't know what to say either. Maybe he believed her. Maybe he didn't.

It didn't matter.

I loaded the bags into the car and slammed the trunk harder than I meant to.

Bethany's venom wasn't new. It was an old, familiar wound—one I had carried my entire life.

Growing up the younger sister by four years, I had always wanted a real relationship with the only sibling I had. I tried everything to win her over—slipping drawings into her notebooks, offering up my favorite toys, searching for any small thing that might build a bridge. I was hopeful. Maybe even desperate. But no matter what I did, Bethany responded with the same thing: scorn or cruelty.

She had resented me for as long as I could remember.

I could still hear the bitterness in her voice when she threw out her favorite accusation, as if it were the gospel truth, "Dad loves you more. He always has."

At the time, I hadn't understood. How could she believe that? All I ever wanted was to love her. But to Bethany, I wasn't a sister —I was a threat. Competition in a war I never signed up for.

Her jealousy grew into a campaign of torment that lasted

years. When we were little, she tripped me for fun, watching with glee as I stumbled. If I passed too close to her chair, she'd "accidentally" knock into me... hard enough to bruise. If I wore something she wanted, or got praised for a good grade, she made sure I paid for it. Punches. Scratches. Cruel words whispered just loud enough for everyone to hear.

But the worst part wasn't Bethany. It was that our parents saw it—and did nothing. I would run to our mom, crying, with bruises on my arms and tears streaming down my face. "Bethany hurt me," I'd say, desperate for comfort. For justice. But she'd wave it off like I was whining about spilled milk. "She's your sister," she'd say, in a clipped and dismissive tone. "She'll be your best friend one day. Just forgive her."

And I did. Every time.

I overlooked the rumors she spread about me at school... the ones that made my friends turn their backs on me. I let it go when she stole my clothes and destroyed them out of spite. I bit my tongue through the names she called me in front of others, and the way she turned every family gathering into a minefield where I was the obvious target.

I kept forgiving because I believed our mom's lie. I believed that one day, Bethany would see me as her sister instead of her enemy.

But that day never came.

Bethany's cruelty only sharpened as we grew older. And our parents kept making excuses. "She'll grow out of it," Mom said.

But she didn't.

Without consequences, Bethany learned she could get away with anything—and she did.

Now, standing in the fresh spring air of this lakeside town, with Bethany's latest performance echoing in my ears and my family's support nowhere to be found, the weight of it all hit me at once.

I leaned against the cool metal of the car, drawing a shaky breath.

Her words weren't the truth. They were just a reflection of who she was—not who I was.

I had spent my entire life forgiving. Forgiving Bethany for her cruelty. Forgiving my parents for their indifference. Forgiving Brad for his disdain.

But I was done carrying the weight of their sins. It was time to fight for myself.

To claim peace.

To claim joy.

To claim the life I should have had all along.

The thought terrified me.

And freed me.

As I looked out across the quiet trees standing tall around the town, I felt it settle deep inside me.

I wasn't that helpless little sister anymore.

CHAPTER 8

Words Unspoken

Sleep hadn't come easy after a day like yesterday. I'd tossed and turned, my thoughts tangled in everything Bethany had said—and everything she hadn't. Her voice, her smirk, the sideways glances at Drucker's... it clung to me like smoke.

I hated that I let it get to me. That after all these years, Bethany still had the power to make me feel like I was thirteen again—awkward, unwanted, not enough.

And the worst part? I'd folded so quickly. Pulled inward like maybe, deep down, I still believed the things they said.

When I couldn't take lying there anymore, I got up and padded into the kitchen, hoping the rhythm of cooking might settle me. Maybe something warm. Simple.

But I stopped short.

Water glistened across the floor, pooling beneath the sink.

My stomach sank.

I crouched down and opened the cabinet doors. A slow leak bled from the pipe, soaking into the baseboard.

Perfect.

I grabbed my phone and texted Sam.

Me: Hey… any chance you're free to stop by for a quick favor?

Sam: Of course. I'll be there soon.

Not even ten minutes passed before I heard the low rumble of his truck outside. I moved to the window just as Sam stepped out. The second I saw him, I felt it—that rush of unexpected relief, like the sight of someone solid when you didn't know how much longer you could stand.

A knock sounded. When I opened the door, Sam was there.

"Morning," he said, his voice low—like he already knew I needed kindness today.

"Everything alright?"

I stepped aside and gestured to the kitchen. "No. Unless you're a plumber."

He gave a lopsided smile and stepped inside. "Let me take a look."

We walked to the kitchen and I pointed at the water. He bent down in front of the open cabinet beneath the sink. As he inspected, he started whistling—a low, easy tune that made it all feel a little less like a crisis.

Sam was nothing like Brad. Brad couldn't change a lightbulb. His hands were only useful for handshakes and holding court in a courtroom. But Sam? Sam looked like he could build a house with his bare hands. Fix anything. Handle everything. And somehow do it without making a fuss.

"It's the drain," he said after a moment, sitting back on his heels. "Simple fix. I'll turn off the water to the sink for now and come back later with the right tools. Just use the bathroom sink in the meantime."

I nodded, grateful. "Thank you. Really."

I grabbed a bucket while he helped wipe the floor dry, and somewhere between the towels and the silence, my throat caught.

A tear slipped out before I could stop it. Then another.

I sucked in a breath, trying to blink them back, but it was no use.

Sam looked up and paused, his expression softening. He didn't ask what was wrong. He just... understood.

He motioned to the kitchen table. "Let's sit."

His voice was gentle.

I sat.

"Want to talk?" he asked quietly, settling across from me.

And before I could stop myself, I did.

The words poured out of me like floodwater. Everything. I told him about Brad, the marriage built on convenience and control. The law firm. The image. My parents and their obsession with perfection. Their silence when I begged for love instead of approval. Their loyalty to everything but me.

"No matter how hard I try, I can't make sense of it," I said, wiping at my face. "They cared more about the image of our family than the people in it. I thought love was supposed to be unconditional. I thought they'd want me to be happy."

I kept talking—about my childhood, about the wedding I didn't want, about losing myself in a life I never chose. It felt like hours. And Sam just... listened.

He didn't cut in with platitudes or try to fix anything. He didn't make it about him. He just looked at me like I mattered.

And maybe that's what undid me most.

When I finally stopped, my voice was raw. I stared down at the table, embarrassed. "You probably think I'm a whack job," I muttered. "I barely know you, and I just unloaded my entire life story."

Sam leaned back, the corners of his mouth lifting slightly.

"No. It takes a lot of courage to walk away from everything you've ever known. Especially when the people who should always be on your side aren't," he said. "I think you're brave."

The way he said it, calm and certain, it didn't feel like a compliment. It felt like truth.

I blinked fast to keep the tears in. "I don't feel brave. I feel... sad."

"I've had offenses in my life, but never from my own family. I can't imagine how that must feel. You deserve so much more." His voice softened as he leaned in, lowering it just slightly. "Sometimes, it's better to be alone than surrounded by the wrong people."

"You think so?" I asked, barely able to get the words out.

"I know so. You might've noticed I'm a bit of a loner," he said, giving me a crooked little smile.

I smiled back, and this time, I meant it. I stood to pour us some coffee, and the conversation shifted gently.

"Don't underestimate yourself, Emerson," he said, his voice soft but sure.

We talked more. An easy, winding conversation that somehow felt both light and profound. We swapped stories and asked questions. I told him about how I used to feel like I had to earn my worth in every room I walked into. He told me about people who had underestimated him. He shared little things about growing up here, about some things he'd had to learn the hard way. Somewhere in all of it, we weren't just talking—we were seeing each other. And it felt like the start of something I didn't want to define yet.

When Sam stood to leave, he hesitated at the door.

"What?" I asked, suddenly aware of the space between us.

His eyes locked on mine—like he was weighing something. Then, just before stepping outside, his fingers brushed against mine. Not an accident. Not casual. A deliberate, fleeting touch. Barely there... but enough to give me goosebumps. Enough to make me wonder if he felt it too.

"I'll see you soon," he said, his tone lighter now. "Assuming your sink hasn't launched a full rebellion by then."

I laughed. And somehow, it really did lift the heaviness in my chest.

I stood in the doorway after he left, watching the empty

road, my pulse still racing. The feeling he left behind didn't fade so easily. And that touch? I wasn't ready to think about that yet.

Later, I sat at the kitchen table with some lunch. Sunlight poured through the windows, warming the worn wooden floors. But it wasn't just the afternoon that felt different. I felt different. Sam's words lingered, giving me something to hold on to as I tried to make sense of the rest of my life.

I didn't have long to think. A knock broke the silence. When I opened the door, there he was again. A smile on his face and a toolbox in his hand.

"Let's fix that sink," he said. "And I figured this place might have a few more surprises hiding."

He raised a brow, and I stepped aside. "Be my guest."

Sam moved through the cabin with purpose, inspecting everything. I followed him, asking questions as he worked, drawn to the way he explained things so simply. He checked the HVAC, the breakers, and he even climbed into the attic. Once he was finished, we made our way to the living room. I grabbed us each a glass of iced tea, and we sat across from each other.

"Is there anything you don't know how to do?" I asked, smiling. "So far, you've been able to fix every problem I've had. A branch in the road, a leaky sink, a lost soul..."

He chuckled. "Years of practice. Life throws enough at you— I try not to make it harder than it has to be."

I nodded. "That's not how I was raised. Everything always felt... complicated. Tense. I guess that's why I never learned great coping skills."

Sam turned serious, looking straight at me.

"Alright," he said, "I'm going to give you a little advice that'll make life easier."

"Are you kidding? Please," I said, intrigued.

He paused for a moment, then leaned forward slightly, his tone thoughtful. "Imagine a zero-to-ten scale of emotions. Zero is peace—calm, happy, grounded. Ten is the worst thing you can imagine. Losing someone you love. A terminal illness. Rock bottom."

"Okay," I said, nodding.

"And most of life doesn't happen at ten. But if you treat every little thing like it is—if you live in constant crisis mode—you'll burn out. Fast. But when you stop and think about where something *really* belongs on that scale, it gives you room. It lets you respond, not react."

My eyes widened. "Oh man. I treat everything like it's a ten."

He smiled. "And when it comes to your happiness," he added, locking eyes with me again, "*you're* the only one who gets to decide."

I tilted my head, taken aback by how much that landed.

He shrugged. "What makes *me* happy? That's up to me. No one else gets a vote. If they don't like it? That's their problem. They don't have to live it."

I laughed, shaking my head. "You really have it all figured out. And I totally do not."

"Not yet," he said, a sparkle in his eyes. "But you will."

His words lingered in the space between us, unspoken and heavy. I felt it—quiet and unmistakable. The kind of warmth that steals your breath, even for only a second.

"How did you get this perspective?" I asked.

He laughed, the sound low and unbothered. "I learned early on not to care what people think. My parents encouraged me to figure out what I wanted in life—and how to get it. I can still hear my mom telling me, 'It doesn't matter what other people think. Including me.' She said it anytime I asked her opinion. It taught me to trust myself."

"Your mom sounds amazing," I said softly. "How wonderful that she gave you such an incredible viewpoint. I wish I had that. I'd be in a completely different situation right now."

Sam's eyes lingered on mine, a small smile tugging at his mouth. "True. But then you might not have ended up here... with me." He winked, and I felt my heart skip a beat.

He sat back, finishing the last sip of his coffee. "I'll leave you with one last thought. Maybe the most important one of all."

I leaned in, curious. "Okay."

That slow, teasing grin curved his mouth again—but he didn't speak.

"Are you going to tell me?" I asked, my voice a little breathless.

He leaned closer, his voice dropping to a near whisper. "I want to make sure I have your full attention."

"I think you know you do, Sam." I blushed.

His smile turned knowing. "No one can—or ever will—knock me off my spot," he said, his eyes never leaving mine.

I tilted my head. "Okay. Explain."

"No matter what anyone says to me, or about me, it will never change how I feel about myself," he said.

I gave a skeptical laugh. "Well, you haven't met my family. They shoot daggers for fun. And you've met Bethany."

"I've dealt with worse. Trust me. There's no flexibility on this," he said, his tone firm. "No one has the power to knock me off my spot. It just won't happen. And you shouldn't let it happen either."

He held my gaze as he continued. "What makes me happiest isn't just knowing who I am—but *being* that person. Whether people like it or not."

He said it with such natural, rooted confidence, that it caught me off guard.

I sat back slightly, wishing I had that kind of certainty—that kind of peace.

"You're *so* different," I murmured, the words slipping out before I could catch them.

His brow lifted. "Is that a good thing?"

"It's a wonderful thing," I said, meeting his eyes. "You're different from anyone I've ever met. You're real. Honest. You have integrity... and you care. Even though you don't have to."

His hand slid over mine. Not performative. Just *present*.

"I appreciate that," he said quietly.

A shift rippled through the air between us—quiet but electric. We didn't move, but something did.

His hand stayed where it was. My breath caught—not just from the kindness, or the weight of his words. But because of *him*. Because of what was happening.

Sam cleared his throat and pulled back slightly. Like he felt it too. "I better take care of that sink."

I nodded, but my heart was pounding as I watched him move. And I realized—this was something more profound. Something that scared me in the best and worst ways.

By the time the afternoon slipped into evening, and Sam packed up to leave, I found myself wishing he didn't have to go.

But he did.

And I was left with the echo of his presence, still settling inside me.

That night, I tried to shake the weight of it. I opened the drawers of Bernice's desk, sorting through old papers, half-filled notebooks, and scraps of ideas. I found some of her poems, the pages worn soft, her writing a mix of elegant cursive and hurried scrawl. Some lines were neat and complete. Others trailed off midthought, like the poem had run ahead of her hand. I traced a faded ink smudge with my thumb, remembering how she used to read them to me aloud. Her voice, warm and proud, made even her unfinished pieces feel whole.

I sank into those memories for a while.

And then I wrote. I poured everything I was feeling onto the page. All the grief. All the tangled threads that were pulling tight in my chest. I wrote until my eyes grew too heavy to keep open.

CHAPTER 9

Mayhem and Moonshine

A few weeks slipped by, and I was finally starting to feel at home. The slower pace, warmer weather, and neighborly people. The way the mornings seemed to stretch a little longer and the conversations never felt rushed. I had been getting out more—visiting the farmer's market, wandering through a small book fair on the square, and spending most of my afternoons tucked away in a corner at the diner or the coffee shop, writing.

More than anything, I was starting to feel calm. Peaceful, even. More than I ever remembered feeling.

Being alone with my thoughts—truly alone—had been uncomfortable at first. Reflecting on my life, my choices, my mistakes. Sitting in the silence I used to fill with noise. But with each passing day, it got a little easier. And then... something strange happened. I started to enjoy it.

It was like I was getting to know myself. For the first time in my life.

With no one around to influence, judge, or pressure me, I was finally free to ask myself what I wanted—without apologizing for the answer.

. . .

The Rusty Skillet was already bustling when I pushed open the door. The scent of sizzling bacon and crispy hash browns made my stomach growl. A warm breeze followed me in, carrying the faint scent of blooming lilacs and freshly cut grass. Spring was just beginning to show off.

Ute was already there, wearing a bright red scarf tied loosely around her neck and a mischievous glint in her eye. Our weekly coffee dates had become my favorite ritual—a steady place in a world that still felt like it was shifting under my feet.

As I slid into the seat across from her, she pushed a muffin toward me. "A little treat," she said with a wink. I smiled and broke off a piece, the sweet smell of cinnamon and blueberries filling the air between us.

We spent the morning lost in easy conversation, drifting from one topic to the next—how she had accidentally entered a pie contest once with a store-bought crust and won first prize, how she'd threatened to ride her bike straight out of town when she was seventeen but only made it two blocks before she realized she had forgotten her shoes.

Ute had a way of making even the most ordinary stories feel like treasures, and somewhere between the laughter and the coffee refills, I felt it again—that unspoken thing between us. A bond I hadn't realized how badly I needed.

By the time I finished the last sip of my coffee, the diner was packed. On our way to the door, I sidestepped a group of old-timers gathered near the entrance, deep in debate over the town council's latest nonsense. Ute leaned in as we passed and whispered, "Nothing gets fixed, but Lord, they sure sound important talking about it."

I laughed under my breath, feeling lighter than I had in a long time.

"Emerson Sinclair!"

I turned, and there he was—Willie Dawson, looking exactly the same as he had back when I used to visit Gram in the summers. Well... maybe with a little more belly and a lot more gray hair.

"Oh my gosh, Willie!" I said, smiling as we hugged. The scent of smoke and aftershave clung to him—some things never changed.

Willie had been the town's resident mischief-maker since long before he retired from the fire department. When I was a kid, he used to sneak me root beer floats and let me "drive" the fire truck from the passenger seat while he steered us down Main Street during the Fourth of July parade. He was harmless chaos. A walking, talking disaster magnet with a heart of gold. If there was trouble being stirred, Willie was usually holding the spoon.

He stood before me now, grinning like he'd just found a stray fifty in his pocket.

"So, ya busy the rest of the day?" he asked, a mischievous gleam in his eye.

"This feels like a setup," I said warily.

"Oh, it is." He shoved a bright yellow paper into my hands.

TUNBRIDGE'S ANNUAL RIDICULOUSLY FUN SCAVENGER HUNT

Saturday at Noon – Meet at the Town Square
Prizes, clues, and bragging rights await
Teams of two

I narrowed my eyes and hesitated. "No."

"Please?" Willie countered, like it was already decided.

I handed the paper back. "Absolutely not."

He smirked and flipped it right back into my hands. "You say that, but I just so happen to be in need of a partner, seeing as mine bailed."

"I wonder why," I deadpanned.

"Oh, don't be like that. It's tradition."

"No, thank you."

Willie gave an exaggerated sigh, as if I were exhausting him. "I expected better from you, Sinclair. Thought you had more fight in you."

Ute gave me a warm hug. "Sounds like a fun day, dear. You could use one of those. You kids be careful now." With a little wave, she headed out the door.

Willie grinned. "You're about to have the best afternoon of your life."

I looked at the paper again. I exhaled slowly. "Fine. But only because I don't want to hear about this for the next six months."

Willie patted me on the back. "That's the spirit! Now let's go win this dang thing." And off we went.

The first challenge? Find a pink lawn flamingo.

"This town has at least fifty," I muttered, scanning the street.

Willie pointed immediately. "There's one."

I followed his gaze and blinked. "That's in someone's front yard."

Willie was already climbing the fence.

"Willie! That's trespassing!"

"Not if I leave a thank-you note!" He dropped over to the other side, snatched the flamingo from the garden bed, and disappeared into the bushes like some kind of feral raccoon. He popped back up a moment later, waving the plastic bird triumphantly.

I groaned. "I swear, if you get me arrested—"

"Relax," he said, tossing me the flamingo. "Tunbridge's finest love me."

I highly doubted that.

Challenge two? Selfie with the mayor's grumpy old dog.

Willie whistled. The dog—a fifteen-year-old Labrador named Captain—barely lifted his head from the porch before going back to sleep.

"Useless," Willie muttered.

I dug into my purse and pulled out a granola bar. The second I crinkled the wrapper, Captain's ears perked up.

Willie scowled. "That's cheating."

I crouched, holding up my phone. "It's strategy." I snapped the selfie as Captain inched toward the granola bar. "And for the record, I have more game than you."

"Please," Willie scoffed. "One lucky bribe does not make you a dog whisperer."

By the time we reached challenge five—chug a mini bottle of homemade moonshine—I was having a full-blown existential crisis.

I eyed the tiny glass bottle in my palm. "Isn't this illegal?"

Willie laughed. "It's Tunbridge. Half the town's been making this since Prohibition."

I sniffed the contents and winced. "It smells like paint thinner."

Willie clinked his bottle against mine. "Bottoms up!" Then, with zero hesitation, he tipped his back in one go, barely flinching.

He exhaled sharply. "It's got a kick."

I squinted at him. "Kick? Willie, this could be used as jet fuel."

I sighed. Then drank. The burn was instant—like my throat had been set on fire. My vision blurred, my lungs screamed, and for a brief moment, I was convinced my esophagus had dissolved.

"Sweet lord, my lungs!" I gasped.

Willie was wheezing with laughter. "Good girl."

Somehow, we were actually doing well.

Clue hunting. Fast talking. Mild cheating.

And then we reached the grand finale.

I unfolded the last slip of paper, staring at the words like they might change if I glared hard enough.

The final challenge was to ride the mechanical bull at The Battered Barrel.

I exhaled slowly. "You've got to be kidding me."

Willie grinned like the devil himself. "Scared?"

"No." I squared my shoulders. "Just regretting all my life choices."

The place was packed. Half the town lined the walls, drinks in hand, hooting and shouting encouragement—or chaos. Someone yelled, "Hold on like he's the last good man on earth!"

When I climbed on, the bull felt higher than it had any right to be. I squeezed my thighs, adjusted the death grip on the rope, and gave Willie one last glare.

The machine bucked.

I held on.

It bucked harder.

I flailed.

My legs flew sideways, my ponytail slapped someone in the front row, and I'm fairly certain I screamed, "I HATE THIS!" right before I slid off like a rag doll and landed in a graceless heap.

People cheered. I think one of them offered me a job.

I got up, dizzy, red-faced, and possibly concussed. Willie just cackled and slapped me on the back. "You did better than Earl last year. He pulled a hamstring and proposed to the bull."

After the scavenger hunt, the whole town funneled down to the marina, gathering at Sundancer for drinks and celebration. I was still buzzed from the moonshine and probably leaking dignity from my fall, but I was laughing. Actually laughing.

An old speaker squealed, and someone from the planning committee called out, "All right, time to announce the winners!"

Half-listening, I stood off to the side, trying to wrangle my hair back into something semi-human.

"And this year's Scavenger Hunt champions are... Willie Dawson and Emerson Sinclair!"

Willie whooped like he'd just won the lottery. I blinked.

"What?"

He threw an arm around me and raised our clasped hands like we were at the end of a wrestling match. "We're legends now!"

"Does this mean we get a trophy? Or at least free fries for life?" I laughed.

Soreness was developing in my thighs from the bull. And then, the crowd parted just enough for me to see him.

Sam.

We locked eyes.

And just like that, the noise faded, and my heart started doing things I disapproved of in public.

He was leaning against the bar, watching me. Grinning. Like he was enjoying this far too much.

"Heard you had an eventful day," he said, voice deep and amused.

I exhaled. "Willie tricked me into public humiliation."

Sam smirked. "Sounds about right."

Willie dropped two shots in front of us.

"Scavenger Hunt tradition," he said. "You survived. Now you gotta survive the shot."

I eyed the amber liquid. "What is it?"

Willie grinned. "Just drink it."

I knocked it back. It burned like hellfire.

Sam watched, amused. "Might wanna pace yourself."

Willie suddenly perked up. "Darts?"

I smirked. "Oh, you're so going down."

I destroyed him. The crowd cheered. Someone whistled.

Willie gaped. "Where the hell did you learn to play?"

I shrugged. "College. You'd be amazed how much free beer I won."

Sam stepped up, smirking. "Alright, let's see what you've got, Sinclair."

I narrowed my eyes. "You sure? I'd hate to ruin your reputation."

His grin deepened. "That's cute. You won't."

And I didn't. Sam obliterated me.

His shots were perfect. Effortless.

I scowled. "That's not fair."

Sam leaned in. "So, what did I win?"

I swallowed. "What do you want?"

His voice dropped lower. "A dance." He nodded toward the floor, where couples swayed under soft lights and something low and aching played through the speakers.

He held out his hand.

And you know what? I took it.

The world tilted a little as he pulled me in—maybe from the drink, maybe from him. His hand found my waist like it belonged there, his other hand catching mine as if we did this all the time. We moved slowly. Closer than we probably should have been.

I could feel the music more than I heard it—low and slow, slipping through my chest. But it was his touch that got me. His thumb brushed the edge of my hip in a quiet rhythm, and every time it did, something inside me fluttered.

I wasn't prepared for how good this would feel. How natural. How right.

I leaned in, just a little. Let my head rest against his chest.

Just for a beat. Just to feel what it was like to belong somewhere.

Then I looked up—just to look. Just for a second. But he was already looking at me.

There was no teasing in his expression now. No smirk. Just this quiet, burning intensity that stole the air from my lungs.

If he said my name right then, I think I would've melted.

We kept moving, slow and unspoken. I didn't want the night to end.

For a second, I thought he might kiss me.

Right there.

In front of everyone.

And I wouldn't have stopped him.

"Are you two gonna keep making heart-eyes, or are we getting another round?"

Laughter rippled through the bar. I snapped back to reality, a flush creeping up my neck.

Across the table, Willie leaned back with a smirk, raising his beer. "I mean, I love a good slow burn, but dang."

Sam huffed a laugh and stepped back—but not before his fingers trailed down my arm, slow and deliberate.

I barely resisted the shiver.

By the time we left Sundancer, I was officially tipsy. Not fall-down drunk, but definitely in the danger zone.

"Okay," I said, wobbling slightly as I stepped outside. "I am... definitely not driving."

Sam snorted. "Definitely not."

"I'm fine," I lied.

"You're adorable when you lie," he said dryly.

"I am not adorable."

Sam just shook his head and slid a hand to my lower back. "Come on. Let's get you home."

The moon hung low over the lake by the time we reached the cabin. I fumbled with my keys, missing the lock twice.

Sam sighed. "Alright, move."

"I can do it," I muttered.

His grin widened. "Sure you can."

Once inside, I kicked off my boots. Sam watched, amused.

"Do you need help getting to bed, too?"

"I'm not a child."

"No," he agreed. "You're a menace."

I ignored him, flopping down onto the couch instead of heading to my bedroom.

"Okay," I mumbled. "Maybe I'll just sleep here."

Sam sighed. Then, to my utter surprise, he bent down and scooped me up.

"Sam!" I yelled.

"Relax. I've got you," he said calmly.

He carried me to bed like I didn't weigh a thing. Like I was his to take care of.

I blinked up at him, suddenly too warm. "Sam?"

His jaw flexed. He tucked me in, brushed a hand down my arm, then—softer than I thought possible—leaned down and pressed a kiss to my forehead.

"Get some sleep," he murmured.

No one had ever treated me like something precious without asking for anything back.

And then he was gone.

Leaving me breathless.

CHAPTER 10

The Weight of Blood

A few quiet weeks passed, each one peeling back another layer I didn't know I was hiding behind.

It's a strange thing—being twenty-eight and realizing you've never truly been on your own. Not in the soul-searching, quiet-morning, nobody-knows-where-you-are kind of way.

I went straight from being someone's daughter to being someone's wife. I was always cared for, accounted for, part of a plan that was already in motion before I ever got to ask what I wanted.

And now?

After all this time, the days were mine. The silence was mine. The choices—messy and beautiful and confusing—were mine.

I felt free. But also... unformed. Like I'd been living in a version of myself built by everyone else. And now I had to figure out who I was without the noise.

I didn't know where to start. But I knew I needed to.

Then came a bang on the door. Sharp. Insistent. It rattled through the quiet cabin like a warning.

My hands froze over the blanket I'd been folding.

Through the narrow glass pane, I saw them.

My mother stood with her arms crossed, gray-blonde hair pulled into a tight bun like always. Her makeup was subtle and expensive. She wore tailored slacks and a cream blouse, a pale blue cashmere wrap draped neatly over her shoulders—like this was just another country club luncheon. My father stood a step behind her, dressed in a sharp navy suit despite the gravel driveway and unpaved road. He looked thinner than I remembered. His grey hair was combed back with precision, his expression distant, like he wasn't here by choice.

"Emerson." Her voice was clipped. She stepped inside without waiting.

Dad followed, dragging a heavy silence in with him.

I shut the door, my stomach twisting. "What are you doing here?"

There was a time I would've run to the door.

When I was little, Mom kept the pantry stocked with my favorite snack cakes and made homemade macaroni and cheese whenever I had a bad day. Dad would scratch my back while we watched TV and sleep beside me during thunderstorms without me ever needing to ask.

That was before the weight of their image became more important than the happiness of our family.

Mom turned, her gaze sharp. "Sit down."

It wasn't a request.

My fingers clenched at my sides, but I sat. They remained standing, looking down at me like judges ready to deliver a sentence.

"We need to talk," she said. "And you need to start thinking carefully about your next move."

I exhaled slowly. "First of all, stop talking to me like I'm a child. I know exactly what I'm doing."

I looked her in the eye. "I told you before the wedding that I wasn't in love with Brad. I told you again afterward. Multiple times." I paused to take a breath. "Marrying him was a mistake."

Mom's lips twitched like she wanted to interrupt. But, for once, she didn't.

For half a heartbeat, I saw the mom who used to cut my sandwiches into hearts and tuck little notes into my lunchbox. The one who brushed my hair and dressed it with pretty bows. But that version of her felt far away now. Like someone I used to know.

For a moment, I thought—hoped—they had come here to be supportive.

"I'm not trying to hurt anyone," I said. "I just want to be happy. Brad deserves real love, too."

She bit her lip, then said, "You're living in a fantasy, Emerson. You've watched too many movies. Read too many romance books. Life isn't a fairytale."

Mom glanced around with thinly veiled disgust. "Hiding away in this... old shed. Tarnishing the family name with a scandalous divorce, associating with people like—" she wrinkled her nose, "the locals."

I took a shaky breath. "I get that you don't agree. Please just support my decision. I need you guys."

Mom didn't even blink. "You need us? You *had* us. But you threw it all away the second you walked out on Brad. This charade has gone on long enough. You need to fix what you've broken."

The words hit like a blow.

I turned to my father. "Dad?" My voice wavered. "Say something. Please. I'm still your daughter."

I remembered when I broke my arm falling off my bike in third grade—Dad had carried me all the way to the car and refused to leave the hospital room until I fell asleep. Mom had brought me chocolate milk and a stack of library books, and told the nurse I was the bravest girl in the world.

Where did those people go?

His gaze flickered—regret? Hesitation? But whatever it was, it vanished.

"This isn't just about you," he said, voice detached. "This

impacts the firm. Brad's future. Our family's standing. You're not just leaving him, Emerson. You're turning your back on all of us."

"Mom, Dad, it's over," I said, my voice calm despite the shake in my hands. "I've already spoken to an attorney. I've filed for divorce. This marriage is over—and nothing you say will change that."

"Well, then. I guess we're done here." Mom said, and they both got up to leave. She didn't even glance back as she brushed past me like I was a stranger.

Dad hesitated at the door—his hand tightening once on the frame—like he might say something. But he only sighed, and the moment was gone.

For a split second, I saw the dad who used to make up bedtime stories on the fly and sneak me marshmallows when Mom wasn't looking. The one who called me "ladybug" and danced with me in the kitchen when no one else was home.

But just like that, he disappeared.

My knees buckled, and I barely reached the armchair before I collapsed. A choked laugh escaped, sharp and bitter, then became a sob. It moved its way up my throat, raw and unrelenting. I clenched my fists, shaking with something I couldn't name. Grief, rage, maybe even relief.

Without thinking, I grabbed the nearest thing—an old porcelain vase—and hurled it at the wall.

The crack of impact split the air. The shatter echoed, splintering through the room, through my chest, through every part of me that had held it all in.

For one breath, it felt like a release. A scream finally unchained.

And for one stupid second, I wanted them to hear it.

To come back.

To care.

Then I looked at the shards. Regret hit instantly. They sat there, jagged and broken, a mirror of everything I felt inside.

The silence returned, thick and consuming. But their words still echoed, ripping through me like shrapnel. I gripped the couch, legs trembling, my stare locked on the floor. The tears came fast. They tore through me, unraveling wounds I hadn't realized were still open.

I had begged them. Laid myself bare—every hope, every desperate need for their love. And they walked away.

The room was too quiet. Too full of what they left behind. My gaze landed on Gram's journal. I reached for it, fingers tracing the worn, intricate cover. Her journal had been my lifeline more times than I could count. She would've known what to say. She always did. Her words echoed in my mind, "Follow your instincts, Emmy."

But my instincts were tangled—knotted with doubt, with heartbreak, and the sharp edge of my parents' words.

I wanted to be anywhere but here. Near the water. Near him. He didn't fix things with words—he just made everything feel less sharp.

I moved to the chair by the window. Moonlight spilled across the desk, turning everything silver. A pen rested on a blank page, waiting.

Unbroken
I begged you to choose me.
Not the image. Not the expectations.
Me.
I asked for kindness,
For love without strings,
For your arms to stay open
When I stopped performing.
But your silence said everything.
The world's opinion mattered more
Than your daughter's happiness.
I tried.
I twisted myself into shapes

You'd be proud of.
I said the right things,
Wore the right smile—
But it was never enough.
I remember the girl who got notes in her lunchbox,
Sandwiches cut into hearts.
A dad who danced with her in the kitchen.
For a little while, I believed
I was loved just for being me.
But that version of you disappeared.
And I've been grieving you ever since.
Now I see the truth—
Of what you are not,
And what I will never be
To you.
But I am not your failure.
I am my own strength.
And I will rise,
Unloved,
But unbroken.

The pen slipped from my fingers. The tears had stopped, leaving behind only a quiet, aching weight. A strange kind of clarity. I would never be their perfect daughter, and maybe that didn't matter anymore. I didn't need their approval to build a life worth living.

The cabin felt different now—not just a place to hide, but a place to start over.

I glanced back at the words on the page. The ache in my chest was still there, but lighter somehow.

I wasn't alone. Not completely. I had Gram's wisdom, this cabin, this sanctuary.

I had Ute. And I had Sam. The thought of him stirred something new inside me—something not rooted in loss, but in hope.

He had seen me—not the broken, desperate version my parents had dismissed, but the person I was trying to become.

And he hadn't turned away.

I exhaled and set the journal aside. My hands were steady now.

Tomorrow, I would keep going.

I would fight for the life I wanted.

CHAPTER 11

The Dock

The morning after my parents' visit, I woke up with anxiety. Their words echoed in my mind. But I knew I couldn't spend another day pacing inside. I'd just keep turning their hurtful words over in my head like stones I couldn't stop tripping on.

I needed air. Peace. I needed the lake.

I'd avoided the dock since I arrived. It was the place that held too much of me. Too much of her. It was where Gram and I would go when the world felt heavy. We'd sit at the edge with our feet in the water and talk about the things I couldn't say out loud to anyone else. Like the time I told her I didn't think I wanted to marry Brad—and she didn't flinch. She simply smoothed her hand over mine and said, "It's okay to want something different, Emmy. It's okay to change your mind." I was nineteen and terrified. And she was the only one who had given me permission to feel it.

But I didn't listen. I thought I was doing the right thing. If I had only trusted myself back then.

I'd talked myself out of going to the dock for weeks.

But not today.

Today, I was done hiding—from them, from her memory,

and from myself. Whatever was stirring inside me had to come out. And that old dock was where it needed to happen.

The morning was warm as I stepped outside. The air kissed with the first traces of sun. Summer had just begun, soft and slow, with long light and the scent of fresh-cut grass hanging in the breeze. The lake was golden and glassy, reflecting the kind of peace I hadn't yet managed to hold. I reached for my phone to snap a photo, then stopped.

Some things aren't meant to be captured—just felt.

The dock creaked beneath my steps. I took off my sandals and sat at the edge, dipping my feet into the water. And I let the quiet wrap around me.

So much had changed in a matter of months. I used to wake up to the skyline of Atlanta, surrounded by luxury and phony people. I was married to a man who thought of me as a trophy, playing a role I never auditioned for. Now, I was here—jobless, alone, and somehow more myself than I'd ever been.

They thought I was having a breakdown. That I was running.

But I wasn't. I was waking up.

It all came into focus the day I sat across from my attorney, Jordan. I had decided to let Brad have the penthouse without a second thought. I only wanted the cabin. Twelve acres of overgrown wild and inherited wisdom. My peace.

Even Jordan had looked surprised when I signed the agreement. I hadn't asked for alimony. I could have—she even suggested I should—but I thought walking away without taking a cent would earn me respect. From Brad. From my parents. From anyone watching.

Ending the marriage had been my decision. I was bending over backward to leave Brad looking better than he deserved. But he was still dragging his feet. Jordan said it was the cleanest split she'd ever seen—on paper, anyway. The rest was just waiting on him.

In the meantime, I still had my severance package. If I stretched it, I had about a year. A year to figure out who I was. What I wanted to do. Maybe I was foolish for dreaming that I could become a writer. But for once, I wanted to live like I believed in something—someone.

Me.

I spent the morning walking the trails behind the cabin, trying to outrun my thoughts. But by evening, I was back on the dock—drawn to the quiet, to the lake, and to the questions I couldn't quite answer.

I watched the sun slip behind the trees and let the silence settle. The first stars emerged—just a handful at first, then more, until they scattered across the sky. I tilted my head back, taking them in, and a familiar warmth filled my chest. Gram had once taught me their names, tracing each constellation with her finger, weaving stories into the night. I searched for comfort in their familiar patterns. Gram had always found peace in the stars.

Tonight, they felt distant and cold.

A sharp breath escaped me, and tears began to fall. At first, they slid silently down my cheeks. Then, the sobs broke loose. I couldn't help it. And I didn't try to stop them.

I'd been trying so hard to move on from my mistake of a marriage and find myself—but I was still so hurt.

Why couldn't my family love me as I was?

Why, after everything, did I feel like a villain?

My fingers tangled in my hair as I let the tears take me under. I didn't hear the footsteps until they were close.

"Hey."

I looked up, startled. Sam stood a few feet away.

He looked at my face—the tear-streaked cheeks I hadn't fully wiped away. His expression shifted into a gentle look of concern.

"What's wrong?" he asked.

I swallowed hard. "Everything. Me." I tried to mask the emotion in my voice.

Sam didn't move at first. He just watched me, like he was

deciding something. Then, slowly, he walked closer and sat down beside me.

He searched my face, as if he could read it.

He must have.

Then, his hand brushed the top of mine so softly, it tickled. His fingers threaded through mine. That simple motion instantly made me feel more calm. We didn't need words. The silence between us felt as if he already knew everything I wasn't saying.

"Talk to me," he said gently.

I hesitated. Letting people in had never felt safe, but something about Sam made it different. He wasn't rushing me. He wasn't pushing. He was just... there for me.

"My parents." I paused. "They came up here yesterday."

He listened, his eyes locked on mine with a calm but intent expression.

"They didn't ask how I was. They didn't care. It was all about them—how I'm ruining their reputation. That I was selfish for walking away. For humiliating them." I let out a breath, my chest constricting. "Like my only purpose was to uphold their image. I just don't understand why the image and Brad are so important to them. More important than me."

I stared out at the water—the ripples moving endlessly, indifferent to everything. "And the funny thing is... I don't know why I'm surprised."

Sam hesitated, as if he were measuring the weight of his words. Then, softly—so softly—he said, "Emmy..."

I jerked my eyes toward him, startled. He called me Emmy. I hadn't heard that name since Gram. I tried to speak, but nothing came out. I just stared at him.

"Sorry," he said quickly, his words rushing out. "I don't know why I called you that. It just came out."

I swallowed hard. "No, please." I looked into his eyes. "I love it."

His grip tightened. "Your parents are supposed to protect you. Love you no matter what. It's unthinkable that they don't."

He exhaled sharply, shaking his head, his eyes holding mine. "And their loyalty to Brad? That's a shame. But honestly? It's a gift to you. It proves what it sounds like you've always felt deep down." He rubbed a slow, deliberate circle on the top of my hand with his thumb. "I know it hurts. But now, you're free."

A flush of embarrassment crept in, and I wished I could take the words back. I felt bad for unloading my drama on him again.

"You must be sick of hearing about this stuff," I said quietly.

Sam smiled with his eyes. "I'm not. You needed to talk, and I'm happy to listen." He paused, his voice turning firm. "I hate what they're doing to you. I wish I could do more."

His words hit something deep inside me. I'd been carrying it for too long. It felt good to finally share it with someone.

"Thank you." My eyes dropped a few fresh tears. "For listening."

Sam smiled—quiet and sincere. "It's what I'm here for."

He glanced toward the house, then back at me with a smirk. "Say the word and I'll start building a stone wall with barbed wire so no one can get to you again."

I laughed—a real one. "Tempting."

We sat there, the silence between us shifting into something else. It was full of understanding—something unspoken, but I felt it. I looked up at the stars. They were brighter now.

I started to feel the stillness of the night. I was so thankful for Sam in that moment. And the security of his arm, as he draped it around my shoulders.

The lake stretched endlessly before us, its surface shimmering under the stars. It made me feel small—but not powerless. I felt connected to something vast and limitless. Unwritten. Far beyond the confining world I'd known. Like I was finally part of something bigger.

"I didn't expect to cry in front of anyone tonight," I admitted.

Sam's lips tilted into a small smile. The moonlight caught the lines of his face, softening his rugged features.

"It's fine," he said.

I let out a long, deep breath.

His expression shifted as he looked out at the water. "I've seen a lot." He hesitated. "Enough to know that people don't cry like that unless they've been hurt. Deeply."

His words felt like a hand reaching out, offering a connection I'd never felt before.

Before I could stop myself, I said, "They always wanted me to be flawless, obedient, and silent. As long as I played the part, life was perfect. Money, luxury, everything I could want. But the cost was everything I am."

Sam let the silence stretch. He didn't try to fill it. He was just... present.

"Maybe I thought marrying Brad would be my escape," I admitted, my voice trembling. "But I just traded one cage for another."

His shoulders tensed. "That was never fair to you."

I fought back tears. "I always hoped things would change. I knew my parents wouldn't love my decision to leave Brad, but I hoped they would respect it, you know? Support me and love me anyway."

His eyes locked on mine, intent and unflinching. The intensity in his gaze made me hold my breath.

"That's not on you," he said firmly. "That's their failure. Not yours."

We sat in silence for a while. It felt peaceful. Almost sacred.

"I've never met anyone like you," I said softly. "You don't judge me. Or expect me to be anything but myself."

He smiled, just a little. "That's how it should be."

He lifted my hand, still connected to his, and pressed my fingers to his lips. The contact was fleeting, hesitant—but it sent a spark through me.

Suddenly, I was aware of everything about him—his breathing, the faint trace of his cologne, the quiet intensity in the way he held me, the way his eyes pierced into mine.

He didn't move right away. Neither did I.

The air between us felt heavy, buzzing with something. My pulse hammered beneath my skin. He stared at my lips, then back to my eyes. I inhaled sharply.

I thought maybe he'd kiss me then. But he didn't. And that was okay. I probably wasn't ready for that anyway. I was just grateful for what Sam gave me tonight.

"I came here hoping to find myself," I said, my voice cracking. "And maybe I am... but the more I uncover, the more I see how broken I've been—and how deeply broken my family is."

Sam shifted closer. "You know that saying—you're either part of the solution or you're part of the problem?"

"Yeah," I said quietly.

He looked at me. "Which were you six months ago?"

"Part of the problem."

"And which are you today?"

I met his eyes. "The solution, definitely."

He nodded. "I can't imagine how it feels. My family was always in my corner. But you have to give yourself a break sometimes. Aren't you proud of how far you've come?"

I paused. "Well, when you put it like that... yes. I am. I never stopped to think about it."

"Take a deep breath. You're fine," he said gently.

And just like that, my tension eased. Maybe the connection and understanding I'd been searching for were finally within reach.

I turned to him. "Sam..."

He looked at me, and I felt the words rise in my throat.

"I'm scared," I admitted. "But I don't want to be anymore."

"You don't have to be," he said softly. "Not with me."

The promise in his words held me. I didn't say anything. I just smiled and leaned into the certainty of his presence as the weight I'd carried for so long began to lift, just a little.

CHAPTER 12
The Turnover

I walked to Ute's that morning. The early sun glinted off of her front windows. Summer had settled in fully now—blue skies, warm breeze, everything in bloom. Her cottage looked enchanting, wrapped in flowers, with crisp white shutters and a brass knocker that gleamed like it had never seen a fingerprint.

Ute opened the door, already dressed for the day in a sleeveless denim shirtdress, gold earrings, and heels that matched the clutch on the entryway table. Her lipstick was flawless. Naturally.

"Come in, come in," she said, waving me inside. "I made the coffee strong enough to stand a spoon in."

I laughed.

"I got some new things," she said, eyes twinkling as she led me toward the living room. "I had a moment of weakness at that new boutique," she said, pulling out two dresses—one blush with a belt that cinched at the waist, the other a navy wrap with embroidery around the neckline. "I can't decide which is more... disarming."

"You're asking me?"

"You have a good eye," she said, handing me a coffee in a delicate porcelain cup. "You just don't know it yet."

I sipped as she tried each one on, doing a slow turn in the mirror while she asked for my honest thoughts.

"Blush feels sweet," I said. "But navy looks like you don't take anyone's nonsense."

Her smile said I'd passed some kind of test.

We lingered over coffee after that, talking about everything and nothing—Ute's new herb garden, how she didn't trust the man who bagged her groceries too quickly, and the fact that her cat refused to acknowledge her unless cheese was involved. And, of course, the next book we planned to buddy read.

I filled her in on the latest with my parents, where I was at with my manuscript, and—as always—she was uplifting and encouraging. I didn't know why, but she thought I was so much better than I was. She constantly reminded me to hold my head higher, and to be proud of the woman I was becoming. And without fail, every time we met, she found a way to say that something about me reminded her of Gram.

Time with Ute always left me feeling comforted. Seen. It was simple, but always genuine.

Later, we decided to run into town together for groceries, and I offered to drive. As I pulled into the lot behind Drucker's, Ute glanced out the window and said, "Oh, Emerson—the farmers market. We should see what they have today."

I parked, and we walked the block to the lawn in front of the town hall and library. The whole square looked like it belonged on the front of a puzzle box—weathered benches, hanging baskets, uneven bricks lining the sidewalks.

"Tunbridge is the cutest little town," I said, adjusting my sunglasses. "It's like time forgot it—but in the best way."

Ute gave a soft laugh. "Oh, you should've seen it thirty years ago. There was a man who used to walk around with a rooster on his shoulder like a parrot. He claimed it helped with his arthritis. No one questioned him."

"That sounds... very Tunbridge."

"It is. And we like it that way. Nothing polished. Just people and stories and chipped paint with character."

We passed a booth with fresh bread, the scent practically pulling us sideways. Children ran barefoot through the grass, chasing each other between picnic blankets. A man in overalls played guitar under a striped tent, and two women argued— gently—about whether the peaches were sweeter this week than last.

Sunlight filtered through the canopy of trees. The booths were simple: white tents with handwritten signs, little chalkboards listing prices, stacks of tomatoes, cartons of blueberries, and honey in glass jars with twine bows. Someone had set out a big tub of lemonade with paper cups and a hand-painted sign: *Take One. It's Hot, Y'all.*

"It's not much," Ute said, smiling as she watched a toddler try to hug a goat. "But it's ours."

Every town had its shadows, but Tunbridge wore its heart on its sleeve. It wasn't pretending to be anything. And somehow, that made me feel like maybe I didn't have to pretend either.

We hadn't meant to stay long, but somehow, we ended up behind the checkout table at a tent, helping a flustered woman named Mae who was juggling a booth, three toddlers, and a pie contest sign-up sheet.

"Just keep the line moving, and don't let the twins eat anything that isn't nailed down," she'd said, shoving a stack of hand-labeled receipts into my hand like I worked there.

And now here I was—selling jars of wildflower honey and peach preserves like it was my actual job.

A little girl in braids handed me two crumpled singles and pointed at the smallest jar. "It's for my Nana," she whispered like it was a secret.

I smiled. "Then she's going to love it."

She beamed and ran off, nearly tripping over her flip-flops.

The simple rhythm of it all—the sun, the breeze, the friendly strangers—loosened something tight in my chest. For once, I wasn't bracing for impact. I wasn't thinking about Brad, or my parents, or what anyone thought of me. I was just there, in a moment that didn't ask anything from me.

Until I heard it.

Two women lingered by the tomatoes, their whispers not nearly as quiet as they thought. One cast a glance my way—sharp, assessing—then leaned in like she had something juicy to add.

I caught the word *"abandoned."* And something like *"poor guy."*

The old ache flared—shame, embarrassment, the sting of being misunderstood.

But I turned my focus back to the little girl with braids and her Nana's jar.

Let them whisper.

I knew the truth now. And it didn't belong to them.

I wiped my hands on a napkin and reached for another paper bag, just as a familiar voice said, "You've got to be kidding me."

I turned.

Sam stood a few feet away, holding a brown paper bag and a bottle of something dark and fizzy. His T-shirt clung to him like it had just lost a fight with the heat, and his eyes scanned the tent like he wasn't sure if he was seeing things.

"You stalking me?" I asked, one brow raised.

He gave a low laugh. "No. I stopped for peaches and found you running a black-market honey operation."

I rolled my eyes, but couldn't stop the smile. "Technically, I'm just covering for a woman with three toddlers and a pie entry to defend."

"Sounds like a hostile takeover."

"I might stage a coup if the samples are good enough."

He leaned on the edge of the table, a grin tugging at the corners of his mouth. "You look different."

I blinked. "Different?"

We locked eyes for a moment. Not searching—just... noticing.

Like he'd memorized the version of me who arrived here and was seeing something shift.

"Lighter," he said simply. "Like maybe today doesn't hurt so much."

The way he said it was like a hand on my back I didn't know I needed. It wasn't a flirt. It wasn't even really a compliment. But it hit harder than either.

I looked down at the honey jar in my hand. "It doesn't."

He nodded, then dropped the bag onto the table and slid it toward me. "I got you one."

I peeked inside. A peach turnover. Still warm.

"You didn't have to—"

"I was gonna swing by later, but... I guess I don't have to now."

I held his gaze, something soft and complicated stirring inside. It wasn't the turnover. It wasn't the way he looked at me.

It was the feeling that if I let him, he'd keep showing up like this—until I believed I deserved it.

"Thank you," I said.

He shrugged. "You're welcome."

He reached up and scratched the back of his neck, like he was weighing something.

"I've got to run back to The Oasis for a bit," he said. "But if you're around later, want to take a walk? Maybe down by the lake. Thought it might be nice to walk off the sugar rush—if you're up for it."

My breath caught—not because of the question, but the way he asked it. Easy. Unassuming. But his eyes never left mine.

"Yeah," I said softly. "I'd like that."

He nodded once, then looked at me in a way I felt more than saw. "Alright. Later, then."

As he turned to leave, he paused beside Ute, leaned down, and kissed her cheek. "See you later," he said, voice low and casual.

"Don't forget the rosemary," she replied, like it was nothing.

I didn't think much of it. Small towns were full of affectionate older women and respectful men.

I watched him go, still holding the warm paper bag like it meant something. Because somehow, it did. That bag might as well have been a flare. Not loud or bright, but impossible to ignore. It was a reminder that sometimes the smallest gestures have the deepest meaning.

"He always was a thoughtful one," Ute said beside me.

I turned. "You know Sam?"

She smiled faintly. "Very well."

I blinked. "How?"

She adjusted her sunglasses, eyes scanning the square like this conversation was nothing special.

"He's my son."

I froze.

For a second, I wasn't even sure I'd heard her right. But the words hung there, unbothered, like they weren't about to rearrange the entire map of my world.

"Wait. Sam... Sam Sterling is your son?"

My brain scrambled to keep up, piecing together every quiet thing she'd ever said, every time she'd lifted me with that unshakable steadiness. Sam's steadiness. Sam's stare. God—how did I not see it? The woman who'd helped me find my voice... had raised the man who made me feel seen.

Ute gave a small, satisfied nod. "He always did like a woman with fire."

My cheeks burned—not from embarrassment, but something else. Something sharp and warm that settled under my skin like a truth I hadn't dared to name.

I nearly dropped the turnover. "Are you—how is that even—why didn't you tell me?"

"You didn't ask," she said smoothly. "Besides, you needed a friend, not a connection."

The air around me didn't shift. It stilled. Like the moment itself was holding its breath.

They weren't just alike. They were carved from the same soul.

And somehow, they both saw mine before I even knew what it looked like.

"Oh my gosh. I should've seen it. You two—you're the same."

Ute smiled, tilting her head. "Flattering. He got my good parts."

My laugh came out shaky. "I can't believe I didn't put it together."

"Well," she said, eyes twinkling. "The best stories reveal themselves when you're ready."

And maybe I was.

Because I hadn't just stumbled into a new life.

I was being handed it—by the only two people who'd ever looked at me and seen the girl underneath the ruins.

The days that followed drifted by in the gentle rhythm of early summer—quiet mornings, soft light, and the occasional flutter in my chest whenever I thought of Sam.

Something had shifted that day at the farmer's market. Not just because of what I learned, but because of how it all felt. Natural. Real. I didn't know what it meant yet, but I couldn't stop thinking about it.

CHAPTER 13

The Storm and the Anchor

The sun sank low, illuminating the lake in amber and gold. The thick heat of the day had lifted, leaving behind the kind of summer evening that begged you to stay outside just a little longer.

Earlier, Sam had stopped by with two cold lemonades in hand, and a familiar look in his eyes. "Walk with me?"

So we did.

We followed the lake's edge in easy silence, the cicadas humming, the water lapping softly at the shore. Just the trees, the curve of the path, and the quiet rhythm of our steps brushing through the summer dusk. Eventually, we ended up at the dock behind the marina.

The boards were sun-warmed beneath us as we sat side by side, legs dangling over the edge, the scent of pine and lake water rising with the breeze. Everything around us felt unhurried. Gentle.

But something in Sam's posture told me this stillness wouldn't last.

"Have you ever felt like you've lived two separate lives?" The words surprised me, slipping out before I fully formed the thought.

Sam's eyes rose to meet the moon's light. "All the time." His voice was raspy and low. "But not in the way you probably do."

I stayed quiet. Just listened.

Sam exhaled slowly, and I sensed something heavy pressing on him. "I had a brother. Caleb. Three years younger." His voice softened. "He had this loud, reckless laugh, like he didn't care who was listening. Everyone loved him."

His jaw tensed, his fingers pressing against his knee. "I thought he was unstoppable."

He stared past me, his voice quieter now. "We were best friends. Shared a room, shared secrets. We did everything together. He could talk me into anything. Once, it was climbing the tallest tree in our neighborhood. I fell and nearly broke my arm. He just laughed and tried to climb higher."

A small smile flickered, but it was gone just as fast.

"I protected him in every way possible when we were kids. When he'd start a fight with someone bigger, when he cheated in a game of basketball, and when he snuck out past curfew. Protecting him was kind of my job, as his big brother." His throat worked as he swallowed hard. "And I tried. God, I tried."

Silence settled in, broken only by the faint, rhythmic croak of frogs near the water's edge.

"But I couldn't protect him from this." His voice dropped. "He was ... good at hiding things. Stuff none of us knew about. Until it was too late."

The implication hit me like a gut punch.

"One night, he didn't come home." Sam's breath came unsteady. "We thought he was with his friends. But deep down, I think I knew. Something felt wrong."

He didn't have to say it. I already knew.

"They found him the next morning," he continued, voice hollow. "In his car. Parked on a back road near our house. He'd... overdosed."

My chest ached.

Sam dragged a hand through his hair, his fingers tightening at the back of his neck. "I replayed every conversation. Every moment. Wondering what I missed."

His voice broke slightly. "Wondering if I could've saved him."

I reached for him, placing a gentle hand on his arm. I saw his eyes glistening in the faint light as they met mine. "I never talk about this," he admitted, voice breaking. "But with you... I don't know. It feels like I can."

I felt the full force of his pain and the depth of his trust. "I'm so sorry, Sam," I whispered. "That must've been incredibly difficult on you and your family."

He gave a nod, pressing his lips together. "It changed everything. My parents, they couldn't cope. My dad buried himself in work, and my mom... she just shut down for a while. It was like losing him took a part of them with him. I just tried to be strong and help my parents through it. But inside, I was devastated."

His words were so vulnerable, my heart hurt for him. I wished there was something I could do to ease the pain that had clearly shaped who he was.

My voice trembled as I thanked him for sharing that with me. "That breaks my heart. I know it doesn't fix anything, but I'm here. I really am."

The weight of his story settled between us—dense and unspoken. The kind of silence that holds more than words ever could. My admiration for him deepened. Not just for the strength he showed—but for the courage it took to let me see what he usually kept hidden.

He broke the silence first. "I've never told anyone... everything."

His voice was calm, but I heard the release in it. Like speaking the truth had unlatched something that had been locked up for far too long.

I didn't try to hide the tears that slipped down my cheeks. I let them fall.

And for the first time that night, he smiled. A real one. Soft and unguarded, like the sun pushing through after a storm. I knew I'd never forget this moment.

The night wrapped around us, quiet and still. For once, I wasn't lost in my own pain. I was just here—with him, holding space for the weight he carried.

Sam's gaze flicked up, thoughtful. "I guess I've learned... some scars are worth sharing. They remind us what we've survived."

"I'm glad you told me," I replied, my voice shaky. "I wish I could've met Caleb. He sounds very special."

Sam nodded, a wistful smile tugging at the corners of his lips. "He was. And I know he would've liked you. He had a way of seeing people, really seeing their character." He paused, and his next words came quieter, almost to himself. "I just wish he'd known how good *he* was."

My throat tightened. "I do know what that's like," I said, my voice breaking. "To carry something that feels too heavy. To replay everything and wonder if you could have changed the outcome."

Sam exhaled, elbows resting on his knees. "A storm can clear the way," he said quietly. "It's rough, but it helps you see what truly matters."

He reached out, resting his hand on mine.

The silence between us was heavy, filled with everything unspoken. Grief. Gratitude. That quiet kind of healing that only happens when someone finally sees your pain and doesn't flinch.

I swallowed hard. "You're the strongest person I know. After everything... you still show up."

Sam shook his head gently. "You just keep going. Even when it breaks you. What else can you do?" He glanced at me, his voice low. "You find something worth holding on to. And you don't let go."

My voice was barely above a whisper. "You do everything with such confidence. You make it look easy. I feel like I'm falling apart."

"You're in the thick of it right now," he said simply. "But you won't stay there. You'll find your way."

My eyes locked with his. Every unspoken word felt like it was clawing its way up my throat. He believed in me. He always had. And that meant more than I could say.

Sam reached up and brushed away a tear I hadn't realized had fallen. His thumb lingered on my cheek, warm and careful, like he was holding something fragile.

"You're not alone," he said quietly. "Not anymore."

There was such a tenderness in his touch. I leaned into it, craving the strength I found in him. Then I shifted, turning toward him, where we sat side by side on the dock—close enough to feel the heat of his body in the summer air. I wrapped my arms around his neck, curling into him, and he drew me in with quiet urgency, one arm around my waist, the other at my back.

We held each other like that—wounded, open, healing.

The ache between us didn't vanish. But it softened. Becoming something we could carry together.

"I'd be lost without you," I whispered.

He exhaled and pulled me in tightly, burying his face in the curve of my shoulder. We held on like that—his arms around me, mine around him.

I thought of all he'd shared—the weight he'd carried alone for so long.

But not anymore.

I reached for him.

And this time, he didn't just let me in.

He held on—like he'd never let go.

CHAPTER 14

F.B.O.W.

It started with the windows.

I opened one. Then another. Then all of them—hoping the fresh morning air might quiet the static still buzzing in my chest.

I hadn't seen Sam in a few days. Not since the dock. Not since his voice cracked and something in me cracked with it.

Then came the call from Jordan. Brad was fighting the terms. He'd decided he was entitled to half my severance package, even though he'd always earned twice what I ever did. Now, he was twisting the narrative, acting like I'd vanished without warning, trying to paint himself as a victim.

And my parents? Still nothing. Not a word.

Yesterday, I didn't leave the house. I wrote like I was trying to outrun something. And maybe I was.

The truth.

The closeness.

The feeling that we were on the edge of something I couldn't yet name.

But this morning, I couldn't sit still.

I wandered the porch twice with my coffee, restless in a way that didn't feel like anxiety. It felt like longing. Like maybe something inside me had already decided it was time to move forward.

So I got dressed without thinking. No makeup. Hair pulled back. I grabbed my keys and slid behind the wheel.

I didn't know exactly what I was hoping for. But I knew where I was going.

The Oasis.

I had only seen it from the lake below—perched high on the cliffs, a breathtaking silhouette against the sky. But I had never made the drive up.

As I climbed higher into the hills, the lake disappeared in my rearview mirror. The road curved through towering trees, sunlight spilling through the leaves in shifting patterns. Then, just beyond the last bend, the woods opened—and it felt like stepping into a dream.

The entrance was mesmerizing. Ivy climbed low stone walls, but the peonies are what stole my breath. They were everywhere —lush, full blooms in every shade of pastel, like pressed strawberries in fresh cream, like spilled rosé on silk, like the soft glow of candlelight flickering against porcelain—spilling over the garden beds, soft and abundant. As if nature itself had woven a love letter in petals, delicate and unspoken, waiting to be read in the hush of the breeze.

Peonies. My favorite. A flower that symbolizes love, resilience, and loyalty.

Lanterns lined the path, their ironwork intricate and timeless. It felt like more than just a beautiful entrance. It felt like a message. Like the universe had left pieces of my heart here long before I arrived, waiting for me to finally come home.

Then, the sign came into view.

THE OASIS ON EMERALD RIDGE LAKE

Carved into a massive wooden slab, the gold lettering was

bold yet elegant, sunlight flickering through the leaves above, casting shifting patterns over the words. Below it, a small bronze plaque caught my eye. Its engraved words were simple, but staggering.

450 FEET ABOVE THE LAKE
THE SUNSET CAPITAL OF GEORGIA

I smiled at the sight, staring up toward the terraces that seemed to spill into the sky. With every turn of the winding road, the view became even more breathtaking.

Finally, I pulled into a spot and climbed out quickly, eager to take it all in. The Oasis stood high above the world, an intricate maze of patios and balconies, each level offering a new perspective of the lake below. Golden light caught on warm stucco and rustic wooden beams, giving the whole place an almost Mediterranean feel—like a lost coastal villa perched above the water. Multi-level terraces cascaded along the cliff's edge, each one lined with wrought iron railings and overflowing with lush greenery, inviting visitors to linger and take in the breathtaking view. This hidden paradise felt suspended between Earth and sky, as if it belonged to both and neither at once.

Before I reached the entrance, my gaze was drawn downward —far below, the lake stretched wide and endless, the morning sun setting it ablaze in a thousand shades of yellow. The marina flickered with movement, boats no bigger than toy models from this height, their wakes cutting delicate trails across the glassy surface. Sundancer bustled with life, people weaving between the docks. Sailboats drifted peacefully in the distance, their white sails catching the light like scattered feathers.

I stood there for a moment, lost in it—the contrast, the perspective, the way everything felt different from up here. The energy, the stillness, the sheer beauty of it all.

Like standing at the edge of the Earth.

As I walked through the parking lot, a soft breeze wrapped

around me, carrying with it the unmistakable feel of a perfect summer day. A path of peonies caught my eye. The sight of them, so effortlessly woven into the landscape, stirred something deep inside me. I wanted to be a part of it. I wanted to belong here.

And, deep down, I had a feeling that I already did.

I made my way toward the entrance, stepping onto a path of weathered flagstone that weaved through the most exquisite gardens I had ever seen. Even more peonies bloomed in soft, ruffled clusters—blush pink, deep crimson, ivory—a riot of color and texture—vibrant blooms twisting around trellises, palm fronds swaying lazily in the breeze, and more ivy creeping along sun-warmed stone walls.

Every corner felt alive, as if the land itself embraced the space, softening the edges of the grand terraces with wild, unrestrained beauty. Roses climbed trellises and arbors, their velvety petals unfurling in delicate whispers of pink and white. Water trickled from tiered fountains, their soft splashes blending with the hum of conversation and the occasional burst of laughter from diners on the terrace. The breeze was thick with the intoxicating fragrance of flowers.

Everywhere I looked, nature and design danced together in perfect harmony. Stone archways framed vine-covered alcoves, where wooden benches sat tucked away, as if inviting lovers to steal a quiet moment together. A pergola stretched along one of the pathways, heavy with ivy and climbing roses, their petals drifting lazily to the ground with the breeze. The entire place felt otherworldly, as if time itself had slowed to a hush, waiting for someone to step into its enchantment and never want to leave.

I stepped inside. The air was warm, filled with the rich scents of slow-roasted herbs and something citrusy I couldn't quite place. The interior was even more beautiful than I had imagined. Light poured in through towering windows, spilling across polished wood floors and stone walls adorned with elegant sconces. The hum of soft music played beneath the gentle clinking of silverware and quiet conversation.

I made my way to the hostess stand, my heart racing a little faster than before. "Hi, I'm looking for Sam," I said, my voice softer than I expected.

The young woman behind the stand smiled knowingly. "Sure. Let me find him."

She disappeared into the restaurant, and I took a slow glance around. Couples leaned in close, and families shared stories over plates of food. It felt like stepping into the middle of an old movie —warm, inviting, a place where memories weren't just made, but cherished.

A moment later, I heard a laugh, rich and easy, carrying across the room.

I turned toward the sound and spotted Sam walking over from the bar, talking with one of his employees. He was grinning with effortless charm. The employee shook his head and mumbled something that made Sam chuckle again. I couldn't hear the words, but whatever was said made him glance in my direction, a big smile spreading across his face.

As they approached, the employee followed Sam's gaze, and then grinned mischievously. "So, this is the famous Emerson," he teased loud enough for me to hear. "Thought she was a myth."

Sam rolled his eyes but looked amused. "Don't start."

I arched an eyebrow. "Famous, huh? Should I be flattered or concerned?"

The employee smirked. "Depends on how much trouble you plan on causing."

Sam shook his head. "Ignore them. They pretend I'm some town mystery."

I crossed my arms. "And are you?"

His eyes twinkled. "Guess you'll have to find out."

He stopped in front of me, his eyes lingering for just a second before he reached out, brushing his fingers lightly against my forearm. "You hungry?"

Before I could respond, he gestured toward the patio. "Come on. Let's get some food."

We stepped onto a terrace and sat at a table overlooking the water. The sunlight reflected off the rippling lake. A few boats drifted gracefully with full sails, gliding smoothly over the deep green water. The view was unreal. The kind that made you feel as though you were on vacation, far away from real life.

A waitress named Celeste approached, pen poised. Sam greeted her, introduced us, and placed our order. "Two sweet teas and two usuals, please."

I smirked. "Confident order. What if I wanted something else?"

He leaned back, eyes twinkling. "Then I'd question everything I thought I knew about you."

I laughed, shaking my head. "Oh, so you think you've got me figured out?"

"Absolutely," he said, tapping his fingers on the table.

I wrinkled my nose and smiled.

Celeste returned with our drinks, setting them down with a knowing smile before disappearing back inside. The tea was cold and sweet, like summer in a glass. Sam mirrored me, his gaze drifting out to the boats.

"This is a whole different world," I admitted. "We must have wandered into some secret resort."

He nodded. "Not bad for a small-town restaurant, huh?"

"Are you kidding? It's unbelievable." I said, smiling. "I can't believe you own this place."

He shrugged. "More like it owns me. But yeah."

I shook my head in disbelief, glancing back out at the lake. "I came to the lake a hundred times as a kid and never knew this view existed."

"You were probably too busy causing trouble," he teased.

I raised an eyebrow. "Excuse me? I was an angel."

Sam gave me a pointed look, full of amusement. "You? An angel? Doubtful."

I grinned. "Fine, maybe a little trouble. But the fun kind."

"The best kind." He lifted his glass.

Celeste appeared and placed two plates on the table. "Two of Sam's favorite salad, with extra chiffon," she said with a smile. A bed of crisp greens, sweet candied pecans, grilled chicken, and fresh fruit glistened under a light strawberry vinaigrette. The side of sunset chiffon, creamy and citrusy, added the perfect touch.

I took a bite, savoring the sweetness of the dressing and the crunch of the pecans. "Wow, that's insanely good."

"It's damn good," he said with a satisfied grin.

Conversation flowed easily, laughter mixing with the gentle sounds of the restaurant. It felt natural, effortless. When his name was called from across the patio, he sighed and stood.

"Duty calls. Sorry to cut this short," he said. "I'll make it up to you. How about... dinner later?"

My eyes met his, and something unspoken passed between us, something full of promise. "Sure. Where?"

His lips tilted in a way that made my stomach flip. "Come by my place at 6 p.m." And he kissed my cheek softly.

As he walked away, I smiled, too. The anticipation moved through me like a warm afternoon breeze.

A few hours later, when I pulled up to Sam's place, I felt slightly ridiculous about how much I had overanalyzed this. I had changed outfits twice, added a touch of lipstick, and then proceeded to wipe most of it off. My stomach had been fluttering since I left the cabin, and now that I was here, I had to remind myself to breathe.

It was just dinner.

With Sam.

Nothing to stress over.

His house sat quietly along the water's edge—a stunning mix of rustic charm and clean lines. Weathered cedar shingles and natural stone gave it warmth, while copper roof accents caught the fading light like fire. Large windows glowed softly from inside. It looked strong. Timeless. Like the kind of place built to last.

The door opened before I could knock, and there he was. Standing in the entryway's soft glow, looking at me as though he'd been waiting all night for this moment. His eyes traced over me, slow and deliberate, as if he was committing something to memory.

"You look beautiful," he said, voice low, intent.

A flicker of heat rushed to my cheeks, unexpected and impossible to ignore. My breath caught for half a second.

He stepped forward and wrapped his arms around me. I felt so secure in his arms. He exhaled, his breath brushing my hair as he pulled back just enough to press a soft kiss to my cheek.

His lips grazed my ear, featherlight, sending a sharp ripple down my spine. Goosebumps lifted along my skin.

He smelled intoxicating, a mix of fresh ocean air, warm sandalwood, and a hint of musk that settled into something both clean and intensely masculine. It was familiar, yet completely unique to him. Undeniably Sam. And it made my head swim.

My pulse stuttered, and for a split second, I thought he might kiss me for real.

"Come on in," he said, stepping back.

I hesitated. "Oh... I thought I was picking you up."

His lips curled slightly, that same secretive smile from earlier. "I thought we'd stay in."

I blinked as I stepped inside, momentarily surprised by the sheer elegance of it all. Candles flickered on nearly every surface, casting a romantic glow over the sleek marble countertops and large windows that framed the lake like a painting.

The table in the dining room was set with fresh flowers and delicate plates, an arrangement you'd expect to see in a high-end banquet hall. Soft music played in the background.

And then, I smelled it. Something sweet and savory all at once. My stomach tightened, but not from hunger. I turned back to Sam, watching him with new eyes.

"You cooked?" My voice came out softer than I expected.

He leaned against the counter, watching me with quiet amusement. "Yep."

"For me?"

His expression didn't change, but there was something behind his eyes. "Yes, Emmy. For you."

I swallowed past the sudden tightness in my throat. "It's all so lovely. No one's ever done something like this for me before."

His gaze held mine for a long beat, something unspoken passing between us. Then he pushed off the counter, walking toward me, closing the space between us inch by inch. "Well," he said, voice low, "it's about time someone did."

I exhaled a quiet laugh, but my heart was pounding fast.

He gestured toward the table. "Sit. Let me take care of you tonight."

I did. And as I watched him move around the kitchen, his presence was fluid and assured, I realized something. This wasn't just dinner—this was something else entirely. Something real.

The meal was incredible. Not just the food, but the way Sam moved around the kitchen, completely at ease. He belonged there as much as he did on the water.

I took a bite of the glazed salmon, and the sweet, savory teriyaki melted across my tongue. I let out a quiet sound of appreciation. "Sam," I said, setting my fork down, "do you have any idea how ridiculously amazing you are?"

He smirked, reaching for his glass. "Really?"

"The marina, The Oasis, the way people respect you..." I gestured at the table between us. "And now this? You're intelligent and gorgeous—that much is obvious. But an amazing cook, too?"

His smirk deepened as he took a sip of wine, eyes gleaming. "You think I'm gorgeous?"

I exhaled a quiet laugh, shaking my head. "Seriously, I don't know one man who can cook. And I don't know *anyone* who can cook like this."

He leaned back, watching me with quiet amusement. "I live alone, and I love food. I figured if I was going to eat well, I had to learn how to make it myself."

"Well," I said, lifting my fork again, "you could open a restaurant."

He let out a low chuckle. "I enjoy cooking for the right company better."

The way he said it made my stomach dip. I focused on my plate, but I could feel his eyes on me, and the quiet weight of the moment pressing between us.

A slow, knowing smile spread across his face. "Come here," he said, standing and holding out his hand.

I hesitated, but something about the way he looked at me—expectant, playful, with just the right edge of challenge. Then, I pushed back my chair and took hold of it.

He led me into the kitchen and then rolled up his sleeves, exposing his muscular forearms. He pulled out bananas, butter, brown sugar, and a few other ingredients.

"We're making Bananas Foster."

"We?" I echoed, raising a brow.

He smirked. "You're my sous chef."

I crossed my arms, raising a brow. "Sounds like a lot of pressure."

He stepped closer, just enough that I could smell him. His voice fell lower. "I think you can handle it."

I watched him move with precision, as I sliced the bananas. Measuring and stirring, he worked with the practiced ease of someone who'd done this countless times.

"You're way too good at this," I said, leaning against the counter as I watched him melt the sugar and butter.

He shot me a grin. "Told you. I like to eat well." Then he grabbed a small butane torch from the drawer.

I raised a brow. "A torch? You own a torch?"

"You sound surprised."

I huffed a laugh. "I just… wasn't expecting pyrotechnics with my dessert."

He splashed some rum on the ingredients in the pan, then ignited it. A flame puffed up and then simmered down. "It's all about the finishing touch."

The brown sugar crystallized into an amber-colored, glassy layer. The scent of rum and butter filled the air, thick and sweet.

Sam was completely in his element, moving with confidence and joy—like this wasn't just about making a meal, but about creating something meant to be experienced.

I swallowed hard, suddenly aware of how close he was, and how natural this felt. Like we had done this before.

He glanced at me, eyes flickering with something unreadable. "You wanna try?"

I hesitated, then took the torch from him, feeling the warmth of his fingers as they brushed against mine. He stepped behind me, voice low and close to my ear.

"Go slow," he murmured.

Focusing on the caramelized surface before me, I pretended I wasn't acutely aware of every inch of space between us. He poured a little more rum.

I flicked the torch on, watching the flame dance over the sugar.

"That's it," Sam said, his voice lower than before.

I exhaled, turning the flame off, and stepped back. I glanced up at him, our eyes met, and for a moment, neither of us spoke.

Then he grinned. "You're a pro."

I laughed, the tension breaking just enough for me to breathe again. "What can I say? I'm multi-talented."

He plated the dessert, handed me a spoon, and we leaned against the counter, sharing bites straight from the dish. It was decadent, rich, unreal.

"Okay," I finally admitted. "This is the most romantic meal I've ever had."

Sam smirked, but there was something softer behind it. "Good. That was the goal."

I glanced at him, my heart kicking up a notch.

After we finished dessert, he led me into the living room, flipping on the turntable.

"Alright. I have an important question."

I settled onto the couch, curious. "Go on."

"What kind of music do you listen to?"

I lit up. "All kinds. I have a soft spot for country, classical, acoustic guitar, and I'm always in the mood for oldies. Pretty much anything that makes me want to dance or question the meaning of life."

Sam pressed a hand to his chest in mock relief. "Wow. That is a range. I respect it."

"Alright, your turn," I said, nudging his arm.

He flipped through his vinyl collection, scanning the titles. "I like a bit of everything. Classic rock brings me back to my college days. But country's really my thing."

I smirked. "Of course it is."

He shot me a look. "What does that mean?"

"Nothing, nothing," I said, all wide-eyed. "I just had a feeling."

He laughed and shook his head, pulling out a vinyl. "Alright, here's one of my favorites. I'm probably going to show my age here."

He placed the record on the turntable, the familiar crackle filling the room before the first few notes poured through the speakers. I recognized the song immediately but couldn't place the artist.

"I know this song," I said, snapping my fingers. "I remember hearing it as a kid. I've heard it a million times. Who sings it?"

Sam glanced at me like I had just deeply offended him. "Elton John."

I gasped. "Oh yeah! Of course."

His lips puckered like he was holding back a laugh. "Elton is, without a doubt, my all-time favorite artist. I've been to four of his concerts." He paused. "His music has been there for me through some tough times."

I smiled. "I love his music."

Sam leaned back, arms stretched over the back of the couch, looking satisfied. "Alright. You're redeemed."

I smirked, tilting my head to look at him. "Sam Sterling, you are full of surprises."

I held his gaze, my breath catching slightly.

There it was again. That shift. That unspoken something humming between us that made my skin prickle.

I swallowed, forcing myself to focus on the music.

He grinned, reaching for another vinyl.

And just like that, the night stretched on, and the air between us became charged.

I leaned my head back against the couch, letting the slow piano notes of a Journey song drift through the speakers. The night had settled around us, warm and unhurried, the kind of quiet that felt easy.

I glanced at Sam as he flipped through his vinyls, the candlelight catching along the sharp angles of his jaw. The thought slipped out before I could stop it.

"Are you seeing anyone?"

He stilled for just a second before setting the record sleeve aside. A slow, amused smile formed on his lips. "Would I be here with you if I were?"

I smirked. "I don't know. Some guys are like that."

He shook his head and sat forward. "I'm not that kind of guy. I think you know that."

I nodded, considering that. "So, no girlfriend? No secret fiancé waiting in the wings?"

Sam chuckled, shaking his head. "No fiancée, no girlfriend, no secret anything."

That surprised me. I studied him for a moment. "Really?"

His brows lifted. "Yeah? Why does that shock you?"

I gestured toward him. "Because you own half this town, you can cook like an iron chef, and you smell really good. And *look at you*."

His grin widened. "You think I smell good?"

"That's the part you focused on?"

"Well, I already knew about the other stuff."

I rolled my eyes, but I couldn't help smiling. "Seriously, though. You're the town's most eligible bachelor. No one has managed to lock you down?"

His expression shifted slightly, something unreadable flickering across his face. "I haven't met the right person." He paused. "And I'm not going to settle."

Sam draped his arm along the back of the couch, his fingertips grazing my shoulder in a slow, absentminded touch. He was quiet for a second, like he was turning something over in his mind. Then he exhaled and glanced at me.

"I've dated," he confessed. "A lot, actually. I've had plenty of relationships. I just couldn't see myself with any of them for the rest of my life. I always thought when I met the right person, I'd know."

He paused, looking at the turntable as the song changed. A slow and smooth song filled the room.

"As I got older, I still dated. I was open to it. But no one ever grabbed my attention. And I started realizing I enjoyed being alone more than I liked going on dates and being disappointed. If I were meant to find someone, it would happen. If not, that's okay, too."

He shrugged, his eyes finding mine again. "I've got a great life. A full one. I would rather be alone than with the wrong person." He took a deep breath. "I made peace with the idea that I might end up alone."

I swallowed, something settling in my chest at the honesty in his voice.

"And you were really okay with that?" I asked softly.

His lips tilted, just the faintest trace of a smile. "Yeah. I *was*."

There was something about the way he said it, something that made my stomach dip. Because the way he looked at me just then... it felt like, maybe he wasn't so sure anymore.

"What about you?" he asked, his voice quieter now.

I let out a short laugh, swirling the ice in my glass. "You know my situation. Not exactly a glowing romantic history."

He watched me, like he was seeing something deeper than I was saying. "Your future can be completely different."

His words settled over me.

I exhaled, shaking my head as I reached for another vinyl. "Alright, DJ. What's next?"

He let it go, flipping through his collection. The moment passed, but it didn't disappear. It settled somewhere deep, waiting.

The music shifted, a slow Kenny Loggins song filling the room, blending into the glow of the candles and the warmth of the moment. I sank deeper into the couch, my head resting against Sam's arm. Feeling the kind of ease I hadn't felt in years. Maybe ever.

"I love this song," I murmured, nodding toward the speakers.

"Me too." His voice was low, edged with something quieter now, something that made my stomach tighten.

I turned my head just enough to meet his eyes. He was already watching me, his expression unreadable, but his eyes—his beautiful, brown eyes—looked like they carried a thousand quiet promises. Like they'd been waiting for something. Or maybe just waiting for me.

The moment stretched, the space between us shrinking by the second. My breath felt tight in my chest, the air suddenly thicker.

His hand drifted to my jaw, his thumb tracing a slow line just below my ear before tucking hair behind it. His touch was deliberate, lingering—as if memorizing the moment.

"Emmy," he said so softly I barely heard it over the music.

My heart slammed against my ribs.

He leaned in, slow enough to give me the chance to stop him. But I didn't.

I couldn't.

Then his lips touched mine—and I felt it. For the first time in my life.

The fireworks.

The rush.

The kind of heart-stopping, all-consuming feeling I'd always been told didn't exist.

The kind of kiss that belonged in movies, or daydreams—except this was real. His lips moved against mine, so gently, igniting something inside me that I hadn't even realized was waiting to burn.

Butterflies? No. This was a free fall—helpless, headfirst.

He tasted like the sweet warmth of rum and something unmistakably him. His hand slipped to the side of my face, his thumb grazing my cheek as he pulled me closer. Like he had been waiting for this, and he wouldn't let me go now that he had me.

I melted into him, my fingers curling into the fabric of his shirt, anchoring myself to this moment.

When he finally pulled back—just enough to breathe—his forehead rested against mine, with his breath gentle against my lips.

I opened my eyes, searching his, needing to know.

I swallowed, my voice barely above a whisper. "So... are you like my boyfriend now?"

His lips curved into that slow, devastating smirk. The one that made my stomach drop.

"F.B.O.W.," he murmured.

I looked at him with confusion.

His smile deepened, brushing another slow, lingering kiss against my lips before whispering, "For better or worse."

I felt my heart stutter, my entire body warming from the inside out.

In that moment, I knew.

I wasn't just falling for him.

I was already his.

CHAPTER 15

Whispers in the Shadows

In the two weeks since that night with Sam, the days had stretched warm and full. I started taking slow walks along the lake in the early evenings, letting the quiet settle into my bones. Once, I even went for a swim—something I hadn't done in years. And one afternoon, on a whim, I walked down to the marina just to say hi. Sam was busy with customers, but his smile when he saw me made the whole trip worth it.

It was simple. Natural. Just enough to keep me floating.

But tonight was something else entirely.

I should've worn something with armor.

The flyer called it the *Summer Nights Street Social*—a simple name for a long-standing tradition. Food, music, lights, and gossip as thick as the barbecue smoke. I remembered coming here with Gram, weaving through booths with a lemonade in one hand and her homemade jam in the other. Back then, it felt like magic.

Tonight, it felt like a test.

Sam was supposed to come with me. But the A/C at The Oasis had gone out—right before the dinner rush—so he had to stay and handle it. He offered to close early. But I told him not to. Told him I needed to do this on my own.

I lied.

Mason jar lanterns hung from the awnings and trees, casting a soft glow across the sidewalk and storefronts. The aromas of baked goods and BBQ blended together. Kids ran from table to table, their laughing drowning out the chatter of adults. It used to feel joyful—a place where names mattered, where people waved from porches and remembered birthdays. I still saw glimpses of that tonight. But underneath the small talk and soft lights, something had shifted. I wasn't just Emerson Sinclair anymore. I was a story, reshaped by rumor.

Some people in the crowd turned to face me, their smiles fading as recognition took hold. Conversations seemed to falter, replaced by strained glances and quiet murmurs. It wasn't blatant, but the whispers carried a weight I couldn't ignore. Like fingers pointing in my direction, I felt them dissecting my every move as I approached the potluck table.

Not everyone turned away. A few familiar faces smiled as I passed—Mrs. Gibbs from the bakery gave me a warm nod, and Mr. Haber tipped his hat like he always used to. But the kindness couldn't drown out the tension.

I set down the cookies and brownies I'd made, my hands unsteady as I reached for a plate. I hadn't even noticed the tremor until that moment.

The voices around me swelled—not to me, but *about* me. I didn't need to listen to know what they were saying. Bethany had made sure of that.

Her social media campaign over the past week had been relentless. She'd painted me as an ungrateful wife who had walked out on her husband without a thought for anyone else. But she didn't stop there. Bethany never just told her version of the story, she always had to embellish it, twisting details into a story so damning that even people who'd known me for years were beginning to question my character.

I felt the weight of their eyes on my back as I filled my plate. Their judgment was palpable, settling over me like a suffocating blanket.

Bethany ensured they never really saw me—neither the girl they used to know nor the woman I was becoming. They saw the villain in her carefully curated tale. And tonight, I was surrounded by an audience all too eager to believe it. A couple of women I didn't know offered hesitant smiles, maybe unsure what to believe, or maybe they were just being polite. But most avoided eye contact.

And now, standing under the warm glow of the lights, the whispers around me cut deep, like splinters burrowing beneath my skin.

"Emerson!"

The voice cut through the chatter, high-pitched and deliberately loud. My stomach dropped. Bethany pushed through the crowd in a crimson dress that clung too tight, bleached hair, and a forced smile. Her jewelry jingled with every step.

"Little sister," her tone laced with mockery only I could catch. "You actually showed up. Color me impressed."

My fingers dug into the plate.

Her grin was all teeth, sharp and predatory, as she gestured toward the crowd with a flourish. "Everyone's been *dying* to see you. It's not every day someone walks out on their husband and then hides out here..." she lowered her voice so only I could hear, "with this *trailer trash*."

I wanted to punch those teeth out of her mouth.

The air shifted as heads turned, conversations quieting to murmurs. I let the silence stretch, let her feel the weight of my stare.

Then, I raised my chin. "I'm not hiding, Bethany. I'm moving on. But you? You're still right where I left you—drowning in everyone else's approval."

She laughed, the sound loud and artificial, meant to draw

attention. "Oh, is that what you're calling it? Moving on? How bold of you."

"I don't owe you an explanation."

Her smile twisted, sickly sweet. "No, you don't. But maybe you owe *them* one." She swept her hand dramatically toward the onlookers. "This is their town, after all. And your little drama is stirring up quite the scene."

"Drama?" My voice cracked, the lump in my throat betraying me. "Anyone who really knows me, knows I avoid drama like the plague. And they know exactly why you're here—to tear me down and steal the spotlight. You're the one desperate for attention, Bethany."

She leaned in, her voice oozing fake concern. "Really? Running away from your responsibilities and hiding from the truth... that's not drama?"

The words hit like knives—sharp, practiced, designed to gut me. Her tone. Her smirk. The gleam in her eyes. It was all perfectly rehearsed.

"Hiding from the truth?" I met her gaze. "You mean the part where I left a marriage that was killing me inside?"

The whispers grew louder, rippling through the crowd like an undercurrent as Bethany ramped up her spectacle.

"Poor Brad," she said with rehearsed sympathy. "He's been so honorable, putting up with her." She turned toward a nearby woman, pulling her into the conversation like a conspirator. "Did you see the video he posted? Just heartbreaking."

A cold wave of dread washed over me as Bethany reached into her purse, her nails clicking against the screen of her phone. "I think everyone should see it," she announced, angling her head to ensure maximum attention. "Brad's side of the story deserves to be heard, don't you think?"

"That's enough, Bethany," a woman near the potluck table said under her breath. I didn't recognize her, but the sharpness in her voice caught me off guard. A few heads turned. One man crossed his arms, unimpressed. It wasn't much, but it was something. Not everyone was buying the show.

The video started playing, and Brad's voice filled the pavilion, smooth and soaked with feigned sorrow. His words were deliberate, painting a picture of a blindsided, devoted husband abandoned by a wife who'd lost all sense of herself. He spoke about my "rash decisions" and "erratic behavior," each phrase twisting the narrative to make me seem evil.

I caught one older man shaking his head, muttering something about how "videos don't tell the whole story." A young mom nearby turned away, visibly uncomfortable. The gasps from the crowd rippled like aftershocks.

I felt their judgment like a physical force. I tried to hold it together, to appear composed.

"Bethany, stop," my voice breaking under the pressure of embarrassment.

But she didn't stop. She thrived on this. Her grin widened, triumph radiating from her as she turned the screen outward for everyone nearby to see. "Oh, Emerson, you've hid enough," she said, her voice dripping with insincere pity. "People want to know the truth."

I couldn't catch my breath. I barely registered the startled expressions or the growing murmurs behind me. My legs felt like they were moving on their own, shaky but determined to get me out of there.

The cool night air did nothing to ease my flushed skin. Bethany's words weighed on me like chains around my neck.

I kept going until I got to the lake. It should have been calming in its silence, but instead, it reflected the chaos within me.

My knees finally buckled, and I dropped onto the dock. I clutched myself with my arms. It felt like the only way to hold all the broken pieces together. I stared out at the water, its glassy surface catching the faint shimmer of the stars above. But the stars felt distant tonight, their beauty hollow and unreachable.

I pressed my palms against my eyes, willing the tears to stop, but they kept coming. I cried until I had none left. My breaths were short and uneven, filled with disbelief. I hadn't come here looking for a fight—I just wanted to remember what it felt like to belong somewhere.

Instead, I'd been ambushed. Shamed. Betrayed. Again.

I came here hoping to rebuild, to find some semblance of peace. But Bethany had tainted even this. I couldn't get her voice, her arrogant smile, or the heartless brutality of her performance out of my head.

The crowd's stares, Brad's lies, Bethany's poison. It was all too much. Maybe I was crazy to think that everything would work out for me. Maybe it was hopeless.

"Emmy."

Sam's voice startled me.

I looked up, and there he was at the dock's edge. The moonlight softened his face, but the concern in his eyes was clear.

With his boots thudding softly against the wood, he walked towards me. He said in a concerned voice, "I got there just as you left. I heard some of the gossip, and then came after you. What the hell happened? Are you okay?"

I wiped my cheeks. "I'm fine."

"You're not," lowering himself to sit beside me.

He didn't push, didn't say anything else. He just sat there patiently. I watched the water, restless under the wind, rippling and shifting like it couldn't find stillness either. The silence between us felt safe, like a pause in the chaos.

I told him what happened.

Finally, he spoke, anger simmering. "Bethany's a piece of shit. This is nothing new."

A bitter laugh slipped out before I could stop it. "She's been pulling crap like this my whole life."

Sam's jaw tightened. "I'll never understand how someone can

treat their own family like that." He stared out at the lake. "She's toxic. I don't care if she's your sister—she's a nightmare."

"She doesn't think of me as family," I said, barely above a whisper. "She never has. I was just... the person who ruined her life by being born."

His eyes flashed, hard and sure. "The truth's going to come out eventually. Not that it's anyone's business. But Bethany? She's desperate to keep the spotlight on you so no one looks too closely at her."

He shook his head. "You're above all of it. Her. Brad. Every lie they've told."

A tear fell down my face. Sam caught it and then wiped my cheek dry. And with calm eyes, he turned to face me. "I'm so sorry. You don't deserve any of this."

I shook my head, tears blurring my vision again. "Why am I being punished? All I want is to be happy. And to have peace. For some reason, the universe keeps reminding me that I don't deserve it."

"You can't really believe that," Sam said with a quiet conviction in his voice.

"You deserve peace," he continued, his tone unwavering. "You deserve happiness, love, and every damn thing you're fighting for. Don't let her, or anyone, make you doubt yourself."

His words hit me, stirring something I hadn't expected—hope.

I wanted to believe him. I wasn't sure how to.

He raked a hand through his hair. "I know how it feels to have the entire world feel like it's against you."

I hesitated. "Is that why you moved back here? To get away from it all?"

He nodded, his focus back on the water. "My parents and I moved here... for a change. We couldn't stay in the city. There were too many memories. And this place..." he exhaled slowly. "It gave me room to breathe."

I studied him, the lines of his face, etched with the kind of resilience that didn't need to be spoken to be felt. "It must have been the right move. You're still here."

"And now you are, too." He smiled.

He didn't kiss me. He didn't need to. Just sitting there, holding space for me while the rest of the world closed in, that felt more intimate than anything I'd ever known.

We sat there, quiet and close. His shoulder pressed gently against mine, a quiet reassurance. I leaned into it. We didn't say anything, but somehow, it felt like he was holding me together without even knowing how much I needed it.

The world was still spinning. People were still whispering. Bethany was still Bethany.

"If you want me to hunt Brad down and break his knees," Sam said casually, "you just let me know."

A breath caught in my throat—half a laugh, half a sob.

"Tempting," I murmured.

But for once... I didn't feel like running.

I just wanted to watch it all burn.

And maybe build something better from the ashes.

CHAPTER 16

Red Nails and Old Books

As I stepped into The Rusty Skillet, I was sure that the scent of fresh-brewed coffee and warm cinnamon rolls was the best way to start this morning. I didn't have to scan the diner—I already knew where to find her.

Sure enough, Ute was at our usual table near the window, two steaming mugs in front of her.

"Right on time," she said, pushing one toward me. "I'm already on my second cup."

I smirked, sliding into the chair across from her. "You've got a dangerous caffeine habit."

"Don't you start sounding like my doctor." She lifted her cup, eyes twinkling over the rim. "Besides, a life without coffee isn't a life worth living."

This was becoming a thing. Saturday morning coffee with Ute. It had started as a casual invite, but somehow, I found myself looking forward to it each week. The way we talked so easily, like I was someone meant to be here. Not just a woman piecing her life back together, but someone who mattered.

I wrapped my hands around the mug, inhaling deeply. "Alright, what's today's wisdom about life?"

Ute grinned. "Oh, I have plenty. But first, we're getting our nails done."

I nearly choked on my sip of coffee. "Wait—what?"

"You heard me." She leaned back, entirely too pleased with herself. "It will make you feel good. A little pampering never hurt anyone."

I sighed, knowing I'd lost this battle before it even started. "Fine. One manicure. But nothing crazy."

"And a pedicure. My treat." Ute grinned, victorious.

We lingered over coffee, our conversation meandering like old friends, before heading a few blocks over to a nearby strip mall.

The salon smelled like nail polish and acetone. "I never even knew this place existed," I admitted.

Ute was having the time of her life, browsing the wall of nail polish colors.

"Ohhh, look at this one," she said, pointing at a blinding neon pink. "I think it screams *Emerson*."

I made a face. "Absolutely not."

"Boring." She grabbed a rich, classic red instead. "Then at least do this one. You'll feel like a femme fatale."

I sighed, glancing at the shade I'd picked. A muted beige. Safe. Predictable.

Ute tsked. "I should've known."

"What?"

"That color is one step away from clear."

"I like simple," I defended.

She shook her head. "Simple is fine. Dull is unacceptable."

I stared at the bottle, then at her, then back again. And before I could talk myself out of it, I set the beige down and grabbed the red.

Ute beamed. "Now we're talking."

When we finally sank into the pedicure chairs, I let out a slow breath as the warm water swirled around my feet, the gentle hum of the massage chair working out knots in my back. I hadn't expected to enjoy this so much—to feel pampered, to let go for a little while. When the nail tech brushed over the arch of my foot, I jerked instinctively, a surprised laugh slipping out.

Ute's head snapped toward me, eyes wide. "You, too?"

I nodded, biting my lip as she burst into laughter. "Right there?" she asked, pointing at the exact spot.

"Like torture," I admitted, grinning.

She shook her head, still laughing. "Well, at least I'm in good company."

Instantly, something settled between us—a quiet kind of understanding, an easy warmth that felt a little like family.

As the nail tech worked, I hesitated before admitting, "I've actually... never done this with someone before."

Ute's eyes locked with mine.

I shook my head. "Not with my mom. Or sister."

She was quiet for a second before smiling softly. "Well, I had boys. Never had a daughter to do it with."

Something warm spread through my chest.

"Well," I said, swallowing past the unexpected emotion, "you've got me now."

Her smile deepened. "That I do."

The nail tech finished, and I held my hand up, studying the color. The deep red looked foreign on my fingers—bold, striking, completely different from the safe colors I always picked. But I liked it.

We wandered into Queen of Hearts Antiques, a cozy boutique of antique furniture, vintage collectibles, and forgotten treasures. The air carried the scent of aged paper and worn leather, rich with stories waiting to be rediscovered.

"I love this place. I used to come here with Gram all the time," I said, running my fingers over an old wooden desk, the kind that probably saw decades of handwritten letters and lovely stories.

"Best place in town to find something with a little soul," Ute agreed, weaving between shelves. "Oh—wait. Over here."

She led me to a section of vintage books, stacked haphazardly in a way that felt like an invitation to explore.

"Tell me your favorite book," she said. "We're finding you a copy."

"*Pride and Prejudice.*"

Her eyes sparkled. "A classic. Let's see..."

After a few minutes of rummaging, she gasped. "Oh, Emerson. Look!"

I turned—and there it was. A worn, leather-bound copy of *Pride and Prejudice.* The gold lettering was slightly faded, and the pages yellowed with time, but it was still beautiful.

I picked it up carefully, running my fingers over the spine. "It's perfect."

Ute smiled, pleased. "Every writer needs a good muse."

I clutched the book to my chest. Maybe it was silly, but it felt like a sign.

A part of me that I had forgotten—something I once loved, something that still mattered—was finding its way back to me.

We ended the day at Butter & Cream, the local ice cream shop that prided itself on *unique flavors.*

Ute ordered without hesitation. "One scoop of peach pie and one scoop of strawberry balsamic."

My nose scrunched. "You're braver than me."

"Oh, come on. Live a little." She pointed at the board. "Try something weird."

I scanned the options. Matcha. Ube. Vanilla with sweet sriracha sauce. Avocado.

I sighed dramatically. "Fine. Two scoops of lavender honey."

When I took my first bite, I paused. "Mmmm."

Ute grinned. "Good, isn't it?"

I took another bite, letting the floral, creamy sweetness melt on my tongue. "It's *so* good."

She lifted her cone. "To stepping out of our comfort zones."

I tapped my cone against hers.

We wandered through a few more shops, laughed more than I expected, and by the end of it, something in me felt a little lighter.

The afternoon slipped by as I sat in the shade of the porch, lost in a book and the hush of a slow day. The air was thick with summer heat, but the breeze off the lake made it bearable in the shadows. Birds called out lazily from the trees, and the pages rustled softly in my hands.

And then Sam pulled up, stepping out like he'd always belonged there. Faded T-shirt, cargo shorts, and that familiar half-smile.

"Hey, beautiful."

He didn't wait. He pulled me into his arms, his lips finding mine in a kiss that was warm and unhurried, like he already knew I'd had a good day but wanted to make it better.

I melted into him, wrapping my arms around his waist, and breathing him in.

"I met your mom for coffee," I said softly. "She kind of dragged me around town all day—manicures, antiques, weird ice cream."

His brow lifted, amused. "Is that why you look... happy?"

I paused, caught off guard by the word.

Happy?

I thought about the day we'd had.

And I realized—yeah. I was.

"I thought maybe we could watch that movie I told you about. *Murphy's Romance*," he said, his voice soft.

I smiled. "The one you said reminds you of us?"

He nodded. "It's an old favorite. Figured it was time you saw it."

"Deal," I whispered, stepping aside to let him in.

While I made popcorn, he got the fire going—adding a few logs and coaxing the flames to life until the room glowed warm with gold and orange. I brought the bowl over, settled beside him on the couch, and pulled a blanket across our legs.

He pressed a kiss to my temple, then pulled me into his side.

As he threaded his fingers through mine, he glanced down. "Wait—are your nails red?"

I smiled. "Yep."

"Dangerous choice. I like it," he said as he winked.

The movie started, soft and slow. Familiar. Honest.

About halfway through, I laid my head against his shoulder and whispered, "I think this might be my new favorite."

He didn't answer. He just pulled me closer.

The night felt still.

Safe.

Like love.

CHAPTER 17

The Price of Desperation

The bar at Sundancer was quieter than usual, the dinner crowd thinning out, leaving only a handful of patrons lingering over drinks. Warm air drifted through the open doors, thick with the scent of lake water and grilled peaches—one of the chef's latest summer obsessions. I sat at the counter, nursing a Diet Coke while waiting for Sam to finish for the day. The hum of conversation and the occasional clink of glasses filled the space.

Then, a voice broke through the quiet.

"Well, well. A Sinclair daughter at Sundancer. This just got interesting."

I turned, already bracing for some offhand comment about my family, but the moment my eyes landed on the man beside me, my stomach clenched.

He was older, maybe mid-forties, with thinning hair slicked back like he still believed he could pull it off. The type of man who thought cologne could cover up the smell of desperation. His dress shirt was tight across his gut, and his tie was loosened like he'd given up halfway through the day. But it was the gleam in his eyes—the slimy, suggestive smirk—that made my skin crawl.

He extended a hand, his grin widening. "Gunner Lynch." His

voice was all self-importance, as if the name should mean something to me.

I didn't take his hand.

"Your sister and I were close once. *Real close.* That practically makes us family, huh?" he mused, lifting his glass and taking a slow sip.

Ice slid through my veins. "Excuse me?"

"Don't be shy." He chuckled, shaking his head. "You Sinclair girls love to be the other woman, don't you?"

I stiffened. "The other what?"

Gunner smirked, swirling the ice in his glass like he thought it made him look suave instead of pathetic.

"The other woman, sweetheart." He took a slow sip, his eyes gleaming with something smug. "Bethany never had a problem keeping secrets."

He pulled out his phone and tapped the screen a few times before flipping it toward me.

My stomach dropped. A picture of him and Bethany. She was sitting on his lap, laughing, her lips just inches from his cheek. Then another. Her hand on his chest, his arm around her waist, their faces too close to be mistaken for just friends.

He raised his glass again, and that's when I saw it. A wedding ring—thick, gold, and shameless.

"We had a hell of a time," he said, his voice low and conceited. "Couple of years back. Kept it quiet, of course. You know how these things go."

"You're married," I said flatly, my voice barely above a whisper.

He grinned, unbothered. "With three kids."

Disgust pooled in my gut, thick and nauseating, like oil in water. "And you're bragging about it?"

He shrugged, leaning in just a little too close. "I mean, Bethany sure as hell didn't mind. So tell me, sweetheart, you looking for a little fun too?"

Rage ignited in my chest. "Go to hell."

I pushed off the stool and stormed out, my hands shaking as I yanked my phone from my pocket.

Me: I just ran into someone at the bar. Gunner Lynch. Want to guess what he told me?

Bethany: What the hell are you talking about?

Me: Meet me at the cabin. Now.

Bethany: You're being ridiculous.

Me: One more excuse and I tell everyone.

...

Bethany: Fine.

At that moment, I held the upper hand, and I intended to use it.

Bethany showed up in record time. Her stupid neon sedan buzzed up the driveway, spitting gravel as she slammed it into park. She left it running, stepped out, and marched toward the cabin, her expression set in a sneer.

I met her on the porch. She wasn't welcome inside.

"What the hell is your problem?" she snapped.

"I had an interesting conversation tonight with Gunner Lynch."

Her face paled. "Whatever you think you know, you don't."

"I know you had an affair," I said, voice cold. "With a married man. He has three kids, Bethany."

She laughed. "You're delusional."

"And guess what? He wasn't shy about sharing the details. He showed me pictures." I took a step closer, watching the panic flicker in her eyes. "You have spent years trying to ruin me, and now, I get to return the favor. Unless you want me to make a few phone calls, I suggest you start listening."

She hesitated, but only for a second before rolling her eyes. "You think you're so clever," she spat. "Holding this over my head. You've always been a nosy little brat."

"This isn't about me," I shot back. "This is about you. Sleeping with some sleazy married man with a family. So, tell me, Bethany, what's it worth for me to keep this between us?"

For a moment, she faltered. Her lips parted, but no sound came out. Then the mask slipped.

"Don't you *dare* tell anyone," she whispered, her voice no longer venomous. Now pleading.

I smiled. Let her sweat. I crossed my arms. "Well?"

She didn't argue. She knew I had her cornered.

Her chest rose and fell in short, sharp breaths. In a rare moment, Bethany had no words.

"No more lies. No more meddling. No more desperate attempts to ruin me. If I so much as hear your name in the same breath as mine, I'll make sure the whole town knows exactly who you are. Mom and Dad would be thrilled to hear you're sneaking around with a married man. I'm sure they'd love adding you—and slimy Gunner Lynch—to their spotless reputation."

A flicker of panic crossed her face, and for a second, she looked... small. Not the tyrant I had grown up fearing. Just a bitter, insecure woman whose own choices had finally caught up to her.

She swallowed hard. "Fine."

"Good."

She turned on her heel, yanking open her car door. "But don't think this makes you better than me, Emerson. You're still the same pathetic little shit you've always been."

I smiled. "And you're still a lying, cheating fraud."

Her glare seared into me as she slammed the door and peeled out, spraying gravel like sparks. She nearly clipped a truck pulling in at the end of the drive—Sam's. He slammed on the brakes as her car sped off into the dark.

He climbed out, a takeout bag from Sundancer in hand, eyes still locked on the road she'd vanished down.

"Why was Bethany here?" he asked, voice low and tight with fury. He stepped in close, one arm circling me even with the bag between us, and pressed a kiss to my lips—sweet, grounding.

I exhaled. "Some drunk guy hit on me at the bar while I was waiting for you. Total sleaze. I shut it down—but before I could walk away, he told me he'd had an affair with Bethany. A few years ago."

Sam's expression darkened. "Wait. Who?"

"Gunner Lynch."

A low curse slipped from Sam's lips. "Damn Gunner Lynch."

"You know him?"

Sam's jaw tightened, his grip flexing around the bag in his hand. "Yeah. Everyone does. He owns a nightclub over in Fox Hollow. Shady as hell. The kind of guy who would sell out his own mother for a quick buck—and screw anything with a pulse while he's at it."

I shook my head, the pieces clicking into place. "Bethany was the other woman. She was so desperate for a man—any man—to want her, that she latched onto the first one who gave her attention. Didn't even matter that he was married."

Sam dragged a hand through his hair, then leaned in and kissed my forehead. "Sounds about right. So, he hit on you?"

I nodded. "Yeah, that's why I left."

He took a deep breath, and then his jaw flexed. He squinted his eyes and said, "Guess I'm going to have to have a little talk with Gunnar."

He lifted the takeout. "You hungry?"

I poured us some tea. "You're really committed to keeping me fed, huh?"

"Someone has to," he said, brushing his thumb over my

cheek, and then smirked. "You'd run on caffeine and stubbornness otherwise."

As I unwrapped my sandwich, the last of the tension uncoiled from my body. No more Bethany. No more drama.

Just Sam, the scent of tomato soup, and the quiet hum of a night that finally belonged to me.

A week passed like a deep exhale.

The days were long, warm, and soft around the edges—like summer had finally settled in and decided to stay.

CHAPTER 18

Something to Talk About

I'd spent the morning sulking, pacing the cabin, replaying every awful moment from last week's run-in with Gunnar Lynch and that exchange with Bethany. The frustration had poured onto the page nearly every day since. I'd written more in a week than I had in months.

The cabin door swung open before I even registered the sound of Sam's truck in the driveway. He stood there, leaning against the frame—arms crossed, a cocky smirk tugging at his lips.

"Get in the truck," he said.

He stood there like a smug cowboy, all stubble and swagger. I couldn't stop the smile from blooming on my face. God help me.

I narrowed my eyes. "Excuse me?"

"Get. In. The. Truck." He dragged out the words like I was slow to process. "You need a break, and I'm kidnapping you for the day."

I folded my arms, arching a brow. "Is that so?"

"Yep. I won't take no for an answer."

I scoffed. "And what if I have plans?"

He glanced around, clearly unimpressed with the empty cabin and the fact that I was still in pajamas. "Yeah, those plans look riveting. Now, get dressed. Let's go."

I hesitated, but the truth was, I didn't have the energy to fight him. A distraction sounded nice. So, with an exaggerated sigh, I freshened up, got dressed, and followed him to the truck.

The drive started in silence. Sam tapped the steering wheel to the beat of some old country song playing softly on the radio, but he didn't say a word about where we were going. I finally caved.

"Are you going to tell me where we're going?"

"Nope."

"Not even a hint?"

"Nope. You'll have to wait and see."

I huffed, crossing my arms and glaring at the passing trees. The smirk on his face was infuriating.

Thirty minutes later, he pulled into a dirt parking lot next to a rundown dive bar with a flickering neon sign that just read *BAR*.

I shot him a look. "Seriously?"

"Trust me," he said, throwing the truck in park. "You're gonna love it."

Inside, the place smelled like stale beer and cheap cologne. A huge barrel of peanuts sat near the entrance, the floor littered with discarded shells. A pool table rested in the center with the felt worn down from years of play. A jukebox hummed in the corner, and a few locals sat over at the bar, nursing their drinks, and barely glancing our way.

Sam strolled up to the bar like he belonged there. "Two shots of tequila," he told the bartender, sliding cash across the counter.

"Have you been here before?" I asked, taking the shot he handed me.

"I might have hustled a few guys out of money here, back in the day." He grinned.

"Hustled?" I echoed, tilting my head. "Sam Sterling, are you telling me you're some kind of pool shark?"

"Wouldn't you like to know?" He smirked.

Sam sprinkled salt onto the back of his hand, took a slow lick, downed the shot, and bit into a lime wedge. He let out a low, satisfied growl. "Damn, that's good."

I mimicked his moves, but the second the tequila hit my throat, I yelped, sputtering through the burn.

As if on cue, a burly man in a red flannel shirt walked up, pool stick in hand. "Sterling. You still got it, or you turn soft?"

"Hey, Bear. How ya been?" Sam fist-bumped the guy and then cracked his knuckles. "Rack 'em up."

I leaned against the bar, watching in amusement as Sam played. He moved like a pro, lining up shots with effortless precision, sinking ball after ball without hesitation.

After he won the third game in a row, he turned to me, winking. "Wanna give it a shot?"

"Absolutely not," I said without hesitation.

"Scared?"

"I'm just saving you the embarrassment of watching me miss every single shot."

"Come on, Emmy." He held the cue out to me. "I'll even help you."

I sighed dramatically, grabbing the stick. Sam came up behind me, his chest pressing against my back as he guided my hands. His breath brushed my ear. "Relax. Let me show you."

I took a deep breath, trying to focus on the game and not how his body felt against mine. But as soon as I took the shot, I completely missed.

"Wow," I muttered. "That was impressive."

Sam chuckled, shaking his head. "Alright, maybe pool isn't your calling. I'll have to teach you sometime."

Before I could protest, the bar erupted into cheers. I turned just in time to see the karaoke machine light up.

Sam grinned. "You should sing."

"Absolutely not."

"Come on," he coaxed. "I dare you."

I narrowed my eyes. "I don't do dares."

"Fine," he said easily. "Then I double dare you."

I exhaled slowly. He was enjoying this way too much. "Fine. But if I do this, you have to do something I say later."

"Deal."

I stomped to the stage and grabbed the microphone. As the opening chords of "Something to Talk About" played, I shot Sam a glare, and then started singing. I was nervous as hell, and I'm sure it sounded that way.

But halfway through, I stopped caring. I was laughing, the crowd was clapping, and Sam was grinning like he had just won something.

When I finished, I plopped down in the booth, breathless. "Never again."

"That was amazing," he said, grinning ear to ear.

We left the bar and hit the road again, winding through tall pines as the mountains shifted in and out of view. Everything felt suspended in that golden, late-afternoon hush that only exists on back roads. We pulled up to a rustic lodge perched over a lake, like something from an old country postcard. The sign read *Ishnala*.

"What is this place?" I asked.

He smiled. "The best supper club in the state."

I stepped out, taking in the rustic, log-cabin exterior, and the enormous trees standing like sentinels around it. The smell of pine mixed with something rich and buttery drifting from inside.

Sam walked ahead, opening the heavy wooden door, and holding it for me. "Come on, city girl. Time for a real meal."

Inside, the place was cozy and lodge-like, with timbered walls and thick wooden beams. The murmur of conversation layered over soft music. The windows overlooked the lake, and you could see the moon's reflection mirrored by the water.

Sam walked toward the bar, nodding at the bartender like they were old friends.

"You've been here, too?" I asked.

He rested an elbow on the counter, fingers absently tapping against the wood. "Came here all the time as a kid. My parents brought us up to these mountains every summer." His voice softened, a flicker of something in his eyes. "My dad used to let me order a steak the size of my head, even when my mom said I wouldn't finish it."

I smiled, imagining a younger version of him, bright-eyed and full of reckless confidence. "And did you?"

"No." He smiled. "But he never let me feel bad about it."

A waitress showed us to a table near the window, and even in the dim light, the view was stunning. The menu was old-school. Cocktails before dinner, relish trays, and steaks that came with baked potatoes the size of softballs.

Sam skimmed the options. "You trust me?"

I narrowed my eyes. "Uh oh. Why?"

"Because I'm ordering for you."

I huffed. "Sam—"

His eyes gleamed. "Trust me."

I sighed, but some part of me liked this.

Liked the way he took charge without steamrolling me.

How he seemed to know exactly what I needed before I did.

I liked how he opened my mind to things the old me would have stubbornly refused to try.

And I liked how excited he was to share the things he loved with me.

When the food arrived, I took one look at the plate and immediately regretted that trust.

"Oh no." I stared at the appetizer in front of me. "What is that?"

Sam bit back a grin. "Escargot. Snails."

I shot him a stink face.

"They're cooked in butter and garlic." He speared one with his fork, and lifted it toward me.

"Please just try it." His eyes twinkled. "They're gourmet."

"I don't know."

"You said that about karaoke," he reminded me. "And then you sang Bonnie Raitt like you were headlining the Grand Ole Opry."

I crossed my arms. "That was different."

My stomach twisted. Not in disgust. In defiance. In the realization that I'd never let myself be challenged like this before.

He dipped the fork closer. "One bite. Here, put it on a piece of sourdough."

I clenched my jaw.

He leaned in, voice dropping to a near-whisper. "Prove me wrong."

My lips parted at the challenge, my heartbeat kicking up for reasons that had nothing to do with snails. I held his gaze, stubborn, then—before I could talk myself out of it—snatched the fork and popped the damn thing into my mouth.

Salty. Buttery. Not at all slimy.

I chewed slowly, narrowing my eyes at him.

"Well?" He was full-on smirking now.

I swallowed. "It's ... not that bad."

His smirk widened. "See? It didn't kill you."

"Don't get cocky."

"Too late."

Dinner stretched on, filled with easy conversation, laughter, and stories about his childhood—he and his brother daring each other to do crazy things, his dad teaching them how to fish, his mom always warning them to be careful, even when they were already knee-deep in adventure. It was the kind of night I hadn't had in... well, ever. Simple, real, fun.

By the time we left, my stomach was full, and my cheeks ached from smiling so much. The air was warm and still, the stars stretching endlessly above us. I wrapped my arms around myself, inhaling deeply. "That was... wonderful."

He grinned, unlocking the truck. "I'm glad."

I climbed in, sinking into the seat, feeling looser and more relaxed than I had in forever. But as we drove, something flickered in Sam's expression. He glanced at a sign on the side of the road. Before I knew what was happening, he hit the blinker and turned down a narrow road. It curved hard, the trees crowding in like a dare.

I jolted forward. "Uh, what are you doing?"

He smirked. "Taking a detour."

"A detour to what?"

He nodded ahead. I followed his eyes, then immediately stiffened. That's when I saw the sign...

No.

No way.

A massive sign loomed ahead, lit by the glow of spotlights.

MOUNTAIN ZIP LINE ADVENTURES
Open Until Midnight

I turned to him, horrified. "Sam."

He was already parking. "It'll be fun, I promise."

I snapped at him. "I just ate snails. That was my *out of my comfort zone* quota for the night."

He leaned closer, grin downright devious. "One ride."

"No."

"Just one."

"Not happening."

He reached for his door handle. "Guess I'll have to carry you, then."

My mouth dropped. "You wouldn't dare."

His eyes glinted. "Try me."

My pulse jumped, but I yanked off my seatbelt and shoved the door open before he could make good on that threat. I stepped onto the gravel, heart hammering. "You're an actual menace."

With a victorious grin, he shut his door, and we started walking. "I've been called worse."

I huffed. "One ride."

His gaze flickered over me, amused. "One."

We signed the waivers and got suited up with helmets and harnesses. Sam looked completely at ease. I, on the other hand, was regretting this.

I inhaled, glancing up at the towering wooden platforms above. This was fine. I was fine.

I was going to die.

Sam nudged me forward. "Let's go."

Now, standing at the edge of the platform, I gripped the harness straps, and stared out at the expanse below. The wind rushed through the trees, making the whole world feel both impossibly vast and terrifyingly small.

"This is insane," I muttered.

Sam chuckled beside me. "You've got a helmet on. You're strapped in. You are perfectly safe."

"That's what they all say before the harness snaps, and someone ends up on the news."

His smirk deepened. "You're stalling."

I was. I absolutely was.

The guide gave me an encouraging nod, one hand on my back. "Ready?"

No.

Before I could second-guess myself, I bent my knees and pushed off.

The world dropped away, the ground a blur beneath me. My stomach lurched, then—

Weightlessness.

The air rushed past, warm against my skin, sharp and clean with pine and mountain air. I stretched my arms out instinctively, the zip-line whistling as I soared. The city, the past, the weight of everything I'd been carrying. None of it existed in this moment.

I was flying.

A laugh burst out of me, wild and unrestrained. Before I

knew it, I was cheering into the night air, adrenaline surging through me like fire.

Too soon, the end platform came into view. My feet hit the padded landing, my legs wobbly but exhilarated.

Sam was already there, grinning as he unhooked his harness.

"That," I gasped, chest rising and falling, "was incredible."

Before I could think, or stop myself, I launched straight into his arms.

He caught me easily, arms wrapping around me, lifting me off my feet with a low, startled laugh.

"See? You're fine," he murmured against my hair, his voice rough and proud.

I tightened my hold around his neck. "Thank you. For this. For pushing me. For making me feel alive."

I finally let go, breathless, my heart still racing. Sam set me back on my feet, but his hands lingered at my waist, steadying me. I met his gaze, still high on adrenaline, on him, on everything.

He grinned, brushing a damp strand of hair from my face. "Told you it'd be worth it."

I let out a shaky laugh, nodding. "You were right."

"Say that again?"

I rolled my eyes, shoving at his chest. "Don't push your luck."

Still laughing, he took my hand and led me back toward the truck.

The truck hummed softly beneath us as Sam drove down the winding backroads, the headlights cutting through the dark. The windows were cracked just enough to cool the lingering warmth from the dive bar's neon haze, and the heat of laughter still caught in my chest. My boots were kicked up on the dash, and Sam's hand rested lazily on my knee, his thumb tracing random shapes against my thigh.

I was still buzzing from the night. The tequila-slick pool games, my begrudging but triumphant karaoke debut, the way

Sam had nearly fallen out of his chair laughing when I almost gagged at the taste of escargot.

"Okay," I said, tilting my head to look at him. "Tell me you planned all that."

He smirked. "Planned what?"

"The most ridiculous, chaotic, absolutely perfect day."

He glanced over, the glow of the dashboard lights catching in his eyes. "Kidnapping you required some strategy, but the rest? That was just luck."

I let out a scoff, nudging his thigh with my knee. "You knew that bar. You knew they'd have karaoke. And don't even get me started on how suspiciously good you were at pool."

Sam laughed, running a hand through his hair. "Alright, maybe I had a few things in mind. But I didn't think you'd actually get up and sing."

I groaned, covering my face. "Don't remind me."

"Oh no, I will absolutely remind you. That was the highlight of my night. You, up there, looking like you were ready to set the whole bar on fire just to escape."

I peeked at him between my fingers. "It was humiliating."

"It was hot as hell," he corrected, squeezing my knee before letting go. "And don't think I didn't notice that you started having fun halfway through."

I sighed, dropping my hands into my lap. "I hate that you're right."

"I'm always right."

"No comment."

The cabin door clicked shut behind us, cutting off the rest of the world. My pulse was still racing—part adrenaline, part Sam.

He reached for me without hesitation, his hands finding my waist, his mouth finding mine. It was instant. Intense. Heat coiled between us, fast and consuming, and every kiss made it more intense.

By the time we stumbled into the bedroom, I was breathless, shaking, caught in the rush of him. His touch was everywhere—deliberate, worshipful, searing.

I felt how much he wanted me in the way his hands lingered, in the quiet hitch of his breath when I whispered his name. But he didn't take.

Instead, he slowed. His lips softened. His arms pulled me in—not to claim, but to hold. His forehead pressed to mine, his voice wrecked.

I smiled against his skin, pressing my hips against his, making sure he felt just how much I wanted this. "What are you waiting for?"

He pulled back just enough to look at me, his eyes dark, hungry, but so damn controlled.

"Emmy..." He took my hand, guiding it between us. "You have no idea how much I want to."

I gasped, feeling exactly how much he wanted me. *Oh wow.*

My heart pounded so hard it hurt.

"See?" His voice was deep, rough, ruined. "I *want* you. But not just for tonight. I want to prove I'm not like the rest."

I stared up at him, my breath catching, my entire body burning.

This man. This incredible man.

I had never felt more important and desired in my life.

And yet, he still wanted me to know that I mattered more than the moment.

A lump rose in my throat.

I lifted a hand, tracing my fingers along his arm. "You are perfect. Do you know that?"

"You've got those rose-colored glasses on again. Seeing me like I'm something more than I am." His smirk deepened. "Not that I'm complaining." He winked.

I pulled him down, our long kiss unraveling every emotion I didn't know how to voice.

And then he pulled me against him, wrapped his arms around me, tangled our legs together, his hand resting over my heart.

As my breathing slowed, my body melted into his warmth. The tension of the day unraveled, dissolving into the quiet rhythm of his heartbeat beneath my cheek.

The laughter, the rush, the thrill, the heat—settled deep in my bones, leaving only this. Only him.

Sam's fingers drew slow circles on my back, his voice a quiet murmur against my hair. "You flew tonight."

A little smile tugged at my lips. "I did, didn't I?"

He hummed in agreement and kissed my forehead. "I'm proud of you."

I moved in closer, sighing against his skin. "Thank you for today."

He just held me tighter.

"Don't let go."

I wasn't even sure if I said it out loud or just thought it, but the second it left my lips, I felt his grip strengthen.

"I'm right here." His voice low and rough. He murmured it into my hair, his fingers rested on my back, anchoring me to him like a vow.

A heavy sigh left my chest as my fingers curled into his side, my body folding into his like it had always been meant to fit. His heartbeat, the weight of him, the effortless certainty that I was safe with him.

I let myself sink into it.

Into him.

And he didn't let go.

He scratched my back with such tenderness that—without even meaning to—I fell asleep in his arms.

CHAPTER 19

The Cost of Pride

August settled in like a deep breath—long, golden days and nights that stayed warm enough to leave the windows open.

A week or two passed quietly. The kind of quiet that feels full, not empty. We found a rhythm without meaning to—slow mornings, shared meals, and touches that lingered a little longer each day. No big conversations. Just presence. Just us.

That morning, sunlight spilled across the kitchen floor as Sam stood by the door, boots half-laced and coffee in hand.

"I'll be down at the marina most of the day," he said, reaching for his keys.

I leaned against the counter, still in his T-shirt, nodding. "Don't forget sunscreen this time."

"Come find me later." He kissed the top of my head before heading out to the marina.

I took my coffee outside, sat on the porch, and watched the breeze tug at the edge of the woods. My heart felt peaceful. For once, it felt like things were clicking into place.

And then I went back inside and opened the mail. A few credit card offers. A catalog. One envelope I didn't recognize. Right then, my phone buzzed.

Jordan.

And that's when everything cracked.

"Emerson, it's Jordan," she said, her tone clipped but not unkind. "I wanted to give you a heads-up."

My stomach turned. "A heads-up?"

"There's a court-ordered hold on all marital assets. Bank accounts, investments, anything acquired during the marriage is frozen until we get a finalized settlement." Jordan explained.

My stomach dropped. "A *hold*? Why?"

"I know it's upsetting, but this kind of freeze is standard. The court does it to protect both parties and prevent any assets from being moved, hidden, or spent before things are finalized. As soon as the divorce is complete, the funds will be released and fully accessible to you."

"Frozen? Jordan, I have no other money," I said, nervously.

A pause. Then, gently, "Well, we can file a temporary support order. It's designed for exactly this—spousal support, funds for basic living expenses during a pending divorce, that type of thing."

I pressed my fingers to my eyes. "No."

"Emerson, I know how you feel, but it's not a weakness. It's a legal mechanism."

I straightened, my voice firmer than I felt. "I want the *only* next thing filed to be the final divorce documents. I signed everything already. Brad's had them for two months. What are we waiting for?"

Jordan's sigh came through the line like static. "He's dragging his feet. I don't know why. But I'll find out."

I swallowed hard. "So, what do I do in the meantime? I have $70. No credit cards. No help."

"I can file the support motion today."

"No," I said again, sharper this time. "I'm not giving anyone that satisfaction. I don't need to file a legal document and tell the world that I can't take care of myself. I'll figure it out... on my own."

Jordan hesitated. "Okay. But don't wait too long. You don't have to prove anything to anyone."

But I did. Not to Brad. Not to my parents. To myself.

Once the divorce was final, I'd have access to my account again —but I couldn't afford to wait. I had bills. I needed gas, groceries, basic things to survive.

Most people could call their parents in a moment like this. Mine already knew the situation. My father was an attorney, and they were close to Brad. I had no doubt they'd discussed every detail over their precious gin and tonics.

If they wanted to help, they would have.

They hadn't.

And I wasn't going to ask.

I hung up and opened my banking app.

Access denied. A message popped up: Account restricted.

My stomach twisted like it had been sucker-punched from the inside.

I called the bank. After verifying my information, the woman on the other end said, "Yes, ma'am. Your accounts were frozen this morning per a court order. I'd speak to your lawyer for more information."

That was it.

"What the hell am I supposed to do?" I screamed, slamming both fists onto the table. The force rattled the legs and echoed into the silence around me.

An hour later, I was at the bank, sitting across from a loan officer who was already shaking his head before I finished speaking.

"I'm sorry, Ms. Sinclair," he said. "I can't approve a loan without income."

I could feel the heat rising in my cheeks as he shut the folder. Even the pen on his desk looked more dignified than me.

A sharp pulse flickered behind my right eye, slow and building. I pressed my tongue hard against my molar, and swallowed down the frustration that was rising in my throat. "I own my cabin outright."

His expression didn't change. "Unfortunately, with no income—"

I pushed back my chair before he could finish. "Thank you for your time."

The words stung as I walked out. Humiliation burned in my throat, in my chest, under my skin. I caught my reflection in the glass doors—hollow eyes, tight lips, my shoulders curled inward like I was bracing for another blow. I used to walk into places like this with confidence. Now, I just looked small.

Fine. If no one was going to help me, I'd help myself.

I needed a job.

Now.

I drove straight to the marina and stood outside, my stomach in knots. I hated this. Hated needing something from someone. Hated asking. Being at the mercy of a yes or a no. But I didn't have time for pride. I didn't have time for applications, interviews, or waiting on polite rejections. My degree meant nothing right now, and neither did my experience as a writer. I needed money— fast.

I inhaled deeply and stepped inside.

The boat rental office smelled faintly of motor oil. The floor was sun-bleached and smooth like driftwood, the walls lined with photographs of families posing on boats and fishermen holding up their catches.

Behind the counter, Marley was typing. Her short brown hair was tucked behind her ears, and her dark-rimmed glasses perched on her nose. She didn't look up until I stopped in front of her.

"Can I help you?" she asked, her voice clipped, the tone of someone with a lot to do and not enough time.

"Are you hiring?" I asked, trying to keep the nerves from my voice.

That got her attention. She paused, leaned back in her chair, and tilted her head slightly. "You looking for work?"

I nodded.

She sighed, shifting a stack of papers aside. "Wish I could help, but we're full up. Deckhands are covered. Office is covered. Sorry."

The rejection landed like a blow to the gut.

I gave a small nod and forced my voice to stay even. "Okay. Thanks anyway."

I turned to leave, the heat of humiliation creeping up my neck like fire under my skin.

"Emmy?"

I froze.

Sam.

His voice came from behind me, thick with confusion. I forced myself to turn, to look back at him like I wasn't unraveling inside.

"Hey! What are you doing here?" he asked, stepping out of the back office.

I lifted my chin, bracing myself. "Looking for a job."

His eyes flickered, taking me in, his brows pulling together. "Here?"

"Just... hit a snag," I said, too casually. "Needed something fast."

I folded my arms—an instinctive defense against the way he was looking at me. Too closely. Like he was seeing something I didn't want him to.

"What? It's honest work."

Something shifted in his expression. A realization. A piece falling into place.

"You don't have to do this," he said quietly.

I stiffened. "Yes, Sam, I do."

The words cut through the space between us.

His eyes moved from me to Marley. "I can make room."

"No." My voice came out too sharp, but I couldn't let him do that. I couldn't let him fix it. "I don't need your charity."

Sam stilled. His eyes locked on mine.

"It's not charity," he said carefully. "It's a job."

"No, Sam. It's you making space for me where there isn't any." I swallowed hard. "I appreciate it, but I have to do this on my own."

Something unreadable passed across his face. He wanted to help—to take the weight off my shoulders. I could see it. But I didn't give him the chance.

I turned and walked out. The second the door shut behind me, I wanted to scream. Just once. Just loud enough to shake something loose.

I wasn't going home—not without a job.

I drove into town and went door to door. The antique store had just hired someone. The library only had volunteer positions. The hardware store wasn't hiring. Each rejection landed like a shove. Another reminder that I was not the person I used to be.

I stepped into The Rusty Skillet. My feet ached, my pride was in tatters, and I had exactly zero options left.

It smelled like freshly brewed coffee and sizzling eggs. Everyone knew everyone here, and that realization made me hesitate. I used to come here for Sunday breakfasts with Gram. Lately, for coffee with Ute. I used to slide into a booth and sip from a mug while someone else refilled it. I never thought about the girl behind the counter—the one with sore feet and a fake smile. But now? Now I was about to be her.

This was a mistake.

But then I saw the HELP WANTED sign taped to the register, and pride didn't matter anymore.

I forced myself forward. "Are you still hiring?"

The woman behind the counter, Dixie, barely looked up. She looked to be in her sixties, and her silver hair was clipped up in a twist that matched her no-nonsense stare.

"You got experience?"

"Yes," I said. A lie.

"I can learn fast." Not a lie.

She exhaled through her nose, still unimpressed. "Can you start tomorrow?"

I blinked. "You don't want a resume or anything?"

Dixie finally looked up. Her eyes were sharp and assessing. "Do you want the job or not?"

I swallowed. "Yes."

"Good. Wear black. Be here at 6 a.m."

And just like that, I had a job—and no idea what I had just gotten myself into.

By 10 a.m. the next morning, I had spilled an entire pot of coffee, broken two glasses, and been yelled at by Dixie. Twice. By noon, people started recognizing me.

"Wait," a woman at table four whispered. "That's Emerson Sinclair."

I felt the shift in the air. The whispers. The looks. I kept my head down and kept moving. By 1 p.m., I was ready to quit.

My back ached. My hair stuck to my neck. My apron was stained. I had never felt smaller. But then I looked at the tip jar. $26. And that was $26 more than I had this morning.

So I stayed. Because I had no other choice.

By the time my shift ended, my body ached in places I didn't know could ache—my arms from carrying trays, my lower back from standing too long, my fingers sore from scrubbing sticky syrup and ketchup from tables.

I stepped outside into the night air, exhaustion pressing down on me like a weight. The town was quiet, streetlights casting long shadows across the pavement. My car sat in the back lot, the only one left. I climbed in, gripping the wheel, staring out at nothing.

I had made it through the first day. Barely. It had been a disaster. I dropped a plate of food, mixed up several orders, and nearly tripped over my own feet more times than I could count. I wasn't built for this. But I needed the money. So tomorrow, I'd do it all over again.

I turned the key. The engine sputtered to life.

Tomorrow.

The second I pulled into the driveway, I knew I wasn't alone. The porch light was on. A soft glow spilled from the windows, cutting through the darkness.

Sam.

I let out a long breath before stepping out of the car. My clothes smelled like coffee and grease. Every inch of me was drained.

I climbed the steps, pushed open the door—and there he was.

Sam stood in the kitchen, stirring something on the stove. The cabin smelled warm, and rich—like garlic, butter, something slow-cooked and hearty. A quiet hum of music played from his phone on the counter.

He glanced up the second I walked in, his eyes sweeping over me. He said, "Hi, beautiful." He didn't ask how my day was. He didn't need to.

I dropped my bag on the table, exhaling sharply. "I don't deserve you."

"Yes you do." He turned off the burner, wiping his hands on a towel. "Sit."

I should have argued. Should have insisted I was fine. But my body had other plans. I sank into the chair, my limbs heavy, the tension in my shoulders slowly unwinding.

A moment later, Sam set a plate in front of me. Pasta, steamed vegetables, and fresh bread. Real food. Comfort.

I picked up the fork and took a bite, the warmth spreading through me. I hadn't realized how empty I felt until now.

Sam pulled out the chair across from me, watching, waiting.

After a few bites, I finally met his eyes. "I was awful," I admitted. "I spilled an entire tray of drinks. Forgot orders. Messed up so many things. My feet hurt."

His voice softened. "I hate that you're going through this."

I swallowed against the tightness in my throat. "Me too."

He said it carefully, like he already knew I'd refuse. "I know you know this, but I want to help. Job, money, *anything*. I know you're too proud to let me—but just say the word, I'm happy to."

I swallowed hard, my fingers curling into the hem of my shirt —grateful, but unwilling to take it.

For a moment, neither of us spoke. The cabin was quiet except for the slow ticking of the old clock, the low hum of music.

Then Sam stood. "Come on."

I frowned. "What?"

I hesitated, but he was already pulling me to my feet. My legs protested, my muscles stiff, but I let him guide me toward the bathroom.

The tub was full. Warm, bubbly water, scented with something light and clean. Candles flickered on the counter. A fresh towel was folded on the edge.

I pressed a hand to my chest, I was overwhelmed with emotion. "Sam..."

He just shrugged. "Just relax."

I turned to him, my eyes burning. "You're making it really hard not to fall in love with you, you know that?"

Something flickered in his expression, something deep. He lifted a hand, brushing his fingers lightly over my cheek.

"Good," he murmured. "Because I'm already there."

I sucked in a breath, my chest tightening, my exhaustion momentarily forgotten.

He gave me a small, crooked smile, then kissed my forehead. "Now, get in before the water gets cold."

I did. And for the first time all day, I relaxed. And then, I slept hard, exhaustion sinking deep into my bones.

When morning came, I felt a little less like I'd been run over. It was time to grind through another day.

The morning rush had been steady but manageable. I was starting to get the hang of things—or at least, I hadn't dropped anything. That felt like progress.

Until I looked up and saw her.

Bethany.

She walked through the door like she owned the place. She strutted up to the counter, eyes gleaming with amusement, then gave me a slow, exaggerated once-over before smirking.

"So it *is* true," she said, voice syrupy. "I heard you joined the working class, but I didn't think you'd go for something quite so... degrading. Do you scrub the toilets, too?" She laughed, delighted with herself.

Not her. Not today.

Her eyes sparkled with the kind of satisfaction that came from kicking someone already down. She took her time, dragging out the moment. "I think I'll get an oat milk latte. Low-fat. With extra caramel and extra whipped cream. To go."

I didn't blink. I grabbed a styrofoam cup and filled it. "One black coffee. Cream's on the counter."

Her smirk faltered. "That's not what I—"

I leaned in, just enough for only her to hear. "I can spit in it if you'd like extra flavor."

Her eyes widened, teeth gritting together, lipstick smudged in the corners of her mouth. I smiled sweetly. "No? Just the coffee, then?"

Bethany stepped closer. "You know, since you're desperate for cash, I could hire you to sort my lingerie drawer. You're good at sifting through messes, right?"

I lifted my chin, matching her gaze. "And I know you're super insecure. But I don't go around pointing it out in public."

Her smirk cracked—just for a second. She steadied herself quickly, flipping her hair over her shoulder. "I'm just glad I got to come see this for myself. This is exactly how I always thought you'd end up."

I leaned in again, lowering my voice. "Careful, Bethany. It would be a shame if the whole town found out what happened with Gunnar Lynch."

I turned back to the register. "That'll be $2.50."

She didn't move to pay. Instead, she slowly reached into her purse and pulled out a crisp $100 bill. With a flourish, she set it down on the counter like a declaration.

The room felt smaller.

I could feel people watching, waiting to see how I'd react. The humiliation burned in my stomach. I stared at the bill, my fingers twitching, aching to throw it back in her face. But I didn't.

I counted out her change, and set it on the counter. She didn't take it. Just looked at it like it was beneath her. Then, with a satisfied hum, she turned and walked away.

But just before she reached the door, she hesitated. Barely a flicker of doubt. Something hollow passed behind her eyes, a second of vulnerability she quickly masked with another toss of her hair before walking out like it never happened.

The money sat there.

I didn't touch it.

My fingers slowly unclenched from the rag in my hands. My heart was still pounding, but the diner kept moving around me, full of people who didn't care about what had just happened. I turned back to the register, punched in the next order, and called it out. My voice didn't shake. My hands didn't tremble.

Because no matter what, I had to keep going.

That's when I saw him.

Sam.

He stood near a back booth, half in shadow, arms crossed. He'd seen it all—every word, every fake smile, every insult I'd swallowed.

Damn it.

I hadn't even noticed him come in. His eyes flicked from the bills on the counter to my face. He didn't say anything at first. Didn't move. He just stood there, with his hands in his pockets, and let the silence hang heavy in the air.

Then he spoke. "Do you want me to throw that in the trash, or do you want the honor?"

I let out a dry laugh. "Tempting."

He didn't smile.

I hated that he'd seen it—that he knew exactly what I was feeling. I turned my attention back to the counter, scrubbing at an imaginary stain. "I don't need to hear it from you too."

"Hear what?"

"That this is beneath me."

His expression changed instantly. "Don't put words in my mouth, Emmy." His voice was low, firm. "I don't think this is beneath you. I think it's bullshit that you have to do it in the first place."

I kept wiping the counter, letting the motion distract me. "It's just a job, Sam."

"It's survival," he said quietly.

The words hit harder than I expected.

He exhaled, dragging a hand through his hair. "I hate this," he muttered. "I hate watching you go through this. I hate that they get to walk in here and act like they still have power over you."

Something inside me tensed. For a second, I almost let myself unravel. Almost.

He let out a slow breath, tapped his finger once against the counter, and turned to leave. But just before he reached the door, he stopped.

"Hey," he said.

My pulse jumped. He didn't turn around. Didn't look back.

"Yeah?" My voice was soft, barely audible above the hum of the diner.

A pause.

"You're stronger than them. Always have been."

His words hit like a spark in a dark room. My grip tightened around the rag, but I didn't move. I just stood there, with my heart hammering and his voice echoing in my head.

Then he was gone.

The diner noise rushed in, too loud, too normal. I stared at the door for a long second before exhaling sharply and turning back to the counter. The change from the hundred-dollar bill still sat there, untouched.

I grabbed a Sharpie, wrote "Keep the change" in all caps across one of the bills, and taped it to the wall behind the register.

A reminder.

Then I moved—because like it or not, I still had a fight to win.

The next few weeks passed in a blur of black coffee, syrup-sticky tables, and aching feet. I took every shift Dixie would give me— mornings, doubles, weekends—anything to stack a little money and prove to myself that I could do this. It was exhausting. Humbling. Sometimes humiliating. But I kept showing up.

I learned the rhythm of the place—the regulars who wanted their eggs a certain way, the early birds who tipped well, the teenagers who didn't tip at all. I learned to dodge Dixie's sharp tongue and laugh off the comments about how Emerson Sinclair had fallen from grace. And somewhere in the middle of that mess, I stopped hating it.

A little.

I liked the quiet clatter before sunrise. The older couple who always held hands over their coffee cups. The way strangers started becoming familiar. The way people here were patient with me—

even when I dropped things, forgot orders, or spaced out from sheer exhaustion. They saw me. Not the version I used to fake... but the real me.

And then there was Sam.

No matter how long the shift or how badly the day went, he was always there. Sometimes with soup. Sometimes just with nothing but silence and open arms. But always, he was there. He'd come by for coffee, or lunch, and tell me I was doing great. He knew how hard it was for me to be seen like this. To start over. To work this hard for so little.

But he never made me feel small.

He made me laugh when I was too tired to smile. He made sure I had enough to eat. And when the world felt heavy, he gave me that look—like I could do anything. Like I already was.

We didn't have much quality time together, but the time we did have? It mattered. Late-night porch swings. Movies with me half-asleep on his chest. And the way he always pulled me close, like I was still soft even when the day had hardened every edge.

Still, something gnawed at me. That quiet ache for more.

I missed writing. Missed the quiet pulse of my fingers on a keyboard, and the freedom of getting lost in the words. I missed feeling like I had something bigger to offer the world than fast coffee and polite smiles. But I didn't have time for dreams right now. I had bills. I had pride. I had a point to prove.

So I got up. Every day. And I worked.

Because starting over is messy, but it's also honest.

I was tired. I was sore. I was broke.

But I wasn't broken.

CHAPTER 20

The Great Pie War of Sterling and Sinclair

It had been eight days since my last day off, and somehow, it already felt like a different life. We slept in, tangled in blankets and each other, the morning quiet stretching like warm taffy. Sam had something planned, but he wouldn't say what. All I knew was that I hadn't stopped smiling since coffee.

The moment we stepped onto Main Street, I knew I'd made the right call agreeing to this. It was only my second time at the farmer's market, but it already felt familiar—the hum of conversation, the easy rhythm of a town that knew itself. It wasn't just a row of produce stands. It was a whole experience. More festival than errand, and it had a way of making you slow down without realizing it.

Fresh bread and cinnamon rolls filled the warm summer air, mingling with the crisp scent of ripe peaches and sun-dried herbs. Booths stretched as far as I could see, offering everything from handwoven baskets to jars of homemade honey. A bluegrass band played somewhere off to the side and their music weaved through the crowd.

Sam reached for my hand. His grip was warm, familiar, and completely natural.

A woman in a sunflower apron offered us samples. Sam handed me a slice of peach before taking one for himself. The moment the juice hit my tongue, I groaned. "Yum!"

Sam popped a slice into his mouth, chewing slowly. "Delicious."

He grabbed a small bag and handed the vendor a bill.

We moved from stand to stand, picking out fresh veggies, local honey, and a loaf of homemade sourdough that still radiated warmth from the oven. Every few minutes, Sam ran into someone he knew. Locals who patted him on the back or teased him about work. And every time, he introduced me.

Not as a guest. Not as his neighbor. But as Emerson. His girlfriend.

The word landed softly, yet it felt enormous.

When we reached the end of the market, I was feeling pretty satisfied with myself. I had fresh food, Sam's hand wrapped around mine, and the lazy hum of small-town life wrapping around me like a favorite sweater.

I was starting to *understand* this place. Feeling the pull of something *real*.

And then we turned a corner and I saw a sign flapping in the breeze.

PIE-EATING CONTEST—SIGN UP NOW!

I laughed, shaking my head. "Wow. This town really leans into small-town stereotypes, huh?"

Sam smirked. "Yep."

I took another step, but he didn't move. When I glanced over my shoulder, he was grinning.

No. Hell no.

My eyes narrowed. "Sam..."

He rubbed the back of his neck. "Sooo... funny story..."

The loudspeaker crackled. "Next up—Sam Sterling and Emerson Sinclair!"

My jaw dropped.

Sam's grin? Wicked.

"You son of a—"

He gave me one last knowing look before tugging me toward the long table that was set up under the shade. A row of pies waited in front of us, along with a lineup of other contestants. Thick, deep-dish blueberry pies, their golden crusts flaky and perfect. The crowd cheered, clapping and calling out names.

I turned on Sam. "You signed me up?! Without telling me?!"

He shrugged, all innocence. "Figured I'd spare you the anxiety."

I glared. "I hate you."

He grinned. "No, you don't."

We sat side by side, hands behind our backs, as the referee explained the rules. I was still fuming, barely listening. Sam? Smug as hell.

The countdown began.

"3..." I side-eyed him. He winked.

"2..." I vowed revenge.

"1—GO!"

My face met blueberry pie.

The crowd roared. Sam dove in with no hesitation, eating like a man who had trained for this moment his entire life. Me? I was drowning—pie filling was in my nose, on my cheeks, and in my hair. I tried to take a bite but snorted mid-laugh, choking on sugar.

"Come on, Em," Sam teased between bites. "You're embarrassing me."

I glared, face sticky with blueberries. "I. Will. Kill. You."

"Not if you choke first."

And then—Sam, the competitive bastard, bumped my elbow. On purpose.

My face planted into the pie.

The crowd lost it.

I gasped, spluttering pastry. "You—"

But before I could retaliate, Sam kept going, winning by a single bite.

The announcer declared him the champion, raising his pie-covered hand as the crowd cheered. I? Murderous.

He turned to me, grinning. "Tough break, Emmy."

I narrowed my eyes... and smashed my entire plate onto his face.

The crowd erupted.

Sam wiped blueberry filling from his cheek, his slow smirk downright dangerous.

"Oh, you're in trouble now."

I took one step back.

He lunged.

I sprinted.

He chased.

And somewhere between ducking behind a vendor's stall, a near-collision with a kid holding a balloon, and the madness of being pursued through the market by a very determined, pie-covered Sam, I did something I hadn't done in a long time.

I laughed *hard*.

I was alive in this moment—breathless, giddy, not caring who was watching, not thinking about rumors or whispers.

As Sam finally caught me, wrapping his arms around me, we were a sticky, laughing mess. Then he kissed me.

It was quick, unexpected, and tasted like sugar and blueberries. But the way he did it—like he just had to—sent my pulse into overdrive.

And then I realized—it wasn't just the thrill of the chase, the heat of the moment, or the way he kissed me.

I really, really loved this man.

Sam was still laughing, his arms wrapped securely around me, his breath warm against my ear. My heart was racing—not just from the pie-covered chaos, but from the way he held me.

I felt him shift slightly, his chest rising and falling with laughter. "You good?" he murmured, his lips just a little too close to my skin.

I tilted my head back to meet his gaze. "I'm covered in pie, my pride is in shambles, and my stomach hurts from laughing. So, yeah. I'm good."

His mouth curved. "Next time, I'll let you win."

I gasped, smacking his arm and leaving a sticky smear of blueberry goo behind. "Let me win? Coming from the guy who almost choked to death on pie crust."

Sam smirked, completely unbothered. "Still beat you."

I narrowed my eyes. "Because you cheated."

His hands tightened slightly on my waist, the amusement in his expression flickering into something slower. Something different. His gaze dipped to my lips, then back up—lazy and unhurried. "I just wanted to see you like this," he murmured, voice lower now.

I was suddenly very aware of how close we were, how solid he felt against me, how his fingers were still gripping my hips like he didn't really want to let go.

I swallowed, breathless. "Well. Guess I'll have to try harder next time."

Sam grinned. "I'll be waiting."

Before I could fall too far into him, a snotty voice cut through the moment.

"Well, that was quite the performance."

I didn't even need to look to know who it was.

Bethany.

Sam's grip tensed slightly—just enough to remind me he wasn't going anywhere.

His sigh was low and controlled, but it had an edge. I knew he was biting his tongue.

I finally turned my head. She stood there with her usual

pinched expression, arms crossed, like she was personally offended by our very existence. A few ladies stood nearby, whispering, darting glances in our direction.

The old me—the Emerson from several months ago—would have felt small. She would have worried about what they were thinking. And she would have felt the need to explain herself.

But I wasn't that girl anymore.

Instead, I leaned into Sam—just slightly, just enough to make a point—and flashed the sweetest, most saccharine smile I could muster.

"Jealous you missed out, Bethany?" I cocked my head. "You know, I think blueberry pie would be a great color on you."

Her face cringed.

"Enjoy your little show," she sniffed, then marched off, heels sinking into the grass with every step.

Sam let out a low chuckle, his hands still resting on me. "Damn, Emmy." His hands tightened just enough to make me feel it. "Remind me never to get on your bad side. That was kind of ruthless... and hot."

I scoffed, but my stomach fluttered anyway. "Oh, please."

"Come on," he said, nudging me toward the market stalls. "You owe me ice cream for humiliating me."

"I think you did that all on your own." I laughed, shoving him lightly as we fell into step together.

The tension faded. The moment softened. And just like that, we were back to us.

Monday came like a slap.

My schedule at the diner doubled. I hadn't even clocked in before the scent of burnt coffee, fryer grease, and exhaustion clung to my skin. My feet already ached.

"Double shift today, eh?" Dixie asked, sliding an apron across the counter with a raised brow.

I nodded.

"Poor thing," she muttered.

That's what I was now—a poor thing.

I tied the apron around my waist and got to work.

Tray after tray. Order after order. Silverware clattered. Plates scraped. Customers grumbled. My muscles screamed, my back throbbed, and every time I wiped down another table, the resentment burned hotter.

No one cared who I used to be. That I once had a career. That I was good at it. To them, I was just the girl with the apron and the tired smile.

By the end of the second shift, I was barely upright.

I was wiping down my last table when I heard it—Sam's low whistle from the doorway.

"Damn, Emmy," he called out. "Is it legal to look that good in grease-stained polyester?"

I rolled my eyes, half-laughing. "Keep talking like that and you'll be bussing tables."

"Only if I get to wear the matching apron."

I threw a balled-up napkin at him. He caught it mid-air, grinning.

Somehow, even covered in ketchup and sweat, he still made me feel like the main character.

And that was more than enough to keep going.

CHAPTER 21

The Work of Becoming

I woke up before the sun, too restless to sleep. Something had been pressing on my chest all night—not pain, exactly. Just a pull. A quiet ache to do something for the man who keeps doing everything for me.

I left it on the seat of his truck before the sun came up. Folded, creased, no envelope. Just my messy handwriting on lined paper, held down by a pack of gum.

Dear Sam,

I don't know how you do it—see through me without needing me to explain. And every time I start to doubt myself, you're already there, holding me up.

You never turn away. Never ask me to be anything but honest. You don't rescue. You don't run. You just stay.

You've taught me that strength can be quiet. That love doesn't push or pull—it holds.

You've made the heavy days feel lighter, the quiet ones less lonely. And even when nothing around me makes sense, you do.

Because of you, I don't feel like I'm starting over. I feel like I'm finally becoming.

You've changed everything, Sam. And I'll never be the same because of you.

Thank you for being the safest place I've ever known.

-Emmy

He'd find it when he left for work.

When I got home that night, there was a small mason jar on the porch. And inside it? A single peony and a note scribbled on the back of a napkin.

JUST KEEP BEING YOU. I'M NOT GOING ANYWHERE.

And somehow, that touched me more than a hundred roses ever could.

. . .

The next morning, the past came calling.

The call came just after 8 a.m. I almost didn't answer.

"Hello?"

A beat of silence. Then—

"Emerson."

My mother's voice—polished as ever, but with a hint of something else beneath it.

Hesitation, maybe. Or guilt.

I waited.

"We were hoping to see you," she said. "For lunch. Tomorrow, if you're free."

I leaned against the counter, letting the silence stretch between us. She didn't call to catch up. She never did. This had an agenda. It always did.

"Why?"

"We've been hearing from Brad. He said things are... still unresolved. That the divorce isn't finalized yet."

I blinked. My jaw tightened.

She continued, voice calm but deliberate. "We just think a conversation might be helpful. A chance to hear you out. And for you to hear us."

I let out a quiet exhale. "Now you want to hear me?"

There was a pause—the kind that said she wasn't used to being challenged. Then, like she hadn't heard me at all, she added, "We can meet anywhere. Your father's schedule is more open now."

That stopped me. "More open?"

"He's stepping back from the firm," she said.

"What? Why?"

"He's scaling back. Semi-retiring. It was the right time."

Just like that. My entire childhood was wrapped up in that law office. Every holiday we spent with clients. Every skipped birthday. Every demand, every illusion of perfection was anchored to that firm. And now, he was just... stepping back?

I said nothing.

"We'll have more time," she added lightly. "It might be good for all of us."

"I'm not coming."

"Emerson—"

"I'm working. I have a double shift at the diner."

Silence.

"And honestly? I'm proud of that."

I didn't let her interrupt.

"I'm working hard. Earning every dollar. Showing up even when I'm utterly exhausted. And it's showing me exactly who I am. So no, I won't be meeting you for a lecture wrapped in polite brunch. I'm busy building a life I actually want."

I continued, "And I know what you're going to say. That I haven't thought this through. That it's not too late. That I can still fix this. But I'm not broken. And this doesn't need fixing."

A pause.

"You're *married*," she said quietly. "You made a commitment."

"It never should have happened," I replied. "And if you're being honest, you know it's true."

Another silence. Heavier this time.

"You're living in the middle of nowhere. In an old cabin. Waiting tables in a diner."

"Yes, I sure am," I said softly. "And I'm the happiest I've ever been. I'm finally becoming who I was meant to be. And I'm in love with someone who loves me completely. All of me. Not the pretty face or the image—but the real, imperfect me."

"You're not serious," she said, eyebrows lifting. "You think this is love? With someone new?"

Her voice faltered. Like the idea hurt her.

"Brad is still your husband. And he's waiting for you to come to your senses. And so are we."

I almost laughed. "I came to my senses the day I left."

I hung up before I changed my mind.

I didn't cry. I didn't pause. I didn't let her voice echo longer than it had to.

Some people are born into support. Others learn to survive without it.

I had learned. The hard way.

By mid-afternoon, the grease on my arms felt permanent. My hair clung to my neck, my socks were damp from spilled mop water, and the burn on my wrist from the toaster oven was beginning to blister. I'd been on my feet for hours, running refills and side orders for people who couldn't even look me in the eye.

The soles of my off-brand sneakers were worn so thin I could feel every crack in the tile beneath me. My apron strings cut into my waist, and my back screamed like it had forgotten how to rest.

"Is that the Sinclair girl?" someone whispered near the register.

I didn't flinch. I didn't even look up.

"She used to be so put together," the voice continued. "Heard she walked away from a fortune. Now she's clocking in like the rest of us. Bethany said it was some kind of meltdown. Can you imagine?"

A flush crept up my neck, hot and prickly. My jaw clenched so tight it ached.

Then a hand waved me over—table seven. Mr. Carmichael, a widower who came in every Thursday and ordered the same thing: oatmeal, extra brown sugar, black coffee, two sugars on the side. He looked at me briefly, then slid something across the table.

A folded five-dollar bill and a little yellow candy from the dish by the door.

"You're doing great, sweetheart," he said. "Keep your chin up."

I blinked. Nodded. My throat tightened so hard I couldn't speak.

And then I turned away before I fell apart.

By the time I made it home, I couldn't feel my feet. There was a deep scrape on my knuckle I didn't remember getting, and a purple bruise blooming on my hip from where I'd bumped the counter. And I hadn't eaten since sunrise. But something inside me—something small and stubborn—was still flickering.

The cabin was dark except for the dim light above the stove. Sam had fallen asleep on the couch. My clothes still smelled like fried onions and syrup. I hadn't even showered. My eyes burned and my spine felt like it had been swapped with rebar, but the ache wasn't enough to stop me.

My laptop sat open on the kitchen table, glowing like it was daring me to try.

So I did.

It wasn't much. Just a few paragraphs. A scene that had been playing in my mind like a secret I wasn't allowed to tell. But once I started, it poured out like breath I'd been holding too long.

A woman at rock bottom. A woman who walked away from everything—family, image, a picture-perfect life—and still hadn't figured out who she was yet. She was raw, uncertain. But she was learning. One line at a time.

I didn't know if it was for a book. I didn't even know if it was good. But it was mine.

Sam woke up and found me there—barefoot, hunched, and a mess of syrup stains and raw words.

He didn't ask. Just leaned against the counter and watched me for a beat. Then, softly, "You're writing again."

I nodded, fingers still hovering over the keyboard.

His voice dropped even lower. "You look beautiful like this."

I let the silence answer him. Because this wasn't a version of me. It was just me. And somehow, that was finally enough.

This wasn't a comeback. This was a birth.

The next few weeks passed like a slow rebuild—still tender, but steady.

It was September now, but still hot and relentless. The kind of heat that clung to your skin and made every small task feel earned.

I worked. I wrote. I rested when I could. And Sam was there through it all—constant, thoughtful, quietly championing me in all the best ways.

There was always a hot meal waiting when I got home. Sometimes, a bubble bath was already drawn. Notes left on the mirror. Coffee set out before I even opened my eyes. He made sure we had time together—even if it meant sitting at the diner from breakfast through lunch just to be near me.

Love no longer felt like something I had to chase.

It found me. And it stayed.

CHAPTER 22

Sticky Fingers and Secret Grins

I t started with a knock. Two quick taps. Then silence.

I groaned from the couch, still half-dead from my shift at the diner, a heating pad on my lower back, and a bag of frozen peas on my knee. I hadn't planned on moving again until dawn.

The knock came again.

"I swear, if that's Bethany with another fake apology—"

But when I cracked open the door, there he was.

Sam. Holding two mason jars of something suspicious and wearing a smirk that spelled trouble.

"Get dressed," he said. "We're going to break the law."

I blinked. "I'm sorry... what?"

He lifted the jars. "Technically, it's homemade peach moonshine from a customer who may or may not have a federal warning against him. So yes. You, me, this questionable liquid, and a small fire. Let's go."

"I'm in pajamas."

"You won't need much. Just bring that attitude and maybe a sweater."

I narrowed my eyes, but my mouth betrayed me with a grin. "Give me five minutes."

. . .

Fifteen minutes later, we were hiking through the woods behind the marina. Sam carried a small backpack and a ridiculous amount of confidence for someone wearing boots and hauling a fire pit.

"This feels a lot like murder," I said. "Are you sure this isn't one of those Dateline setups?"

"If I were going to kill you, I wouldn't bring snacks," he said, lifting a Tupperware of chocolate-covered pretzels.

"Fair."

The clearing was small—nothing but a patch of earth, a few flat rocks, and a rusty folding chair that looked like it had been left by a drifter in 1978. But above us, the stars were wild and bright. Untamed.

Sam built the fire with ease. Ten minutes and a spark later, orange flames crackled to life, licking the edge of the night. He handed me one of the jars and sat beside me on a log, close enough that our knees brushed.

"Here's to questionable decisions," he said.

I clinked my jar against his. "And the men who make them irresistible."

The first sip hit like a punch and a kiss at the same time—sweet, then sharp, then warm all the way down.

I coughed. "Agh! That's paint thinner in a prom dress."

He laughed, full and deep. "Told you it had bite."

Sam stretched out behind me, one arm braced on the ground, watching the flames with that quiet intensity I was starting to crave more than sleep.

"Tell me something stupid," I said.

He raised a brow. "Stupid?"

"Yes. Something pointless. No emotional landmines. No past trauma. Just... give me dumb facts."

He thought for a second. "I hate raisins. I think they're a betrayal of grapes."

I burst out laughing, nearly choking on moonshine.

"Your turn," he said.

I grinned. "I once had a crush on the guy who played the voice of Simba in *The Lion King*. Not Matthew Broderick. The kid version."

Sam blinked. "That's oddly specific."

"I was six. He had range."

He was still laughing when a rogue spark shot from the fire and landed on his thigh.

"Shit!" He leapt up, swatting at his shorts, then glared at the flame like it had insulted his mother.

"You okay?" I said between gasps.

He nodded, then pointed at the log. "You're officially fire captain. I've been demoted to snack patrol."

Then, we roasted marshmallows. Badly.

He dropped his first one in the fire and blamed the stick. I lit mine on fire and tried to pretend it was on purpose. The third round ended with melted sugar on my chin, which Sam leaned over and wiped with his thumb—slow, deliberate.

Our eyes caught.

Something shifted.

"I like this," I said quietly.

He didn't smile. Didn't tease. Just looked at me like the sky was getting jealous of how I glowed.

"I like this, too."

The quiet stretched between us.

Then he pulled something from the backpack—a pack of sparklers.

"You brought fireworks?" I whispered.

"The label says 'novelty item.' That's not a crime. That's a good time."

He lit the first one and handed it to me. I held it high, watching the gold sparks shoot into the air, a mini galaxy in my hand.

"Wish for something," he said.

I looked at him, the firelight painting him in shadows and starlight.

"I don't need to."

He didn't kiss me—not yet. But he took the sparkler from my hand and tossed it into the fire, his fingers trailing down my wrist, curling around my waist.

We stood like that, two rebels with sticky fingers and secret grins, dancing on the edge of everything.

I was still laughing when Sam stepped in behind me, his arms slipping around my shoulders, pulling me back against his chest. The firelight flickered against the curve of his jaw, casting everything in gold and shadow. The air was thick with summer—warm earth, smoke, pine, the faint sweetness of whatever flower had opened for the night.

He leaned in, lips brushing the shell of my ear. "You always look this beautiful when you're covered in ash?"

I turned to face him. His eyes were on me—smoldering, focused, the kind of look that pinned me in place and made the world fall away. My breath caught.

"I didn't pack pajamas," I whispered, barely joking.

"Didn't plan on sleeping." His hand slid up my spine, fingers tracing skin beneath the hem of my shirt, slow and deliberate. "You want to go back to the cabin?"

I shook my head. "No."

"Then come with me."

He looked like he was going to kiss me, then paused, grinning.

"You still tasting prom dress and paint thinner?" he quipped.

I laughed, breathless. "A little. That stuff could kill a rhino."

He leaned in, lips ghosting over mine. "Then I'll have to give you something better to remember tonight by."

Sam took my hand and led me into the trees—just far enough for the firelight to fade into memory. We found the blanket he'd tossed in the truck earlier and stretched it beneath a canopy of stars, the night pulsing warm around us.

He didn't rush.

His hands explored like they were learning, not taking. Like he had time. Like he knew we did.

Every kiss was a promise. Every touch a question.

It wasn't about what we *did*. It was about what we *almost* did. What we held back. What we built.

We weren't planning to sleep out there. But we'd been talking for hours, our limbs tangled, his heart beating steady beneath my cheek—and somewhere between kisses and confessions... sleep just found us.

But love couldn't erase the past.

And when morning came, I still had to face it.

CHAPTER 23

The Girl in the Third Chair

If I hadn't left, I would've died living someone else's life—polished, perfect, and quietly miserable. That was the cost of staying.

The drive into the city that morning felt strange, like stepping back into a version of myself that I barely recognized.

That old life—the penthouse, the image, the silence I'd learned to survive—felt like it belonged to someone else. Like it had all happened a lifetime ago.

And still, my hands gripped the wheel like I was bracing for impact.

But today, I stood before a judge and ended the lie.

No tears, no pleading.

Just the quiet, final truth—cold, unflinching, and long overdue.

30 minutes later, I walked out of that building more myself than I'd ever been.

That's all it took to unravel years of pretending.

A signature, a silence. A door closing behind me.

Brad didn't look at me. I didn't look at him.

We weren't enemies. We were nothing. And somehow, that was worse.

Outside the courthouse, I stood on the sidewalk as the wind moved through me.

The sun was too bright. The noise of the city too sharp.

But I stood still. I let it hit me—the finality.

The freedom.

The beginning of something real.

The cabin was mine. My bank account was mine.

Everything else, I left behind.

I didn't ask for a cent. Didn't want the pieces of a life that never fit me in the first place. All I took was my car, my clothes, and the parts of myself I'd fought to get back.

And I would never look back.

Because what I had now was worth more than anything he ever gave me.

I had me.

Walking down the courthouse steps, I pulled out my phone and texted Sam.

Me: It's done.

Sam: Congratulations. You're finally free. Now set something on fire.

I stared at the screen and laughed—sharp, sudden, real.

Not because it was funny.

Because it was permission.

Two chains snapped that day—the marriage that had caged me, and the job that had carried me through.

I wasn't surviving anymore. I was finally choosing.

I never had to file that temporary support order Jordan offered. Never had to call my parents and beg for help. And never leaned on Sam, even when he would've carried the whole weight without blinking.

The diner didn't save me. But it did something just as important.

It reminded me that I could start over. That I could do hard things. That I didn't need to be rescued—I just needed to keep showing up.

And somewhere between the blisters, the double shifts, and the sting of judgmental stares, I found a version of myself I didn't want to lose. The one who doesn't quit. The one who earned her freedom.

One shift at a time. One tip at a time.

One breath at a time.

I shoved open the doors of The Rusty Skillet. The door swung shut behind me, and for once, it wasn't a weight dragging me down. Today was different.

Today was my last shift.

With a grin, I set a box of donuts on the counter. "If I'm working one last shift, we're doing it on a sugar high."

Dixie barely looked up from the register, but I caught the slight twitch at the corner of her mouth. "You sure you wanna quit, Sinclair?"

I leaned my elbows on the counter and smirked. "Yeah. But today? I'm working for free."

That got her attention. She finally glanced up, arching a sharp brow.

I laughed, shaking my head as I grabbed an apron from the hook by the kitchen. As I tied it around my waist, I caught the amused expressions of the regulars.

"Never thought you'd last, but hell if you didn't prove us wrong," Alfred grumbled as he stirred sugar into his coffee.

"Yeah," Jed chimed in. "You remember her first day? Damn near dumped a whole tray of plates right in my lap."

"You could've used the wake-up call," I shot back, grinning.

The joshing continued, but it was all in good fun. It was warm, like family teasing each other. And somewhere along the way, this place had become exactly that—something real. Something I had been a part of. Something I had gotten good at.

The orders rolled in, and I moved with ease between the tables, refilling coffee cups, balancing trays, and laughing with the customers. I could feel the difference. The first day I'd walked in here, I was drowning. But now? I was in control. This job wasn't beneath me. It had grounded me. It had reminded me that working hard wasn't a weakness—it was something to be proud of.

By the time my shift was nearing its end, a strange feeling settled over me. Not sadness, exactly. More like gratitude.

I stopped by the counter where Dixie was totaling receipts. "Guess this is it."

She glanced at me over the rim of her glasses. "Guess so."

A beat of silence passed before she spoke again. "You ever need a job, Sinclair, you know where to find me." She paused. "Not that you'll need it. You're made for more than this."

Warmth bloomed in my chest. "Thank you for everything, Dixie. I'll be back. Just on the other side of the counter."

She gave me a quick nod before returning to her work, but I didn't miss the way her lips pressed together, just the slightest bit softer than usual.

I stepped outside, inhaling the air tinged with the last breath of summer. The season was shifting—summer's heat lingering, but autumn was whispering on the breeze.

And then I saw him.

Sam was leaning against a sleek, powerful blue and white rocket on two wheels. His arms were crossed over his broad chest, and a smirk playing at his lips. He looked like trouble, and every bit of it begged me to come closer.

I slowed, my eyes flicking from the machine to the man who looked way too sexy beside it. "I didn't know you had a motorcycle. And here I thought I had you all figured out," I said, surprised.

His smirk deepened. "It's not just a motorcycle. It's the king of sport bikes." He tapped the sleek frame with his fingers. "1,000cc of pure power between my legs."

I bit my lip.

"What are you doing here?" I asked, arching a brow as I walked toward him.

"Thought you could use a celebration."

I leaned my head. "And what exactly are we celebrating?"

"Freedom." He tossed me a helmet. "Now get on."

My heart pounded, a mix of nerves and anticipation swirling through me. I glanced at the bike, then back at him. "I don't know..."

Sam leaned in just enough for his voice to drop. "Do you trust me?"

My breath hitched. "Yes."

I climbed onto the bike, and there was only one thing to hold onto—him. I wrapped my arms around him, my fingers gripping the fabric of his jacket.

Before I could process the moment, he revved the engine—a low, thunderous growl that surged into a razor-sharp scream, splitting the night wide open.

And then, we were flying.

I didn't just feel the wind. I let go of everything that ever held me back. And as Sam opened the throttle, I realized—we weren't escaping anything. We were flying toward everything I never thought I could have.

The bike shot forward, the front wheel lifting briefly off the ground. My breath caught, a rush of wind stealing it away as my stomach dropped like I was plunging down the first drop of a roller coaster. My pulse pounded, my chest tightening with the dizzying mix of thrill and anticipation.

Sam leaned into a few turns as we tore down the road, the acceleration sending a jolt through me. I squeezed him tighter, my muscles tensing as the speed left me weightless for a split second before the next surge forward.

"Sam!" I gasped, gripping him tighter, the thrill stealing my breath.

He let out a deep chuckle, his voice vibrating through me. "Like it?"

The world blurred around us, the air whipping through me. It wasn't just about the speed. It was about the freedom, the sheer untamed exhilaration that set fire to every nerve in my body.

After what felt like both an eternity and a split second, he slowed, guiding us toward a secluded overlook. He cut the engine, the sudden silence making my pulse feel impossibly loud. The town stretched below us, the lake reflecting the golden glow of the distant streetlights.

I jumped off the bike and pulled off my helmet, sucking in a deep breath. My hands were shaking, not from fear, but from the sheer intensity of it all. "That was—" I exhaled sharply. "Insane."

Sam smirked, swinging his leg over the bike as he stood to face me. "You should see yourself right now."

The way he looked at me—like he could barely restrain himself—sent a shiver through me, igniting something deeper. He stepped closer, hands braced on either side of me against the bike, and his lips crashed against mine, fierce and unrelenting. Heat surged through me, a desperate, all-consuming hunger. I pulled him closer, tasting the thrill of the ride still lingering on his lips.

He grabbed my hips, a low rumble in his chest as he pulled me against him. His body pressed solidly against mine, demanding, and I let myself sink into him—into this wild, reckless moment that felt like everything I'd been craving. Then, just as suddenly, he pulled back, breath ragged, his forehead resting against mine as his fingers flexed against my side.

I groaned, gripping his shirt. "You drive me crazy."

His chuckle was dark and knowing. "Good."

He stepped back, running a hand through his hair, his chest still rising and falling fast. "Let's go home and get cleaned up. I'm taking you to dinner."

Catching my breath, I whispered, "Where?"

His smirk returned, slow and sinful. "You'll see."

My heart was still racing from the ride... my body still humming from his touch. The wind whipped around us, alive and electric.

I didn't move when he pulled up to the cabin. I held on, breathing him in. The engine idled. He shifted slightly, his voice low and steady. "Go get dressed." He hesitated. "And wear something comfortable. Very casual. I'm going to run to my place for a few things. I'll be back in an hour."

I slid off the bike, lifting my chin. "So bossy."

His smirk was slow and deliberate. "You must like it." He winked and revved the engine.

"I sure do." I smiled with excitement.

As soon as I got out of the shower, I saw a text.

Sam: I miss you already. Be there soon.

I traced my fingers over the screen, rereading the words like they were something to hold onto. God, this man. I pressed my phone to my heart, biting back the ridiculous, lovesick grin taking over my face.

Me: Hurry up, handsome. I miss you more.

When Sam came back, I was ready. I threw my damp hair into

a messy twist, and slipped into a worn t-shirt and soft shorts. No makeup. Just me.

The second I opened the door, Sam's gaze swept over me—like he was taking inventory of something precious. "Wow," he murmured. His voice was low, almost reverent. "You're glowing."

He didn't move at first. Just looked at me like I was the answer to something he didn't know he was asking.

Then he stepped forward. His hands cupped my face, his kiss soft at first—anchoring, worshipful. It deepened slowly, like we had all the time in the world. His fingers slid into my hair. Mine gripped his shirt like I didn't want him to go anywhere.

When we finally pulled apart, his thumb brushed the corner of my mouth, almost like a secret.

"You're everything," he whispered.

Then he kissed my temple and whispered, "Come on."

He laced his fingers through mine and led me to the truck.

Sam parked on his driveway, but didn't say a word. Then, he grabbed a blanket from the back seat, we got out of the truck, and came to my, holding out his hand.

He led me down a narrow path, the ground soft beneath our feet. The horizon bled slowly into dusk—like a quiet surrender—by the time we reached the lake's shore. We stopped at a small clearing behind the trees—private, hidden, quiet. There was a fire pit already crackling. Two chairs sat in front of it. A third was off to the side, facing the lake. A bottle of wine rested in a small tin bucket of ice, two glasses beside it. Lanterns flickered along the branches, casting golden light through the trees.

It was magical, in the most unexpected way.

"Sam..." My voice caught. "You did all this?"

He shrugged like it was nothing. "You've had a hell of a week."

I let out a shaky laugh. "That's one way to put it."

He handed me a glass and sat down, stretching out his long

legs toward the fire. I joined him, wrapping the blanket around my shoulders. The heat from the flames felt good against my skin.

We sat in silence for a while, watching the fire dance.

Then Sam said quietly, "You're free."

I smiled. "I know. I still can't believe it."

"It's done. How do you feel?"

"I feel… like I finally righted a wrong. Like I took my life back. And also"—I laughed softly—"I'm really glad I don't have to be at the diner tomorrow for a double shift."

He grinned. "I'm so damn proud of you."

I looked at him, my throat tightening. "I couldn't have done it without you."

"That's ridiculous," he said, shaking his head. "You did every bit of this without me. Why do you always sell yourself short like that?"

I gave him a half-laugh, half-glare.

"You chose your own happiness. You went against everything people expected of you. Was that because of me?"

I shook my head. "No."

"I wasn't the one clocking in every day at the diner. I wasn't the one untangling your life, line by line. That was you."

"I meant—"

Sam leaned in slightly, voice softer now. "You were brave. You stood up. You showed the world who you are. I just got to witness it. I got to watch you rebuild everything. Little by little. Every single day."

I couldn't speak. My chest ached in the best way. My eyes blurred with tears I didn't bother to wipe away. And then I noticed the third chair again—the one slightly off to the side, angled toward the lake. I gestured toward it, voice quiet. "Are you expecting someone else?"

Sam's gaze followed mine. His mouth lifted, just barely. "She's already here."

I frowned, confused.

He looked back at me, eyes steady. "I thought maybe she deserved to sit with you one last time. The girl you used to be."

Something cracked in my chest.

He continued, softer now. "I know she did what she had to do to survive. She smiled when it hurt. She kept the peace. She played their game. But she's tired now, Emmy. She's been trying to let go for a long time."

My eyes welled, the tears sliding silently down my cheeks.

"She got you this far," he said. "But she's not the one who's going to carry you the rest of the way."

I reached for the second glass, poured a small amount of wine, and set it gently in front of the empty chair. The fire popped behind us.

Then I lifted my own glass.

"Thanks for getting me here," I whispered, voice shaking. "But I've got it from here."

We clinked glasses in the quietest toast I'd ever made.

And something inside me finally... let go.

Sam didn't speak again. He just pulled me into his arms, wrapped the blanket tighter around us, and let the fire burn.

CHAPTER 24

Undone

It had been a month since the divorce was finalized. I settled into a peaceful routine of reading and writing every day, working on the cabin, weekly coffees with Ute, and a lot of fun in the sun by the lake. The days were still warm, but the nights had started to carry the first hints of fall—crisp edges in the breeze, the scent of leaves just beginning to dry.

The moon's silver light shone on the lake—its dark expanse stretched endlessly beneath the night. Sam and I had driven out to a secluded lookout, far from everything, just the two of us and the quiet hum of the summer night.

I leaned into him, his warmth sinking into me as the rhythm of his breathing smoothed out the knots in my chest. We sat on the hood of his truck, watching the water, letting the silence say the things we weren't ready to. When he kissed me, it was slow, unhurried, deep. Like he wanted me to feel it long after the moment passed.

At some point on the drive back, exhaustion pulled me under.

A shift in the air woke me. The truck had stopped. The familiar scent of pine and lake water filled my senses, and I realized we were home.

Before I could stir, I was wrapped in strength—strong arms, a solid chest, a heartbeat against my cheek.

Sam was carrying me.

The smooth motion of his steps lulling me halfway between sleep and wakefulness.

I mumbled against his chest. "Why are you carrying me?"

"Carrying you off like a proper damsel in distress." Sam let out a quiet laugh, his breath stirring my hair. "Because you're exhausted. I figured you'd rather wake up here than face plant in the driveway."

I peeked up at him, my lips curving. "Such a gentleman."

His smirk deepened. "Would you rather I had thrown you over my shoulder like a sack of potatoes?"

I gasped dramatically. "You wouldn't dare."

His smirk deepened. "Oh, I would. And I still might."

I narrowed my eyes. "Put me down."

Sam just adjusted his grip and kept walking. "Nope. Too late. You're already the damsel."

I let my head roll to the side, blinking up at him. "So... you just carry women around like this?"

Sam leaned in slightly, his smirk unmistakable. "Only the difficult ones."

I let out a mock gasp, placing a hand over my heart. "Excuse me?"

"You heard me." He ran his knuckles lightly down my arm. "You're small, but you're feisty. Like a feral kitten."

I swatted at his chest.

His grin turned wicked.

A slow wave of awareness spread through me, but I kept my eyes closed, letting myself sink into him. His steps were careful, his grip firm but gentle, as if he was carrying something precious.

· · ·

He adjusted his hold, nudging the door closed behind him with his foot. He walked us to the bedroom, and when I felt the mattress beneath me, I finally let my eyes flutter open.

Sam was crouched beside me, watching me in the dim light with an intensity that stole my breath.

I swallowed hard, my voice softer now. "You didn't have to carry me."

A slight smile touched his lips, but his eyes stayed fixed. "I wanted to."

My pulse did a slow, lazy roll.

His fingers grazed my cheek, brushing back my hair. "You okay?"

I nodded, but my body betrayed me, leaning into his touch like I needed it.

Something shifted in his expression—a flicker of something deeper, darker... hungrier.

"You should get some rest," he murmured. But he didn't move. Neither did I.

The silence stretched between us, thick with a hundred unspoken things.

I was exhausted but not tired. Not in the way that mattered.

I licked my lips, and Sam's gaze dropped to my mouth. The tension snapped so tight it felt like a live wire between us.

I could end this now. Pull away. Say goodnight. Let exhaustion win.

But I didn't want that. Not tonight.

I let out a shaky breath. "Sam."

I swallowed... my pulse thudding in my throat. "Please."

That was all it took.

He exhaled—and then he moved. Sharp. Hungry. Like that one word shattered every bit of control he had left.

In one smooth motion, he pulled his shirt over his head.

Lord help me.

His big shoulders, hard muscles, and golden skin stretched over strength. He was beautiful in a way that felt almost unfair.

Sam caught my stare and smirked.

I dragged my eyes up to meet his, heat rushing to my face. "You're ridiculous."

The smirk faded, replaced by something sharper. Something raw.

I reached for the hem of my sweater and pulled it over my head. His breath caught.

I knew that look.

I loved that look.

I unbuttoned my jeans.

His voice was hoarse. "If you take those off, I won't be able to stop."

My fingers paused. I looked him in the eye. "You better not stop."

That was it. His restraint snapped.

In one motion, he had me in his arms, my back against the wall, his mouth inches from mine.

"Say it again," he whispered.

My hands slid down his chest. "Don't stop."

He kissed me—possessive and consuming, like he needed to memorize the taste.

His hands gripped my waist, holding me in place like he couldn't risk letting go. I felt every inch of him—heat, strength, and control just barely held in check.

I tugged at his waistband, aching for him. But suddenly, he pulled back.

Chest heaving, pupils dark. His voice rough with restraint. "Emmy."

I blinked, breathless. "What?"

He rested his forehead against mine, his breath shaking. "We need to slow down."

My body was on fire. "Seriously?"

He smirked, lips brushing my temple. "I just... want to take my time with you."

My whole body flushed.

"Shower?" he murmured.

I nodded. "Oh yeah."

He took my hand and led me down the hall. No rush. Just this undeniable tension between us.

Steam filled the bathroom as he turned on the water, but he didn't touch me right away. He just looked at me. Like he was taking in every inch.

I shifted, self-conscious, arms twitching toward my body— but he stopped me gently.

"Don't," he said softly. "Let me see you."

His hands slid over my skin—slow, reverent. His lips brushed below my ear.

"You're perfect," he whispered. "You have no idea how much I love your body."

The insecurity melted away.

"I just... I want you," I breathed.

His voice was gravel. "I've wanted you. So. Damn. Bad."

Before I could blink, he lifted me into his arms. His mouth trailed fire across my skin as he stepped into the shower, water cascading down around us.

The heat didn't come from the water. It came from him—his mouth on my neck, his hands exploring every curve like I was a secret he'd waited a lifetime to uncover.

"I need you," he said, voice rough against my skin.

"Then show me."

He kissed me again—deep, relentless. His hands slid down my thighs, lifting me effortlessly, pinning me against the tile.

His body fit mine like it was meant to. Every motion, every sound, every kiss sent another wave of heat spiraling through me.

"You feel perfect," he rasped, forehead to mine. "Like you were made for me."

"I love you," I whispered, barely a breath.

He froze.

Then his mouth crashed into mine.

"You have no idea," he murmured, voice frayed and tight like he could barely hold himself together. "No fucking idea how much I love you."

His rhythm was deep and deliberate. His hands claimed me, held me, anchored me. His mouth left a trail of fire down my throat.

"I've dreamed about this," he murmured. "About you."

"Me too," I breathed.

When we finally broke together, it wasn't just release. It was *everything*. A burning away of everything that came before.

He held me there, wrapped around me, his lips at my temple.

"If this is a dream," he whispered, "don't wake me."

CHAPTER 25

The Rain and the Pages

I t had been a few weeks since that night—since I first said I love you, with nothing between us but truth and skin.

Life didn't explode afterward. It didn't twist into some dramatic new chapter or sweep us into a whirlwind. It just settled —eased into something more certain.

Autumn had deepened, wrapping the world in gold and fire. Mornings came slower, with mist rising off the lake and the scent of woodsmoke in the air. The trees burned with color, like the whole world was letting go and somehow becoming more beautiful because of it.

Sam and I had found a rhythm. Late mornings tangled in sheets, slow afternoons at the lake, dinners barefoot on the porch, trading laughter under string lights. There was a quiet joy in it I hadn't expected. It wasn't boring. It wasn't routine. It just felt... peaceful. Right.

But even happiness, I was learning, has its own kind of weight.

The kind that presses in when everything is still. When the noise quiets long enough for the old dreams to whisper again.

. . .

A storm rolled in without warning—low clouds stretching like bruises across the sky, the kind of gray that made everything feel heavy and still. Rain hammered the roof of the cabin in steady sheets, softening the edges of the world. It was the kind of day that asked nothing of me.

Maybe it was the rain. Or the hush it pulled over the world.

But something cracked open in me.

Not pain. Not grief. Just... remembering.

I had love. Peace. A home that finally felt like mine.

But somewhere beneath the quiet, something stirred—not discontent, just a part of me I hadn't touched in a long time.

The part that used to dream.

Lately, I kept hearing Gram's voice in my head, soft but certain, "Don't forget the part of you that dreamed before the world told you who to be."

And I realized—it wasn't restlessness.

It was readiness.

I didn't get dressed. Didn't brush my hair. Just wrapped myself in a blanket, made tea, and wandered through the back bedroom where Gram kept all her old things. Boxes of dusty linens, more books, old photos, brittle newspaper clippings... and then—tucked behind a stack of vintage recipe binders—I saw it.

A thick binder. Yellowed pages inside. The first line typed, the rest handwritten in Gram's careful, cursive script.

Chapter One

I stared.

Gram wrote a book?

I sat on the floor and flipped through it. Pages filled with long-ing, grief, and strength I didn't know she had ever put into words.

It wasn't finished. The final page trailed off mid-sentence, as if the words had simply stopped showing up for her one day. Or maybe she gave up... maybe she thought it didn't matter.

Tears pricked my eyes.

It did matter. It *should* have mattered.

I looked at the page still in my hand. Gram's words were faded, but certain.

She must've had a dream. And somewhere along the way, she set it down.

I wondered if anyone knew. If she had ever told anyone.

"Why didn't you finish it?" I whispered, running my fingers over the faded ink. "Did you think no one would care?"

My throat tightened. I imagined her sitting here alone, writing in the quiet—maybe hoping someone would one day find these words and understand.

"I care," I whispered. "My dream started with you, Gram."

I grabbed my laptop, opened a blank document, and stared at the blinking cursor like it was a heartbeat.

At first, it was just noise—random notes, flickers of characters, scraps of dialogue with no home. But then a sentence came. Then another. And just like that, I was in it.

So deep I didn't hear the rain stop.

When I finally looked up, five hours had passed.

But I wasn't tired. I was on fire.

Even after the rush faded, it wasn't enough. I didn't just want to write—I wanted to *live* in it. I wanted a life built on words. A purpose that was mine.

I didn't want to just start a story.

I wanted to finish one.

Really finish it.

For me.

And just as that thought settled, a familiar voice crept in— quiet, doubting, persistent.

Who do you think you are?

It wasn't cruel. Just quiet. The kind of doubt that wears a softer mask.

It wasn't that I didn't want it—I did. More than anything. But wanting and believing are two very different things. I didn't have a plan. I didn't have experience. I didn't have a résumé, or a deadline, or a guarantee that anyone would care.

But I had this longing—this pull.

And maybe that was enough, for now.

I slipped into a sweater, grabbed my keys, and decided to stop by the library before heading to the store. I wasn't sure what I was looking for—maybe inspiration, or maybe just someone else who understood the hunger to create something that mattered.

The moment I stepped inside, the scent of old pages and quiet purpose wrapped around me like a memory. I wandered the aisles slowly, letting the stillness sink in.

"Emerson?"

I turned toward the voice and blinked.

A woman stood at the end of the row—late twenties, strawberry blond hair twisted into a messy bun, a small nose ring glinting beneath the pendant lights.

"It's me—Natasha Charnin. Remember me?" She raised her eyebrows. "We used to play in the woods together when you visited your grandma in the summers."

I laughed before I could stop myself. "Tasha!" And I hugged her.

"You always made me be the villain." She laughed.

"And you always escaped!" We both laughed.

We talked—about Gram, summer swims, and how time had both stretched and folded. I told her just a little about the past year. She didn't flinch or gossip. She just listened. And when I told her about my dream of writing, her eyes lit up.

"You know," she said, "we just started a local writing group.

It's small—just a few of us. We meet here on Tuesdays. You should come."

I said yes to something that had nothing to do with survival.

I said yes because I wanted to.

I wrote the time down in my notes app before I could talk myself out of it. It wasn't a commitment. But it was a step.

CHAPTER 26

Crooked and Perfect

"You're making me do *what*?"

I held up the reservation email on my phone. It's art with wine. You'll love it."

Sam stared like I'd suggested we reenact *Dirty Dancing* in front of his coworkers.

"There's wine," I coaxed.

"Wine is good. The rest feels like community service." He laughed.

"Sam."

"Fine. But if someone is going to try to grade my art, I'm filing a report."

The place was called "Sip & Splatter." The sign on the door had glitter paint, fairy lights, and a poorly drawn wine glass with googly eyes glued to it. Sam looked like he was walking into a crime scene.

"I take it you've never been to a paint-and-sip night," I said, barely hiding my grin.

"I do math," he said, holding the door like it might bite him. "Not macaroni art."

I kissed his cheek on my way in. "Relax, Picasso. It's just paint, not surgery."

Inside, couples were already seated at long wooden tables, sipping wine and clutching paintbrushes like weapons of emotional expression. Each easel held half of a blank canvas. The night's theme: Sunset for Two.

"I hate how metaphorical this is already," Sam muttered as we sat.

"Which is exactly why I brought you," I said, setting down my purse. "I deal in emotion. You deal in geometry. Together, we will create very mediocre art."

Sam studied the prompt—a glowing sunset split straight down the middle. Both canvases held half the sky, half the water, and the sun somewhere in between. The challenge was to make them match just enough to belong together—but still look like their own.

I shrugged. "You're the engineer. Handle the logistics."

The instructor—Jolene, per her rhinestone name tag—offered us our first glass of wine and a cheerful pep talk about "painting from the soul." Sam looked like he wanted to ask if souls had measurable output.

Thirty minutes in, mine looked like a dreamy watercolor postcard. Sam's looked like a binary-coded sunset having an identity crisis.

"You realize the water is not supposed to be purple, right?" I asked, squinting.

"That's a shadow layer. For depth," he said with faux authority.

"I dipped my brush in coral and reached across the table to swipe a streak down his nose. "Consider that emotional growth."

He blinked. "I will retaliate."

"Oh, I hope so," I said, squinting at his brushwork.

A second later, I had a splatter of blue on my collarbone.

"Sam!"

"Balance," he said, entirely too smug.

I grabbed the gold paint.

Jolene cleared her throat from the front of the room, giving us the look reserved for disruptive children and mildly inebriated couples.

"Do not challenge me, Sterling," I whispered, flicking a dot of yellow onto his forearm.

"I built a deck with a dislocated shoulder," he said, eyebrow raised. "You're not the toughest thing I've handled."

I snorted. "You can't even draw a straight horizon line."

He looked at our shared "masterpiece." He wasn't wrong. My sun looked like it had regrets. His water looked like it had feelings.

We laughed so hard my ribs ached.

Eventually, the war ceased. Mainly because we were out of wine, and Jolene threatened to separate us. Sam wiped the paint from my chin with his thumb, slower than necessary. His hand lingered. His eyes lingered longer.

"You two are adorable," said the woman at the next table, her paintbrush hovering mid-air.

"She started it," Sam said, pointing at my coral-covered hand.

"He's emotionally repressed," I replied.

"So we splatter," Sam finished.

The woman laughed, shaking her head. "Honestly? Marriage goals."

I didn't correct her.

We stared at the canvases in silence for a full minute. Then Sam said, "Switch with me."

"Surrendering your half already?" I asked, grinning.

"Let's just say your radiant chaos is holding up better than my moody little lake," he said, rubbing the back of his neck with mock shame.

We swapped sides. He mimicked my color blending. I attempted a canoe—it looked like a sad banana.

"Remind me never to take up realism," I muttered.

"You're killing it in abstract optimism, though."

"This is fun," I said quietly, gesturing to the mess, the moment, all of it.

His gaze didn't move. "Yeah, it really was."

The night ended with us holding our two canvases outside the studio. When placed side by side, the sun aligned just enough to pass for intentional.

"It's crooked," Sam said.

"It's perfect," I said.

"I'm hanging it in the garage." His deadpan delivery only made me laugh harder.

"I'm hanging it in the living room." I crossed my arms. "Front and center."

He raised a brow. "We don't negotiate, do we?"

"Nope." I kissed his cheek. "But you're lucky you're cute."

He reached for my hand, fingers lacing through mine, paint smudges and all.

"You know I'd paint with you anywhere, right?" he asked.

I smiled. "I know."

And just like that—paint-streaked, wine-warm, and grinning like idiots—we drove home with two terrible paintings and one perfect night.

We didn't talk about the future that night. We didn't need to. It was in the laughter, the paint-streaked kisses, the way his hand never let go of mine. But joy like that doesn't need to shout. Sometimes, it just settles in quietly—deep in your bones—until one day you realize it's still there, long after the laughter fades.

Two Halves, One Heart

I let my head rest against the cool window as Sam drove, the hum of the truck smoothing out the chaos in my mind. The further we went, the quieter everything became. The weight of the past year. With each mile, I felt it slip further away—if only for a little while.

He lifted my hand, brushing a kiss over my knuckles before setting it back in my lap. "This weekend is ours."

The Blue Ridge Mountains stretched out around us, painted in bold, breathtaking strokes—rust, amber, gold. Every ridge was alive with color, as if the hills had been set on fire in the softest way. Dogwoods blushed deep red beneath the glowing canopies of sugar maples. Sunlight spilled through the trees in golden shards, catching on drifting leaves that twirled lazily to the ground. A smoky blue haze softened the peaks in the distance, and the crisp air smelled of woodsmoke, pine, and something wilder—earthy and untamed. It felt like we were driving straight into a painting. One only October could've made.

The further we drove, the quieter the world became—the hum of the town's gossip fading into nothing but the purr of

Sam's truck, the country station on the radio, and his low voice singing along.

I exhaled, anticipating a relaxing weekend. Sam's hand reached across the console, fingers wrapping around mine, his grip warm and steady, as always. I turned to look at him. He didn't say anything, but he didn't have to.

After another turn, the chalet came into view. I was breathless.

Nestled against the mountainside, it was effortlessly beautiful. Clean lines and rustic wood, a wraparound porch that overlooked the valley below. A place built for peace. Something inside me loosened.

"You never told me you had a place like this," I said, my voice softer than I intended.

Sam smirked, putting the truck in park. "I was waiting for the right time to bring you here."

I swallowed past the sudden warmth blooming in my chest as I climbed out. The air was cool, and scented with pine.

Sam grabbed our suitcase, along with some grocery bags from the back seat, and led me up the steps. The door creaked slightly as he pushed it open, revealing a space that was purely him. Minimalist and strong, with rich wood tones and large windows that let the last bit of daylight spill inside. The fireplace sat cold and empty. Within moments, Sam had stacked logs inside, striking a match and coaxing flames to life. The glow flickered across the room, warming the space instantly.

I dropped onto the couch, tucking my feet beneath me. It felt surreal being away for the weekend. Sam moved around the kitchen, unpacking groceries, and setting things into place— enough food for a few days. My heart twisted at the thought. He had planned this, knowing I needed an escape before I even realized it myself.

For a moment, we just sat there with the fire crackling, the tension easing. Then he passed me a glass of wine, his voice low. "Tell me what's going on in that head of yours."

My fingers curled around the stem. I blinked hard, eyes suddenly full.

"I'm scared it's too good," I admitted quietly. "That if I stop holding my breath, I'll lose everything."

He didn't speak right away. He just watched me like he was choosing his next words carefully.

"I get it," he said. "Some nights, I wake up and wonder if I'm dreaming this, too." He paused.

"But I'm not. And neither are you. This is real, Emmy. And I'm not going anywhere."

The silence stretched, but it wasn't heavy. It was comfortable in a way that settled deep inside.

Sam set his glass down and stood, disappearing into the back room for a minute before returning with a small box in his hands. He sat beside me again, handing it to me without saying a word.

I blinked... my heart hammered as I opened it. Nestled inside the velvet box was a delicate gold necklace, its pendant shaped into a perfect heart. One side shimmered with deep blue sapphires, the other glowed with brilliant diamonds.

My birthstone. His birthstone.

Us.

Separate, yet inseparable. Bound together.

He fastened it around my neck, his touch lingering at the clasp. "Yours, mine, always."

His voice stayed low. "I had it made for you." His eyes held mine.

"You know what you are to me?" His voice was certain. "You're the softness in a hard world. You pull me out of my head with a simple look, a laugh, or a touch. I reach for you without thinking, like it's instinct."

He paused.

"You make me feel chosen. Respected. Needed. And I love taking care of you—not because you need me to, but because I *get* to. Because it's the greatest damn honor of my life."

His hand brushed my cheek.

"You look at me like I'm brilliant. Like I'm unshakable. Like nothing could touch you with me beside you. And the way you adore me?" His voice broke just slightly. "Emmy, it makes me feel ten feet tall. Like there's nothing I can't do—because I know you believe in me. Because you love me that way."

My fingers traced the stones, their weight settling against my skin like a pledge.

Emotion pressed like a clenched fist in my throat. "Oh, Sam."

Tears stung my eyes as I pressed my fingers against the pendant, feeling the profound meaning behind it. "You are..." I shook my head, searching for the right words. "Incredible."

He shrugged like it was nothing. But it was everything.

I turned, throwing my arms around him, and pressing my face against his chest. "Thank you. I absolutely love it."

Sam pulled me closer, his voice a whisper against my hair. "I'm glad."

I let my eyes close, breathing him in.

His voice was low, rough, like the words had been carved from somewhere deep inside him. "From the second we met, it was you."

Silence stretched between us, thick with something more profound than words.

There was a time I thought no one would ever choose me— not really. Not without conditions. Not without masks.

With a pounding heart, I forced down the lump in my throat. "I've spent my whole life trying to become what someone else needed. But you... you saw me. You accepted all of it—the mess, the moods, the weight I carry—and never once asked me to be anyone else."

My voice shook. "You've stood by me through everything. The family stuff, the emotional wreckage, and you never pulled away. You made it better—just by being there. Just by being you."

Sam's eyes didn't waver. He didn't interrupt. He let me speak like he knew how long I'd been holding it in.

"I don't know what I did to deserve that kind of love," I whispered. "But I know I'm never letting it go."

His lips brushed mine—barely there. "You showed me who you were. That's all it took."

I shattered.

"I was always searching. For something that felt like home. And you are it." My voice cracked. "Every mistake, every challenge, every moment I thought would break me—it led me here. To you. To us. And if that's what it took... I'd go through it all again."

He pulled me into his arms, holding me so tight I could feel his heartbeat against mine. "By the way. *I'm* the lucky one."

The two days in the mountains had been perfect. A stolen moment outside of reality for just the two of us. We had woken up slowly, wrapped around each other, as the sun spilled through the windows. Sam had cooked for me. Simple, delicious meals that tasted better because his loving hands had made them. I read him some of my poems—including one I'd written just for him, for this weekend.

WHAT LOVE REALLY IS
You never asked me
to be less
so you could feel like more.
You never tried
to fix the broken parts—
just held them
like they were whole.
You saw me
when I still wore the mask.
And stayed
when I began to take it off.
Love isn't loud.

It doesn't shout,
or demand,
or chase.
Sometimes—
it just shows up.
Over and over.
Until you finally believe
it's real.
And because of you,
I do.

After I read the poem, Sam didn't speak at first. He just looked at me.

Like the words had carved something open in him that he wasn't ready to close.

"Emmy... no one has ever written something for me. Not like that."

He reached out, brushing his fingers along my wrist.

"You could've handed me a thousand gifts, and none of them would touch this."

A pause.

Then softer.

"You saw me. And you put it into words. I don't know how you do that, but... wow."

He smiled, eyes glassy.

"I'm gonna carry that with me for the rest of my life."

I didn't speak. I couldn't. I just reached for him—and in that moment, something settled between us.

That weekend, we laughed, talked, and made love... and I finally let myself go completely. I let myself exist without expectation. It was peace. It was love. It was everything I didn't know I could have.

The fire burned low, casting flickering shadows across the

walls. Outside, the mountains stretched out beneath the night sky—endless and quiet. But inside, it was just us. Just this.

With a sure grip, Sam pulled me to my feet. No words.

He led. I followed. A slow dance to nothing at all.

My cheek rested against his chest, his heart beating beneath my ear. His arms tightened around me. One hand smoothing up my back, fingers tracing slow circles against my spine. It wasn't just comfort—it was something deeper. Something that said *I'm here. I've got you. No matter what comes next.*

The quiet settled between us like a slow exhale. And then he pulled back just enough to tilt my chin up, with his thumb brushing across my face. His gaze searched mine, something heavy and knowing behind those gorgeous brown eyes.

Then he kissed me.

It was slow but intense, like it could've been the last time—even though we both knew it wasn't.

My body was warm from the heat of his, the fire, and the moment.

He led me to bed, pulling the blankets over me, and brushing a slow kiss to my forehead. And then he climbed in beside me, tucking me against his chest... holding me the way only he could. Strong, sure, like nothing in this world could shake us.

And as I drifted off, my fingers wrapping around the pendant at my throat, I knew something with absolute certainty.

This was real.

I curled into his chest, the pendant cool against my skin. But somewhere beneath the quiet, something whispered—don't get too comfortable.

CHAPTER 28

Peace Born of Pain

I t had been almost three weeks since the mountains.

Since the necklace, the dancing, and the kind of quiet that doesn't come around twice. And while part of me wanted to live in that moment forever, real life had crept back in—slowly, gently, and very much welcomed.

I'd started attending Tasha's writing group once a week at the library. The first time, I sat in the back with a death grip on my notebook and didn't say a word. But something about the room —the smell of paper, the warmth in people's voices, the feeling of being surrounded by others who *needed* to write—settled something in me. I started to feel increasingly connected to this little community of aspiring authors.

After a few weeks, I wasn't just attending—I was showing up as *me*.

Reconnecting with Tasha had been easier than I thought it would be. Coffee with Ute, which used to be every Saturday, had shifted to every other week—life had gotten busier for both of us. I'd also started slipping into the back row at a small church down the road. Nothing formal. No fanfare. But the stillness of it quieted something inside me. It was the kind of quiet that made the noise of life easier to carry. Which made what came next all the more welcome.

Last Tuesday, a new woman named Hazel joined the group. She was at least seventy-five, with fire-orange glasses and a bright yellow beret that didn't match a single other thing she was wearing. She introduced herself with one sentence, "I'm Hazel. I write smut, but classy."

Tasha snorted her coffee.

Hazel then read a passage from her latest "gentleman's novella," which included the phrase *throbbing legacy.* When the room fell silent, she looked up, completely unfazed.

"What? You think because my knees are shot, that my imagination is, too?"

The entire room burst out laughing.

I did, too. I felt like I belonged in a room where I hadn't earned it with fake smiles or perfect posture. Just *words.* Just the real me.

Later that night, Sam and I were on the water.

Under the moon, the lake was like glass. The boat rocked gently, the only sound the soft ripple of water against the hull. Sam and I sat in the middle of it all, a vast nothingness stretching around us like the entire world had gone quiet.

I pulled my sweater tighter, the cool autumn air brushing my skin like a quiet reminder that everything was changing. "It's so quiet out here."

Sam nodded, staring out at the horizon. "Yeah. That's why I come out here when my head gets too loud."

There was something about his voice tonight. It was lower, and more measured. He wasn't just talking. He was on the edge of something more intense. I could feel it.

After a long silence, he finally said, "You ever think about how fast life changes?"

I glanced at him. "All the time."

He exhaled, his grip tightening around the wheel. "I used to think I had all the time in the world. Thought I could race through life, chase after every thrill, and still have years to figure out the rest."

I leaned in slightly. "And then?"

Sam let out a slow breath, his jaw tensing before he spoke. "I landed my dream job fresh out of college. Head engineer at Hughes Aircraft in L.A. It was everything I thought I wanted. Fast cars, a flashy bachelor pad, racing motorcycles on the weekends... you name it. I was living the dream, or so I thought."

The corners of his mouth twitched, a humorless attempt at a smile. "Then I got the call." He hesitated. "My dad had pancreatic cancer. It was aggressive. They gave him weeks."

It knocked the air from my lungs. I reached out instinctively, placing my hand lightly on his arm. He didn't pull away, but his body was tense, as if he were holding back something heavy.

"I dropped everything," he continued, his voice thick. "Packed up my life in a day and flew back here. Everything that I thought mattered—my job, the fancy car, the beachfront condo—felt meaningless. The only thing that mattered was being with him."

He appeared to be lost in thought. "I sat with him for weeks, watching him fight through a pain no one should have to endure. He never stopped blaming himself for Caleb. Said a better father would have saved him. He carried that weight to his last breath."

Tears burned behind my eyes, unbidden. "That must have been unbearable."

"It was," he admitted. "But it changed me, too. Watching him suffer made me realize how fragile everything is. Life, love, all of it. I'd been living like I was invincible—like nothing could touch me. But sitting there with him in those weeks, I saw how fast it can all slip away."

I let his words settle in, watching the way the moonlight painted silver streaks across the water. "You gave up everything for him."

"I'd do it again in a heartbeat." His voice was firm, unwavering. "When he was gone, I couldn't go back to the life I had before. I didn't want to. The constant rush, the competition, the noise. It all felt hollow. So, I slowed down. Moved back here. Started living a life that felt... real."

His words stirred something deep within me... a yearning I couldn't quite name. "That's why you're so calm," I said, almost to myself. "You've faced the worst."

He gave a soft laugh, though there was no humor in it. "I've learned to let go of the things that don't matter. The people, the moments, the things that bring you peace. That's what makes life worth living."

I swallowed hard, my heart aching for him. "I admire you, Sam," I said quietly. "I don't know how you can be so positive after the things you've gone through—losing Caleb and your dad."

"You've walked away from everything you've ever known, stood up to people who tried to break you." He touched my hand. "That takes a kind of courage almost no one has."

For so long, I had felt small, powerless against the tidal wave of my family's expectations and a marriage to Brad built on image. But Sam didn't see me that way. He saw someone resilient.

The silence between us stretched, thick with meaning. His fingers slowly folded into mine. Something about being out here, surrounded by nothing but water and stars, made everything feel raw—honest.

His gaze drifted toward the shore. "My poor mom has had to endure so much." His jaw tightened slightly, his throat working like he was swallowing something heavy. "Losing my dad, my brother... she carries a lot of weight. She's incredible."

I glanced at him. "She really is. She carries herself like the world never touched her, but you can see it in her eyes. The loss. The grit. And somehow, she still shows up for everyone."

Sam's expression softened. "Yeah. She's the strongest person I know."

"You're a good man, Sam," I said quietly. "And a wonderful son."

He studied me for a long moment, then gave a small, grateful nod. The world felt too vast, the weight of it pressing in—but he didn't have to carry it alone.

We sat there, floating in the stillness, hands still linked. The grief, the truth of it all, settled between us—not crushing, not his burden alone, but shared.

I squeezed his fingers. Then, without hesitation, I shifted closer, wrapping my arms around him.

Sam stilled for half a second, then exhaled against my hair, his hands sliding up my back, pulling me in. His uneven breath warmed my temple.

I didn't say anything. I didn't have to.

I just held him closer.

And this time, I was the one holding him together.

CHAPTER 29

Dreams on the Water

The air had that late autumn chill that made you crave a fire, a blanket, and someone's arms around you. Our hands brushed as we walked toward the marina, laughter still lingering from something ridiculous Sam had said earlier.

Everything felt light. Easy. Like the storm had passed, and we'd somehow come out the other side with clearer skies and steadier hearts.

The lake stretched out before us, its surface sparkling under the late afternoon sun. A light breeze carried the familiar calm that always settled over me here.

But tonight, there was something different about Sam. His posture was the same—relaxed, hands in his pockets, easy stride—but there was an energy simmering beneath it, like he was waiting for something.

When we reached the docks, I felt the pull. The hum of boats, the energy of people at Sundancer, and the cliff-side silhouette of The Oasis, standing watch over it all.

Sam veered toward his office, pushing open the door and motioning for me to follow.

"Come on," he said, his voice quiet but firm.

Curious, I stepped in behind him.

The space was sleek yet lived-in, with a wall of windows over-looking the water. It was undeniably his—streamlined, purpose-ful, and comfortable, yet functional. It smelled faintly of cedar and fresh air, with a hint of leather from the worn chair behind his desk. Shelves lined the walls, filled with nautical charts, model boats, and a few framed photos.

The whole room carried a quiet sense of control—smooth wood floors, the faint vibration of a distant boat engine, the soft clink of glassware from Sundancer.

But my eyes locked on the table in the center of the room.

Blueprints, digital renderings, contracts, and plans. It wasn't just a marina expansion. It was something bigger.

I blinked, stepping closer. "What are you working on?"

He leaned against the edge of the table, watching me carefully. "This is the next phase of The Oasis."

I ran my fingers over the smooth blue paper, tracing the outlines of the familiar structures—Sundancer, the marina, the cliff-side restaurant—but there were *new* elements, too. Larger docks. More slips for local boaters. An extended deck off of Sundancer for live music and community events. An expanded garden space nestled into the cliff-side gardens.

"You're expanding?" I breathed, taking it all in.

Sam nodded, a small smile tugging at his lips. "For the people who live here. For the ones who love coming here. I don't want to turn it into some resort or money-grab destination. I just want to make it even more useful and special."

I swallowed, forcing myself to look at him. "When did you start working on this?"

"I've been considering it for a while," he admitted, rubbing the back of his neck. "But I didn't think it was worth pushing for until recently."

I frowned. "Why?"

An unreadable look held in his eyes as they met mine.

"Because for a long time, I wasn't sure it mattered. I figured this place was already good enough. But then you showed up. You got me thinking about what this place means to the people here. It's an important place for our community. People love being here. And I want them to enjoy it even more."

I went back to the plans, glancing at the details. The stone pathways winding through the new gardens, an arbor set against the backdrop of the lake, and the dock stretching wider to accommodate the growing needs of the people here.

"Sam... this is incredible." My voice was barely above a whisper.

He studied me for a long moment before speaking. "You really think so? I have a solid plan. I just need to fill in some details. Any ideas?"

I let out a small, shaky laugh. "I know exactly what you should do with that huge new garden space. Weddings. Wow, can you imagine? Outdoor ceremonies right under the new arbor, the lake stretching wide beneath them, and twinkling lights woven through the trees. At sunset? And then the expanded patio could be used for receptions—dancing under the stars, with champagne flowing. They'd be legendary."

His eyebrow lifted slightly. "Weddings? Huh. I never even thought about that. But now that you mention it... yeah. Tunbridge would love it. The best wedding venue right now is the town square, and this view blows that out of the water. With the expanded gardens, we'll have all the space we need. It's perfect."

Excitement surged through me, the possibilities unfurling like something waiting to come to life. I turned to him, eyes wide. "And it doesn't have to stop at weddings. Picture live music drifting through the gardens on warm summer nights. Twilight dinners beneath strings of lanterns. Cozy fire pits where people gather with drinks, wrapped in blankets as the season shifts. This is so exciting."

His expression shifted, something thoughtful settling into his features. He tapped a finger against the blueprints, nodding slightly, like a piece of the puzzle had finally clicked into place.

"I love those ideas," he said, his voice quieter now. "That's what this was missing."

His fingers brushed against mine on the table. "You."

I swallowed, suddenly hyperaware of the space between us. The warmth of his skin, the weight of his gaze.

He didn't say anything. He just looked at me for a minute, like he was thinking.

And I realized something, too.

I didn't just admire Sam for what he had built.

I admired him for who he was.

For the way he believed in something bigger than himself.

For the way he had unknowingly taught me that I was capable of more.

The weight of it settled deep—this place, his vision, the way he made me feel like I was part of something special. Like I belonged. And maybe that's why, as we stepped out of his office into the warm night air, something between us felt different. We weren't just caught in each other's worlds anymore. We were building one together. Dreaming, side by side. And I wanted to celebrate that—with him.

Sam had fire in his eyes. The kind that told me this night wasn't ending with a polite goodnight at my doorstep.

From the moment we stepped into the night, the space between us changed—like a match waiting to be struck.

At Sundancer, he sat close—closer than necessary. His thigh brushed mine beneath the table. His fingers grazed my wrist in a way that felt casual, but wasn't. His arm rested along the back of my chair, his fingers brushing my shoulder, slow and gentle.

I leaned towards him, smiling.

We both knew exactly where this night was heading and still let ourselves enjoy the slow, delicious burn.

Then his fingers brushed the nape of my neck—barely there, but searing.

I shivered.

His smirk deepened.

I took a sip of my wine, trying to settle the heat crawling up my spine, but it didn't work. Not when Sam was watching me like he could read every thought in my head. Every dirty, wanting thought.

The food was good, but I hardly tasted it.

The conversation was easy, but I hardly heard it.

Because the only thing I could focus on was him.

By the time we left Sundancer, the tension between us had stretched so tight, so razor-thin, that the second I stepped inside the cabin, I knew.

I met his intense gaze, feeling the blood hammer in my temples. "Are you going to keep looking at me like that?"

His voice was a low, rough rumble, like distant thunder. "Like what?"

"Like you're about to take me apart."

His eyes pierced me. His hands flexed at his sides.

And then he moved.

The kiss was instant—hungry. The hours of restraint between us had finally snapped. He lifted me effortlessly, my back hitting the wall, my fingers digging into his shoulders.

And in that moment, I wasn't thinking. I was *feeling*.

His hands on my skin. His mouth on mine. His breath at my neck.

We didn't speak. We didn't need to.

What happened next wasn't rushed, and it wasn't careful. It was everything. It was raw and reverent. Like he was discovering me—not claiming me. Like I was letting him see everything I'd never shown anyone else.

We didn't make it to the bed. The firelight wrapped around

us, flickering across bare skin and whispered promises. And in that heat, I stopped thinking about who I had been. I stopped hiding.

I let go.

I gave him every part of me.

And what he gave in return unraveled something I didn't know was still tangled inside me.

When it was over, neither of us moved. We just stayed there, wrapped in each other, our breathing slowly falling into the same rhythm.

Sam's fingers traced the curve of my shoulder, featherlight, like he needed the reassurance that I was still here—that this had really happened.

I looked up and his eyes were already on mine. He didn't speak. He didn't need to. He just held me tighter, like he couldn't get close enough, like the silence between us meant more than anything words could carry.

And somehow, even as my body still trembled from what we'd shared, I already ached for more.

Then, without warning, he pulled me even closer. His mouth brushed my ear, his voice low and reverent. "You are my love."

I exhaled, my entire body melting into him. His fingers drifted through my hair.

Sleep started to tug at me, but before I drifted off, he pressed his mouth to my hair and whispered, almost to himself—

"Mine."

I didn't resist the word.

I breathed it in like it had always belonged to me.

CHAPTER 30

Still Not Chosen

I hadn't spoken to my parents in months. Not since before the divorce was final. And then—out of nowhere—a text.

> Mom: Would you meet me for coffee
> sometime this week? Please?

I stared at it for a long time, thumb hovering over the screen. My first instinct was to delete it. Ignore it. Pretend it never happened. But something about that one word—*please*—threw me. It wasn't like her. So, I agreed.

We met at The Rusty Skillet. My mother was already sitting when I walked in, but she looked... different. Her hair—once always twisted into a tight, immaculate bun—now fell softly around her shoulders. She wasn't wearing one of her flashy silk scarves or oversized sunglasses. No pearls, no designer blazer, no power heels. Just a soft sweater, jeans, and a quiet look I didn't recognize.

She stood when she saw me. And to my surprise, my mother looked real. More than she ever had in all her polished, pristine armor.

I slid into the seat across from her. "Hey."

She nodded. "Thank you for coming."

A long, awkward silence passed between us.

Then, finally, she said, "Your father's not practicing anymore."

I blinked. "Yeah. You told me that a few months ago."

Her eyes flicked down. "Yes, I suppose I did. I just... I guess I didn't understand what that would mean. Not really."

I waited.

She folded and unfolded her napkin, like her hands needed something to do. "All those friends I thought we had, and the couples we vacationed with, sent Christmas cards to every year? They've vanished. Like we were never even there. Apparently, without the invitations, the power lunches, and the name on the firm... there's not much left to admire."

A flicker of something moved through me. It wasn't satisfaction. It wasn't vindication. It was just... strange.

Hearing her say it out loud—finally seeing the emptiness of the world she once worshipped—it made something shift.

Maybe for the first time, she wasn't looking down at me from the glass castle.

She was standing in the rubble beside me.

I said nothing. I didn't need to.

She took a breath. "I thought they cared about us. About me." Her voice cracked slightly, but she pushed through it. "But I think they cared more about what we represented. And now that your father isn't Richard-the-attorney, our status is gone."

She trailed off.

I studied her face, searching for the angle. For the guilt trip. For the part where she'd say *you were right* and expect me to fill in the blanks.

But it didn't come.

Instead, she said, "I think I'm beginning to understand what it felt like for you. Not the same, of course, but... similar. The isolation. The judgment. The silence. I've been trying to imagine how much worse it must have felt for you—having it come from your own family."

That landed.

She looked up. "I was cruel, Emerson. I judged you when I should have listened. And I did it for the approval of people who don't even remember my name now."

I exhaled, slowly. "It always felt like love came with conditions," I said, voice low. "If I didn't fall in line, the strings got pulled."

She nodded without hesitation. "I know."

"And if we went back in time... I don't think you'd do anything differently."

She paused, lips pressing into a thin line. Then she nodded slowly. "You're probably right."

That stunned me more than any apology.

She reached for her coffee, then paused. "But I'd like to try. Not to be perfect. Not even to be forgiven. Just... to be better. A better version of the mother you had."

I didn't speak. I let the words sit there, steeping in the space between us like they might change the air.

Then I looked at her. "If you mean that... then we have to talk about the part you've always avoided—Bethany."

Her eyes flicked—not surprise, exactly. Just a shift. A tightening.

"She's still doing it," I said. "Lying, being manipulative, trying to turn people against me. She moved here just to watch me fall apart. And you know it. You've always known what she's like." I insisted.

My mother sat still.

"You watched it for years," I said, voice unsteady. "The way she bullied me and tore me down. The hateful things she did. And you never stepped in. You never told her to stop. You never even said it was wrong."

"I didn't think—" she started.

"No," I said. "You didn't. Or you didn't want to. And that silence? It gave her permission."

She looked down, fidgeting with her napkin again like it might hold the right response.

"I spent my childhood thinking I was the problem. Bethany was cruel, and you defended her. She was jealous, and you excused her. Somehow, you always felt sorry for *her*, but you never saw *me*. You just told me to keep the peace. Like I didn't matter."

Tears burned behind my eyes, but I didn't let them fall.

"If you still won't call what she's done *wrong*—if you keep coddling her, and pretending not to see it—then nothing has changed. Not really."

Her voice was quiet. "She's my daughter, too."

I nodded. "I know. But so am I. And I deserved your protection."

Her eyes lifted.

"Letting one child destroy the other—just because it's easier not to choose—is not love. Mom, you chose a side when Bethany hurt me. You didn't choose me then. And you didn't choose me with Brad. Even now, I don't think you understand what real healing would take."

My voice wavered, but I didn't look away. "You want to stay neutral. Safe. But that silence tells the world—and Bethany—that it's still okay to mistreat me. That I'm still the one you'll sacrifice to keep the peace."

I sat back. "You want the best of both worlds. And while I want to move forward... I don't think you're ready to finally choose me. And if you can't do that, then I don't know how this ever gets repaired."

I let the words land. I needed her to feel them. To sit in them.

My mother's expression didn't change. But she didn't argue. She didn't defend. And maybe that was the closest thing to any kind of truth I was ever going to get.

We didn't speak after that.

We stood at the same time. She hesitated again, like maybe this time she'd hug me.

She didn't. And neither did I.

We walked out into the crisp autumn air in silence. She went left. I went right.

I didn't look back. But I wanted to.

In the car, I sat for a minute with my hands on the wheel, the weight of her words circling like smoke.

I didn't know if she meant it. I didn't know if she'd change.

But for once, she hadn't asked me to be anything other than who I was.

And that was something.

Not everything.

But something.

CHAPTER 31

Unbroken

November had arrived with a quiet defiance—cold, clean, and bracing. The air had grown sharper, the leaves now brittle and wind-tossed.

Sunlight illuminated the wooden floors through the cabin windows. I sat at Gram's old desk, the fire crackling softly behind me, my fingers hovering over the keyboard. My breath caught as I reread the email for the hundredth time.

Dear Ms. Sinclair,
We are pleased to inform you that your poem, Unbroken, has been selected for publication in our upcoming anthology. Your work capti-vated us with its raw emotion and stunning imagery.
Congratulations on this well-deserved recognition.
Regards,
Margot Ellison
Senior Editor, Crestwood Literary Review

I pressed a hand to my chest, feeling the rapid thud of my heart beneath my palm. My words had found their way into the world.

"No way!" I burst out, excitement crackling in my veins.

I had spent years writing in the shadows, never daring to believe that my voice mattered. But someone had read my work. Someone had felt something because of it.

"What's up?" Sam's voice pulled me back, but my eyes stayed locked on the screen. He leaned against the doorframe.

I swallowed hard, my emotions all tangled up in my throat. "It's happening," I whispered. "They're publishing my poem."

For a few seconds, he just stood there, watching me like he was absorbing every piece of that moment. Then, in the blink of an eye, he was across the room, lifting me off my chair and spinning me around.

"I knew this would happen!" he said, laughing as he set me down. His voice was bright with pride, and edged with certainty and conviction. His hands framed my face, his thumbs brushing over my cheeks. "You're talented. And this is only the beginning."

"It's just one poem," I whispered.

"And the first of many," he corrected, his gaze unwavering. "You're gonna leave a mark. The kind no one forgets."

I let out a shaky breath, trying to absorb the weight of his words. Trying to believe them.

Before I could fully process it, his hands slid down to mine, his grip warm and sure. "Come on," he said, a grin already tugging at his lips.

I narrowed my eyes. "Where are we going?"

"We're celebrating," he said simply, like it was the most obvious thing in the world.

I let him pull me up, laughing despite myself. "How exactly do we celebrate this?"

His grin turned downright wicked. "By jumping into the lake."

I froze. "You're joking."

"Nope," he said, leading me outside like a man on a mission. "New beginnings deserve a leap. And what better way than straight into cold water?"

I laughed, but my stomach flipped. "Sam, it's November. We'll turn into popsicles!"

"All the more reason to make it memorable," he shot back, giving my hand a tug. "Come on, Em."

I let out an exaggerated sigh. "If I say no, you're just gonna talk me into it anyway, aren't you?"

"Absolutely." He winked.

He led me toward the dock. The air was cold, the sunlight bouncing off the water in shimmering waves. Sam let go of my hand just long enough to reach for the hem of his shirt.

He flexed—just to mess with me—his pecs jumping in response.

Without another word, he took off running, sprinting straight down the dock before launching himself into the air.

SPLASH.

I gasped as the water swallowed him whole, but a second later, he resurfaced, shaking his head like a wet dog.

"Son of a—*that's cold!*" he shouted.

I was laughing at the look on his face. "Serves you right!"

He flicked water at me. "Get in here!"

"Yeah, no thanks."

His grin turned downright devious. "You really wanna start your new career as a writer with a broken promise?"

I blinked. "What promise?"

"You said you were in this with me," he said, voice mocking, teasing, tempting. "So? Prove it."

Damn him.

I kicked off my shoes and took a deep breath, toes curling against the rough wood of the dock. Then I ran.

The second I jumped, my heart plummeted. The wind rushed past me—and then,

ICE.

The lake consumed me instantly, the shock of it stealing the air straight from my lungs.

I surfaced, gasping. "Oh my—!"

Sam had a wicked grin. "Told you."

I shoved water at him. "You're insane!" It was so cold that my skin started to feel like it was burning.

But Sam just stretched his arms out lazily, treading water like he belonged there.

He swam toward me, brushing wet hair from my face. His fingertips trailed down my cheek, lingering. "I'm so proud of you," he said softly.

We climbed out, shivering and soaked, grabbed our stuff, and raced back toward the cabin.

We tumbled inside, dripping onto the floor, breathless and giddy.

Then Sam gave me *the look*.

He grabbed my shirt, yanking it over my head. His fingers skimmed my stomach, his touch leaving a trail of fire in its wake.

"Shower," he murmured. "Before you freeze."

Steam wrapped around us as we stepped under the spray, the cold still clinging to our skin. His hands slid over my back—less about warmth and more about the moment. The kiss came quiet. Then it turned greedy.

He kissed me like he couldn't get close enough. "Is this how you imagined celebrating your big win?"

I wrapped my arms around his neck, breathless, our foreheads brushing as the water slipped between us. "No."

His smile softened as he cupped my face, eyes locked on mine. "Better?"

I didn't answer—I couldn't. But the way my body moved against him said everything.

So much better.

When we finally emerged, wrapped in towels and warmth, the sun had shifted in the sky, stretching amber rays across the lake.

Sam handed me one of his hoodies, and I pulled it on without thinking. It smelled like him—like his yummy cologne and home.

"Okay," he said, ruffling his damp hair with a towel. "Now that you're officially a published poet, and we've made that milestone very memorable..."—he shot me a wicked grin—"what's next?"

I flopped onto the couch and grabbed my laptop. My heart fluttered. I bit my lip and my pulse was racing. Then, before I could second-guess myself—

"My book. I want to finish it. And then publish it," I admitted.

Sam paused, then turned to face me fully. No teasing. No smirking. Just pure, quiet interest.

"Yeah?" he said, sitting down beside me. "Tell me about it."

I swallowed, suddenly shy. "It's a romance novel. About a woman who thought she had the perfect life. But it was a lie. She had to fight to get out, fight to rebuild herself. Figure out who she was. And when she finally does... she realizes she's never felt love —not genuine love. Until she meets this incredible man. And she doesn't just survive. She *chooses*—love, freedom, and most of all, herself."

Sam's eyes didn't leave mine. I felt like he was seeing right through me—because he was. The story was mine.

Slowly, he nodded. "Wow. You *have* to finish it."

A lump formed in my throat. "But what if—"

He shut that down instantly.

"No." His voice was firm, absolute. "No what ifs."

I stared at him.

"Emmy, you have a story that can split the darkness wide open," he continued, voice low. "And if even one person finds themselves in your words, it was always worth writing."

I gasped. That was it. That was the moment. The words I didn't know I needed.

Because he was right... I had to finish it.

. . .

Without hesitation, I opened my laptop and started typing.

Hours passed. The sun slipped lower. I barely noticed. The words were pouring out of me—unfiltered, raw, aching to be told.

After a while, Sam walked over and set down a plate of sliced apples and peanut butter beside me. I looked up, blinking, only then realizing how late it was.

"You've been at it all day," he said softly.

I rubbed my eyes. "I didn't even notice."

His lips quirked up. "That's how you know it's what you're meant to do."

I exhaled, sitting back against the couch. "It's… going to be amazing. I can feel it."

"I know," he said, settling beside me, his hand sliding over mine. "And I can't wait to read it."

"Thank you," I whispered.

He squeezed my hand, his gaze warm and sure. "Always."

I lost myself in the story again. Sam sat across the room, leaning back in the armchair, his long legs stretched out before him.

At some point, he must've dozed off. Firelight flickered across his face while I just watched him.

I had spent my whole life waiting for the other shoe to drop—for love to be conditional, for the rug to be yanked out from under me the second I got comfortable.

But this? This wasn't fragile. This was built to last.

I set my laptop aside and quietly draped a blanket over him. He shifted slightly, half-asleep, and reached out instinctively, grabbing my wrist.

"Come here," he mumbled, tugging me onto his lap. His arms wrapped around me instantly.

I melted into him.

For once, I wasn't afraid of what came next. I was ready for it. And with Sam, I wasn't doing it alone.

I glanced at my laptop, then back at Sam. His eyes held no doubt, no hesitation—just quiet certainty. And I wanted that certainty for myself.

I took a breath. Then, without overthinking it, I turned the laptop toward him.

His brows lifted slightly. "You sure?"

"Yeah." My voice didn't shake. I wanted him to read the last few chapters I wrote.

Sam sat up beside me, his arm brushing mine. "Alright," he murmured, a slow smile tugging at the corner of his mouth. "Let's see what you've got."

His eyes scanned the words as he scrolled, his expression unreadable. The silence stretched.

When he finally looked up, his voice was firm. "Emmy... this is incredible. I swear, I feel like I'm inside the story with her. I love it."

I let out a sigh of relief. I hadn't realized how much I needed to hear that. I pressed my lips together to keep from grinning too big.

This time, I wasn't just ready.

I was unstoppable.

CHAPTER 32

He Sang, I Fell

I waited until we were about twenty minutes from Atlanta before I told him.

Sam leaned back in the passenger seat, suspicious. "Why do I feel like I'm being set up?"

"Because you are," I said, trying not to grin.

He narrowed his eyes. "Is this another paint night? Because my artistic ego hasn't recovered from the last one."

"Nope," I said, shaking my head. "This is bigger."

He raised an eyebrow. "Should I be worried?"

I reached into the center console and handed him the envelope. "Just open it."

He pulled out the tickets and went still. His eyes scanned the text, then flicked to me in disbelief.

"Elton John?" he said slowly, like he didn't believe it.

"Final tour. Floor seats," I confirmed, trying to keep my voice casual.

Sam blinked. "You got Elton John tickets?"

I nodded. "Surprise."

He looked back at the road, shook his head once, then laughed. "You're kidding."

"Nope," I said again, watching the joy spread across his face. "You once told me you've seen him in concert three times."

"Four," Sam corrected with a grin. "But never with you."

"Exactly," I said, resting my hand on his arm. "I wanted to see how you look when you hear 'Daniel' and 'Skyline Pigeon' live."

Sam squeezed my fingers. "You're going to make me cry before we even park."

"I'll allow one tear," I said, teasing. "Maybe two."

The stadium buzzed with life—tens of thousands of voices, a hum of anticipation, the kind of energy you could feel in your bones. We found our seats, which really meant we found the spot where we'd stand once the music started. For now, the crowd was seated, murmuring and sipping drinks, the stage still dark.

Sam looked around, visibly lit up. "This is wild," he said, grinning. "I still can't believe you pulled this off."

More than the stage, it was his reaction that lit something in me. "I figured if I was going to surprise you, I had to do it right."

"Mission accomplished," he said, reaching for my hand.

Then the lights dropped.

The stadium erupted—thousands leaping to their feet in a single breath.

I stood too, but the moment the first chords of "Bennie and the Jets" hit, the crowd in front of me became a wall of backs and shoulders.

"I can't see a thing," I said, shifting uselessly on my toes.

Sam lifted me onto the chair.

"Really?" I asked, hesitating.

"Yes," he said, steadying me as I climbed. "I'll catch you if you fall. And I'll sue the stadium if I don't."

I laughed, balancing on the seat as the music swelled. I wrapped my arms around his shoulders from behind, chin resting near his temple. "Deal."

He looked up at me with a grin so big it practically split his face. What held me wasn't the performance—it was him.

"Incredible," he said, eyes wide, swaying slightly to the beat.

I smiled and watched the way he mouthed every lyric, and the way his whole body moved with the music. This wasn't just nostalgia. This was joy. Pure, unapologetic joy.

He turned and kissed my knuckles. "I still can't believe you did this."

"Yeah," I said, nodding. "I wanted to see your face when he plays the deep cuts."

As the opening notes of "Skyline Pigeon" filled the arena, Sam went still again.

"Oh hell," he murmured.

"Don't cry," I said softly, smiling.

Sam didn't answer—just pulled me tighter, my arms wrapped fully around him.

"I love this song," he said over his shoulder.

"I know," I whispered, pressing a kiss to his cheek.

When the final note faded, and the crowd thundered its approval, he looked up at me.

"I'll never forget this," he said quietly, reverently.

"I won't either," I whispered back.

We stayed like that, wrapped in each other, still swaying long after the music faded. Just two people. One voice. And a memory that would never fade.

After the final encore, after the applause faded and the lights came up, we found a hole-in-the-wall diner two blocks from the arena —one of those all-night places with worn booths, laminated menus, and a neon sign that buzzed like it was trying to stay awake.

We split greasy turkey burgers and drank vanilla milkshakes straight from the metal mixers.

Sam dipped his fries in mine and argued that it was "efficient resource sharing." I told him it was theft.

We laughed until the waitress swung by with a smirk and two more napkins—just to make sure we hadn't passed out from joy or grease.

"I needed this," he said, stretching one arm along the back of the booth.

I leaned into him, warm and full. "Me too."

There was nothing fancy about that booth, or that food, or that moment.

But it felt like magic anyway.

CHAPTER 33

Foundations

There are worse ways to wake up than with a six-foot-something man wrapped around you like a weighted blanket with abs.

The press of his lips lit a fuse beneath my skin. They wandered lower... slower... until breath left my body in a gasp. A low, satisfied growl rumbled against my stomach as his hands tightened around my waist, pressing me deeper into the mattress.

"Good morning to me," he muttered, voice thick with sleep.

I sucked in a breath, my fingers tangling in his hair. "Sam—"

His laughter was low, sinful. "I could wake up to this every damn day."

Sam savored every inch of me before the sun had even risen. When he finally let me catch my breath, my legs were jelly, my body was spent, and my heart was so full it might burst.

I rolled onto my side—breathless—and my eyes still hazy as I took him in. Tousled hair. Bare chest glowing in the morning light. That cocky smirk tugging at the corner of his lips.

I smacked his arm. "You planned that, didn't you?"

His smirk widened. "Nope. Just couldn't resist."

We stayed in bed too long, lost in slow kisses, wandering hands, and the warmth of a morning neither of us wanted to end. But eventually, Sam stretched, grinning like he knew every filthy thought still running through my mind.

"I need to run out for a bit."

I blinked up at him, still coming down from whatever spell he had put me under. "What? Where?"

He smirked. "You'll see."

Before I could question him, he kissed me. Then he got dressed, threw on his boots, and was out the door before I could process what had just happened.

I stayed there a little longer, my body still buzzing—still *his*.

A few hours later, I was curled up on the couch, sipping tea and writing, when the rumble of the truck pulled me back to reality. He pushed the door open with his shoulder, a set of rolled-up blueprints tucked under one arm, a box balanced in the other, and a sheepish smile on his face. His presence filled the space instantly. His eyes landed on me, along with a big smile.

"Hey, beautiful." His voice was like gravel. "Got a minute?"

I glanced at the rolled-up papers in his hand, curiosity stirring. "Yeah."

He set them down on the table, the weight of them was heavier than I expected. I moved closer, drawn in by the quiet deliberation in his movements, the way he was carefully handling something that clearly mattered.

"What's all this?" I asked, my fingers grazing the curled edges of the paper.

He leaned against the table, watching me. "Something I've been working on. For us."

Us. The word sent a shiver down my spine.

He unrolled the papers, and my breath caught.

They were detailed blueprints and renderings of the cabin— reimagined. Every inch was carefully thought out, and refined with precision and care. A bigger, remodeled kitchen. Refinished hardwood floors. A bathroom renovation. A huge wraparound porch addition. Built-in bookshelves. A floor-to-ceiling stone fireplace. Even a complete exterior facelift.

I let my fingers trace the lines, taking in every detail. "Whoa," I whispered, barely able to get the word out.

He pulled out wood stain, marble, cabinet samples, and paint swatches. He had thought about everything.

Then, as if saving the best for last, he reached for a box near the door. And when he opened it—

I gasped.

It was the chandelier. The one I had seen in the antique shop downtown. The one I had stopped in front of, mesmerized by the delicate crystal pieces that had sparkled in the light.

"You remembered?" My voice braking, just slightly.

Sam's eyes softened, his lips curving into something small and knowing. "I remember everything you tell me. Especially the things that make your eyes light up."

Tears slid down my cheeks as I let out a choked, shaky laugh.

"Sam... I don't even know what to say," I whispered.

His hands framed my face, his thumb catching a tear. "Just tell me you're in this with me."

I exhaled sharply, my hands finding his chest. He had been through hell and back for me. Fought for me when I couldn't fight for myself.

And now?

He wanted a home—with me.

Something real. Something strong. Something that couldn't be taken away.

"Sam, I—"

But before I could finish the thought, he reached into his back pocket and pulled out something small and leather-bound—a notebook.

"What's this?" I asked, confused.

"Just some thoughts." He looked almost nervous, scratching

the back of his neck. "Ideas for the cabin. Notes I've made over time. I've been thinking about this for a while."

I opened it, my fingers trembling. Page after page. His handwriting filled every inch. Notes, sketches. And in the margins—

- ASK ABOUT HER FAVORITE PAINT COLORS
- FIND HER CHANDELIER
- MAKE SURE THE PORCH EXTENDS FAR ENOUGH FOR COFFEE AND LOUNGE CHAIRS AT SUNRISE

I pressed my hand to my mouth. I was shaking. Tears blurred the ink as I flipped the pages, unable to process what I was seeing. This wasn't just a blueprint for a house—it was a blueprint for a life. Our life.

I lifted my eyes to his, my breath coming in soft, uneven gasps. "You... really mean this, don't you?"

His fingers wrapped around mine, warm and sure. "Every word."

"Of course I'm in this," I whispered.

His lips brushed over mine. "Good," he murmured.

And just like that, every broken piece of my past felt like it had finally found its place. The air between us had changed—not in a thunderclap kind of way, but in the quiet shift you feel in your bones before your mind can catch up. Like the tide rolling in just a little closer than before. I knew something had shifted between us, and I didn't want to run from it.

Sam was still standing there, watching me with that knowing gaze—the one that saw everything, even when I tried to hide it. The weight of the notebook in my hands was almost unbearable. I looked down at the blueprints again, my fingers trailing over the ink lines, the scribbled notes that had nothing to do with wood and nails and everything to do with us:

- ENLARGE BEDROOM WINDOWS SO SHE CAN SEE THE LAKE FROM THE BED
- BUILD A WALL OF BOOKSHELVES FOR ALL OF HER BOOKS
- FIND THE PERFECT ANTIQUE HUTCH TO DISPLAY BERNICE'S SILVER TEA SET

I tried to get the words out, but I couldn't find them. How could I? How do you thank someone for this? I'd been given flowers. Apologies. Promises. But never this. Never plans. Never permanence. Never the kind of love that was built like a house—measured, crafted, and meant to last. How do you tell someone that this quiet, deliberate care, is the most loved you've ever felt in your entire life?

Sam must have seen it in my eyes, because his grip on my hand tightened, like he was reminding me that I didn't have to find the words... not with him.

"I know," he murmured. His voice was a quiet rasp, rich and raw all at once. He remembered things I never even told him. His love wrapped around me—not just a shield, but a vow.

I exhaled shakily, pressing my hands to my face for a moment before dropping them, meeting his eyes with more certainty than I had felt about anything in my life. "I love it. It's perfect. I want all of it," I said. The words weren't just a decision. They were a declaration.

He grinned, slow and wicked.

I laughed—actually laughed—through the mess of emotions clogging my throat, and Sam took that moment to pull me into him, wrapping his arms around me.

I pressed my face against his chest, letting myself sink into the feeling, and letting myself memorize the solid rhythm of his heartbeat beneath my cheek. This was real. And it was ours.

After a long moment, he tilted his head down, lips brushing against the top of my head.

"Guess we better get started, huh?"

I tipped my head back to look at him. "Where do we even start?"

Sam grinned. "Kitchen's always a good place. It's the heart of the home, right?"

The words hit in a way they probably shouldn't have, because the truth was—I didn't really know what home felt like. I had spent years walking on eggshells in a house that had never really been mine. But standing here, with Sam? I was starting to figure it out.

I nodded. "Yeah. Let's start there."

Sam reached for the blueprints, but before he could roll them up, I saw a small note scrawled in the margin:

– MAKE SURE SHE KNOWS SHE'S SAFE HERE

I blinked fast before he could notice my eyes. His hands settled on mine, gently.

"Hey."

I looked up.

His voice softened. "You okay?"

I sucked in a breath and nodded. "Yeah."

A wicked, slow smirk twisted his lips. "Wanna take a break from blueprints?"

I exhaled a shaky laugh. "Depends."

"On what?"

I grinned and grabbed onto him. "Are we still talking about the kitchen?"

Sam growled. Actually growled.

"Emmy," he warned.

I just smiled, pressing closer. He let out a long, measured breath, shaking his head.

"You are gonna be the death of me."

I laughed softly. "No, I'm going to keep you young."

His eyes darkened, his voice dropping to a dangerous, velvety rasp.

"You wanna know what my plan is?"

A shiver ran through me. "What?"

His lips grazed mine, then my neck, my shoulder.

"To make damn sure you never doubt," he murmured. "Not for a second. Not for a breath…" His teeth grazed my pulse, hands tightening at my waist. "That you belong here."

I swore I stopped breathing. Not just from the words, but from the way they landed.

With a tender touch, Sam swept my hair behind my ear. There was certainty in his stare.

I pulled him down into a kiss, my heart pounding so loud, so fast, so full I swore he could hear it.

"I love you," I whispered. "And I absolutely adore you."

Sam stilled. His arms tightened. Then, in a voice rough and completely raw, he said the only words I ever needed to hear.

"I love you, too. F.B.O.W."

And just like that, I was home.

Not in walls or wood.

Not in blueprints or renovations.

In him.

CHAPTER 34

I'm Not for Everyone

A low hum filled the restaurant as I shifted in my seat, adjusting the napkin on my lap. The place was beautiful—if you liked modern art that felt cold and uninviting. Everything was sleek, dimly lit, and meant to impress. But instead of feeling special, I felt like an imposter. Like we'd walked into someone else's world by mistake. It was pretentious, soulless—everything Sam Sterling was not.

Across from me, Sam sat back in his chair, his fingers drumming lightly against the side of his Old Fashioned. His eyes swept over the room, his expression was blank, but I could feel it. The same discomfort tightened his shoulders... the same awareness that we didn't belong here.

"You're quiet," I said, taking a sip of my wine.

He smirked, but it didn't quite reach his eyes. "I'm soaking it in. Figuring out if I still fit in places like this."

I raised my eyebrows. "And?"

He let out a breath, shaking his head. "Yeah. No. This isn't me."

I laughed under my breath, leaning in. "So, what exactly were you trying to prove, Sterling? That you could wear a suit and tolerate pretentious small talk?"

His smirk widened, his eyes regaining their warmth. "Maybe. Thought I should make sure I haven't become completely uncivilized."

I grinned, but something about the way he said it made me pause. "You're not uncivilized, Sam. You just know what you like."

"Yeah?"

"Yeah. And it's not this."

His gaze lingered on mine, something unreadable flickering there. He picked up his drink, taking a slow sip before setting it down. "What do you say we get out of here?"

I didn't hesitate. "Hell yes."

Sam signaled for the check, and the relief between us was almost laughable. We weren't meant for places like this—for stiff conversations and overpriced entrees served on plates that looked like modern art. We needed something real. Something that felt like us.

When we stepped out into the crisp night air, I exhaled, stretching my arms above my head. "Thank goodness. I was about five minutes away from making a scene."

He glanced at me, amused. "What kind of scene?"

I shrugged. "I dunno. Maybe flip the table. Loudly rank the worst Botox jobs in the room. Call out the guy next to us for wearing a scarf indoors. Trade the sommelier's pretentious pairing for a round of whiskey shots at a dive bar. Really lean into it."

Sam chuckled, unlocking the truck. "Damn shame we left. I'd have paid to see that."

I slid into the passenger seat, kicking off my heels before curling my legs beneath me. "So, where to now?"

He started the truck, his hands gripping the wheel. For a second, he sat there like he was weighing his options. Then he looked over at me. "You hungry?"

I snorted. "After that three-bite entrée? Starving."

He smirked, shifting into drive. "Good. Let's go home."

By the time we got back, I was ready to shed the last remnants of that restaurant. I ditched my dress for one of his sweatshirts and curled up on the couch while he moved around the kitchen, grabbing plates and pulling leftovers from the fridge.

"Hope you're good with chicken sandwiches," he called over his shoulder.

I stretched my legs out and got comfortable. "If it's real food and not a tiny art project on a plate? I'm in."

He smirked, setting a plate in front of me before handing me a drink. Then he dropped onto the couch beside me, stretching his legs out as he leaned back against the cushions. There was something easy about this—about us. The way we fit together without having to force anything.

I took a bite, sighing dramatically. "Alright, spill. What was tonight all about? Why did we even go there?"

Sam exhaled, running a hand over his stubble. "Just wanted to see if I'd changed, I guess."

I frowned. "Changed how?"

His eyes flicked to mine, something hesitant in his eyes. "I used to live in places like that. I was the guy in the suit, making deals over dinner, drinking overpriced bourbon because it meant you were someone important."

I scoffed. "Yeah, well, I like this version of you better."

A slight smirk pulled at his lips. "This is the real me." He sipped his Diet Coke as his eyes moved to the fire crackling in the hearth. "I'm not for everyone, Em. I'm rough around the edges. I'm direct, brutally honest—and sometimes that offends people— but I've never pretended to be something I'm not."

He looked at me then, his voice quieter. "I'm not always a *nice* guy—but I'm a *good* guy."

My chest tightened as I stared into his eyes. I'd known that about Sam from the beginning, but hearing him say it, laying it bare like this, made it hit differently.

"You absolutely are," I said softly. "I don't know how someone like you stayed single."

His head lifted, locking onto me with quiet certainty. "I hadn't met the right person."

Every part of me quieted.

Sam's expression sharpened. "You came along, and I felt it right away. You were different. I had a feeling deep inside."

"Why me?" I whispered.

"You didn't fall at my feet—you made me think. You pushed back when no one else ever had. Challenged me. That grit. You're strength. You have a kind of bravery I didn't know existed. You are everything I didn't know I needed." His eyes locked onto mine, intense and unflinching.

"And man, you're feisty." He let out a low laugh. "You keep me on my damn toes."

Shaking his head slightly, he let out a breath, his voice quieter but still confident. "I used to think maybe I was too picky. I dated plenty of women. But there was always something missing. I wanted someone I couldn't get enough of. Someone who challenged my mind and set my blood on fire. You are both—beyond measure."

"I needed someone who could match me. A woman with passion, with conviction, who stood her ground and didn't give a damn what people thought. Someone who wasn't intimidated by me, who would walk beside me. A best friend I could be completely insane for."

Sam's stare still held mine.

A rough edge crept into his voice, thick with emotion. "I wanted fire. I wanted depth. I wanted the kind of love that burns everything that came before it. I wasn't searching for something easy—I was searching for something real."

It was like stepping into sunlight after a lifetime of cold.

I spent so long believing that Sam was the one holding me up, that he was my rock, my constant. I had never stopped to consider that I could be that for him, too.

He threaded his fingers between mine slowly. Like this moment—this connection—meant too much to risk rushing.

He spoke quietly, but with conviction. "I could've spent the rest of my life alone. I was never going to settle. But when you came crashing into my world, I knew I was done."

Tears burned at the backs of my eyes, but I refused to blink them away. I needed to hear this, to absorb it, to believe it.

He hooked a finger under my chin, tilting my face up as his presence wrapped around me. "I wasn't looking for someone I could live with, Emmy. I was looking for someone I couldn't live without."

I inhaled sharply, the words settling deep, pulling me toward him like gravity.

I felt his arm brush against mine. My pulse thrummed as I leaned in.

I knew what I wanted.

I knew who I wanted.

CHAPTER 35

Blueprints for Forever

Frost clung to the grass, our breath rising in clouds—and for some reason, we ran.

Every once in a while, on mornings like this, we laced up our shoes and jogged the gravel road in silence. Just breath. Crunching frost beneath our feet. And the occasional brush of his hand against mine.

We made it back to the cabin, cheeks flushed and lungs burning. We peeled off layers and stumbled inside to the scent of brewing coffee. While I thawed in the shower, Sam made breakfast—cinnamon oatmeal.

"There you are." He pressed a soft kiss to the back of my neck. "Ready to get this show on the road?"

"What's the plan?" I asked.

"Porch, staining, trim work... remember?"

He handed me a bowl, made just the way I liked it.

"It smells divine. Thank you."

We ate standing at the counter, the windows fogged from the warmth inside, fighting off January's chill.

With one last sip of coffee, we were ready.

. . .

Layered in flannels and jackets, we headed to the hardware store. Sam was in his element—rattling off measurements, inspecting lumber, geeking out over miter saw specs. I followed along, genuinely curious, but mostly just happy to watch him.

"What exactly are we getting again?" I asked, trailing behind him with the cart.

"Lumber for the porch," he said, picking up a cedar plank. "Studs for the bathroom. And..." He shot me a sideways grin. "A new miter saw."

"Oooh," I said with mock awe. "Every girl's dream."

He raised a brow. "You're about to understand why."

Thirty minutes later, I did. Sort of.

We unloaded everything together when we got home. Sam passed me a tape measure and tossed me a confident nod. "Ready?"

I narrowed my eyes. "You're totally going to double-check all my measurements, aren't you?"

"Nope," he said. "I trust you."

I smiled. "That's a terrible idea."

He laughed and bumped his shoulder gently into mine. "Welcome to construction."

We spent the afternoon side by side, rebuilding the porch. Sam was efficient and focused. I was cautious but determined. Every now and then, he'd guide my hands, correct my grip, or offer quiet encouragement when I hesitated.

"Look at that," he said after my first clean cut. "Natural."

I beamed like a kid.

When it came time to stain the wood, we settled into an easy rhythm—brushstrokes moving in time, the smell of cedar thick in the air. The lake glittered behind us, the light catching the surface just right. Everything felt peaceful. Rooted.

Until Sam dipped a rag in stain and swiped it across my arm.

I gasped. "You did not."

He didn't even try to look innocent. "Gotta break in the rookie."

"You asked for it." I grabbed the brush and dragged it across his shoulder.

That started a full-blown stain war. He ducked, I chased, and somehow I ended up pinned between the porch post and Sam's body, laughing and breathless.

"You're covered," I said, looking at the streak down his cheek.

"So are you." His voice was lower now, his gaze dropping to the mess he'd made across my collarbone.

I didn't move. Neither did he.

And then he kissed me—deep and slow, like the world had faded behind the fog of laughter, sawdust, and everything we were building.

When we finally broke apart, he whispered, "We're a mess."

"Yeah," I said, smiling against his mouth.

By sunset, half of the porch was stained, the tools cleaned up, and the sky painted in streaks of orange and gold.

We sat on the steps, side by side, our legs touching, the scent of cedar still clinging to our clothes.

Sam stretched, looked at the boards in front of us, then at me. "Not bad."

I bumped his shoulder. "You mean perfect."

He laughed. "Yeah. Perfect."

And it was.

Not because it was flawless.

Because we'd built it—together.

The next morning, I woke up to a missed call from my mother.

A voicemail.

I hesitated, thumb hovering over the screen. Then I played it.

"Hi. I read your poem—Unbroken. I—I just wanted you to know it hit me hard. You've always had that gift with words, even as a little girl, scribbling poems on napkins and the backs of church bulletins. I'm sorry it took me this long to say it, but... I'm proud of you. I hope you're well. Love you."

I stood there for a long moment, staring out the kitchen window as her words settled. No expectations. No explanations. Just her voice. Soft. Trying.

I slipped the phone into my pocket and stepped back outside, where Sam was waiting by the truck, arms crossed, smile easy.

As we pulled into the parking lot, the marina was buzzing with activity. Boat engines hummed in the distance, and The Oasis loomed above us—beautiful, thriving, and *his*.

But this evening, it felt like *ours* too.

"Alright, boss," I teased as he parked. "What's on the agenda?"

Sam shot me a look as he killed the engine. "You making fun of me?"

"Never." I smirked.

He chuckled, shaking his head as he opened his door. "Come on, troublemaker."

I followed him inside, past the staff already setting up for the day, past the bar where the morning crew was prepping for brunch, and down the back staircase. I had been here before, but usually, I just hung out, waiting for Sam to finish something.

Today, I had a purpose.

I trailed Sam into his office and turned, expecting him to rattle off the day's priorities. Instead, he just watched me—quiet, unreadable, like something was shifting behind his eyes.

"What?" I asked, suddenly self-conscious.

Sam tipped his chin toward the door across from his. "Open it."

I frowned but did as he said. I crossed the hall and pushed the door open.

And my heart *stopped*.

It was a sunlit space with floor-to-ceiling windows facing the lake. An antique writing desk was nestled in the middle of the room, a plush blue chair by the window, and bookshelves already lined with some of my books. A soft cream-colored couch stretched along the far wall, big enough to curl up on. And on the desk, a vase of peonies—soft, delicate, and impossibly perfect.

My breath caught.

A brand-new laptop sat beside them. This was a space built just for me—one I had never even dared to dream of.

"I can't believe it," I whispered.

He leaned against the doorframe, hands in his pockets, watching me with that sweet gaze, like he was memorizing this moment.

"Figured when you're here, you should have a space that's yours."

I blinked fast, my throat tight. "I can't believe you did this."

His lips quirked into a quiet smile.

I stepped deeper into the room, my fingers brushing over the desk, the books, and all of the small, thoughtful details that made it feel like it had always been mine.

Sam's voice was low. "This is you, Emmy. I see it every time you get lost in your writing. The way your face lights up when you talk about your book. Your dream matters to me, too."

A tear slipped free before I could stop it. He had always seen me—but this was more. This was belief. In me. In my words. In my future.

I pressed my fingers to my lips, trying to hold back the wave of emotion. "You remembered all my favorite things," I whispered.

Sam's smirk softened, something deeper flickering in his eyes.

My heart clenched. I turned back to him, swallowing the lump in my throat. "You're incredible," I whispered, blinking hard.

This wasn't just an office.

This was the moment I knew—I wanted to chase the dream —and dream bigger.

Sam shrugged, like he hadn't just cracked my whole heart wide open. "You like it?"

"I absolutely love it."

His smirk faded, replaced by something quiet and serious. "Good. Because you need to finish that book. Publish it. Maybe a dozen more. And whenever you need a break..." He nodded toward the hall. "I'll be right there."

My heart was going to burst.

I ran to him, lifting onto my toes as I wrapped my arms around his neck. "I don't deserve you."

Sam's arms slid around my waist, pulling me close. "You do," he murmured against my temple. "And you're stuck with me."

I pulled back just enough to press my lips to his, pouring everything I felt into the kiss—gratitude, love, the overwhelming certainty that he was it for me.

His grip tightened as he deepened the kiss, slow and deliberate. My fingers tangled in his hair, and for a moment, I forgot where we were.

Suddenly, someone cleared their throat.

I broke away, my face heating as Sam smirked—completely unbothered.

Hudson, the manager of Sundancer, leaned against the doorway with an amused look. "When you two are done making out, I need your signature on a few things."

I covered my face. "Kill me."

Sam just grinned. "Give me five minutes."

Hudson laughed and walked away.

As he disappeared down the hall, I let out a mortified groan. "He's never gonna let me live that down."

Sam chuckled, pressing one last quick kiss to my lips before heading off.

I closed the door to my new office, running my fingers over every surface—trailing them across the desk, the bookshelves, and the plush chair by the window. Dusk began to settle outside, casting long amber shadows across the floor. I turned in a slow circle, drinking it in, my pulse thrumming with something rare and bright. I sank into the chair, smoothing my hands over the armrests, then spun in a full, giddy circle before stopping to press my fingers to my lips.

Because this wasn't just about a dream.

It was proof. That someone believed in me. That I was meant for more than just surviving.

For the first time, I wasn't just hoping for more.

I *knew* I was made for it.

CHAPTER 36

Firelight

For weeks, the invitation had sat on my dresser—taunting me, daring me.

I kept telling myself I hadn't decided yet, but the truth was, I'd thought about it every day. What to wear, what to say, and whether I even belonged there.

It was the night of the marina's annual winter bonfire—music, food, and the whole town gathered under the stars. I held the invitation in hand... heart pounding harder than I wanted to admit.

Town events used to mean whispers. Side-eyes. People who once smiled had looked away like I carried something contagious.

But I wasn't her anymore. Not the girl who swallowed her voice to keep the peace.

Sam leaned against the doorframe, arms crossed. "You want to go?"

I sighed, gripping the counter. "What if it's just more of the same?"

Sam pushed off the frame and crossed the room in three steady strides. "Then we start a food fight. Or a riot. Either way, we're making it memorable."

A startled laugh burst out of me.

He smirked. "What? You think I won't launch a hot dog at someone's head if they deserve it?"

His confidence settled something inside me.

Maybe it wasn't just about what the town thought of me. Maybe it was about what I thought of myself.

And I was tired of feeling this way.

The night was unseasonably warm—low fifties—crisp, but bearable. The kind of cold that made you breathe deeper instead of shivering. The sky was colored a deep indigo, and scattered with millions of stars. The bonfire crackled at the heart of the marina, flames twisting upward, sending embers drifting like fireflies set loose. Laughter and music rolled over the water, the glow flickering across the lake's surface—like the shimmer of a struck match, brief and electric, alive for just a moment before vanishing into the night.

People gathered in tight circles, hands curled around mugs of cocoa and spiked cider, with flames dancing in their eyes. Someone was roasting marshmallows. Laughter cracked through the cold like firewood. I recognized nearly everyone. Some faces turned toward me, some friendly, some expressions unreadable. Others kept talking, like I wasn't even there.

I braced myself.

Sam slid his fingers through mine. Not just comfort. A statement.

We stepped forward together.

A hush swept through the crowd like a ripple in still water. It wasn't loud, wasn't dramatic, but I felt it. Like the moment right before a wave crashes.

Someone approached me—Margaret, her smile proud. "I saw your poem in the paper. It was beautiful."

One by one, voices joined in. Someone whistled. A couple of guys out on a dock raised their drinks. Margaret was grinning from ear to ear, giving me a small, proud nod.

Then—one I didn't expect.

Susan Draper.

The same woman who had side-eyed me in Drucker's, and had whispered to her friend at the bakery the first time I showed my face in town. She waved and walked over. "That piece in the paper… 'Unbroken'? It stuck with me."

I blinked, throat tightening, because—this wasn't what I expected. Not even close.

"Wow, thank you."

Then, suddenly, a voice pierced the noise. "Hell yeah, Emerson, the writer!"

I turned, heart in my throat.

It was a guy I'd seen before but never met.

"Glad you came!"

The feeling hit me so hard it nearly took me off my feet.

They weren't whispering. They weren't avoiding me.

They were *with* me.

Something shifted deep in my chest, like a tightly wound spring finally uncoiling. A sensation so unfamiliar it almost startled me.

Sam squeezed my hand. When I looked at him, there was nothing but quiet pride in his eyes.

I wasn't an outsider anymore.

I had been forged in the fire, and these people—my people— saw it.

And then—

"Seriously?"

The sneer cut through the moment like shattered glass.

Bethany.

Of course.

She stood at the edge of the bonfire, a blight against the warm glow. Her lips were painted in some desperate shade of superiority, puckered in barely concealed disgust.

She let her eyes drag over me. "Didn't expect to see you here. Thought maybe you'd moved to a commune or disappeared entirely."

I didn't answer. Just stared.

Bethany's smile twisted. "So it's really over? You didn't even fight for anything... did you?"

When I didn't respond, she kept going. "Brad still has the penthouse. And the Porsche. And the house in Aspen."

She tilted her head, voice syrupy and sharp. "And you got what, again? A cabin in the woods? A coffee-stained diner uniform and a handyman with a rusty truck?"

She laughed loud enough to draw a few curious glances. "From gala girl to ghost town. It's poetic, really."

I stepped closer. Calm. Clear.

"And yet I'm happier than you'll ever be."

That wiped the smirk from her face.

I didn't yell. I didn't flinch. I just looked her in the eye and told the truth.

"You built your entire identity on envy and manipulation. You spent your life begging for attention, and tearing people down just to feel taller. But the charade's over. Everyone here sees you now—manipulative, dishonest, and pathetic."

I took a step closer.

"You tried to break me. But I'll always rise above you. Always."

Bethany blinked.

"You don't scare me anymore," I said, my voice like glass. "You are nothing. But I think you already know that."

And then—

A slow clap broke the silence.

Margaret stepped forward.

"I don't think you were invited," she said smoothly.

Bethany let out a sharp, mocking laugh. "Since when is this your town, Margaret?"

Margaret smiled. "Long before you... and long after you."

A murmur of agreement passed through the crowd.

Bethany scoffed, shifting uncomfortably. Then she took a step towards me.

And then, the final blow.

Ute stepped out from the shadows, like she had been waiting for this moment for a long time.

I stilled.

I had never seen her look quite like this. Like a woman who knew exactly how much power she held.

She stepped in front of me, shielding me, her posture straight. Her voice sharpened to a lethal edge.

"You should leave, Bethany," she said.

Bethany let out a dry laugh, flicking her gaze over Ute with an unimpressed sneer. "And who the hell do you think you are?"

Ute didn't blink... she didn't falter.

"I'm Sam's mother."

Her gaze stayed locked on Bethany, unwavering. "And Emerson is my family. You are not welcome here."

Bethany blinked. Once. Twice. Her mouth opened, then closed.

And then—she snapped.

"Oh, spare me the soapbox," she spat, her voice cracking at the edges. "You think any of these people actually like you? You think they've forgotten who you really are?" She turned to the crowd, wild-eyed now. "You're all such hypocrites! You used to laugh at her, just like I did!"

She pointed at me like it was supposed to mean something. "You're not some saint, Emerson. You're a mess in a pretty dress. Always have been."

Silence.

She let out an exaggerated laugh, like she could still win them back. "She abandoned her family. Her marriage. *Remember*?"

She turned back to me, the desperation in her smile sharp as glass. "This won't last. You'll screw it up—because deep down, you know you're just like me."

I didn't move. Didn't blink.

Then Ute stepped forward—closer this time, ice in her voice.

"No, Bethany. She's nothing like you. And everyone here knows it."

That's when it broke.

Bethany's face twisted. Her mask slipped. "You're all pathetic!" she shrieked, eyes darting wildly as people turned away from her. "Every single one of you!"

And then—

"Heard Gunner Lynch's wife finally filed for divorce."

Bethany froze mid-step.

A voice cut through the quiet like a blade. He stood by the docks, one hand in his pocket, the other holding his beer.

"Maybe you can stop sneaking around now, huh? Make it official."

A few people snorted. One woman choked on her cider.

"Bet his kids'll love that," someone else added—low, but loud enough.

Laughter spread like wildfire.

Bethany's face drained of color. Her jaw twitched. Her mouth opened—but nothing came out.

That flicker of panic behind her eyes? It wasn't just embarrassment.

It was the end of her audience.

And this time, she knew it.

She spun on her heel and disappeared into the dark without another word.

For a long moment, no one spoke.

Then, someone cheered.

And just like that, the spell was broken.

A wave of laughter rippled through the group, and suddenly, conversation picked up again. Like the moment had never happened.

But it had.

I turned to Ute, eyes stinging, overwhelmed by the kind of loyalty I'd stopped believing in.

She smiled.

I had a mother who was trying.

And now, I had another—standing right there—who never had to. She claimed me. Stood up for me. Without hesitation.

It felt like a gift.

Warmth bloomed where hurt used to live.

Sam's fingers tightened around mine.

The world moved around us. People were still drinking, still laughing, and still talking about Bethany getting what she deserved, but I wasn't there with them. I was here, in this moment, in this firelight, with the man I loved and the mother who had just defended me.

Ute turned back to me, her gaze softening.

"You were always meant to be here, my dear."

The words landed deep, like roots settling into soil—like something inside me had been waiting to hear them my entire life.

I wanted to say something, anything, but the emotion clogging my throat made it impossible.

Instead, I nodded.

Then Ute pulled me into a hug, wrapping me in such tender affection—the kind that said you belong, that you're loved, that you're home.

A breeze kicked up from the lake, sending the fire crackling higher.

Sam's lips quirked, but there was something deeper in his expression—something that told me he knew exactly what this moment meant to me.

Ute stepped back, giving us space, but her presence stayed anchored inside me.

Sam's hand slid up my arm, slowly, gently, soothing me in the moment.

Something light and sweet filled the air. Music. Someone had picked up a guitar and was playing it near the fire, the low strum was humming under the laughter and conversation. It was soft and easy, wrapping around the night like a memory being written in real-time.

The weight of everything that had just happened was still there, pressing against me—but there was something else, too.

Peace.

I leaned into Sam, letting my body relax against his rock-solid presence.

The fire crackled.

Across the lake, water stretched black and still, stars reflecting like scattered diamonds.

Beside me stood the very people who once whispered and condemned me—now, they were choosing me.

I had been bracing for rejection. For judgment. Instead, I had been given a place to belong.

The music shifted, a familiar song drifting through the air—something old that made people want to dance barefoot in the sand.

Sam turned his head slightly, looked down at me, and said in a low, tender voice, "Dance with me, Emmy."

The firelight flickered in his eyes, something mischievous glinting behind all that charm.

I shook my head, but was already letting him pull me forward.

A few other couples were dancing, swaying to the music, and suddenly, it didn't feel so crazy. It felt like something I had been waiting for without even knowing it.

Sam's hands found my waist and I lifted my arms around his neck.

The music played. The lake stayed quiet.

The town that had once swallowed me whole, had just lifted me up.

I swayed with him, feeling his heartbeat, my cheek resting against his chest.

"I'm so glad I came," I murmured.

Sam pressed a kiss into my hair, voice low and certain. "Me too."

I closed my eyes, letting myself sink into the moment.

CHAPTER 37

Winter Reckoning

I t had been a few weeks since Sam started the renovations, and the kitchen was already taking shape—new cabinets in, fresh paint on the walls, progress humming beneath everything. December had settled in hard. The trees were bare, the lake crusted with frost, and the air carried that frigid edge that only winter brings. We'd fallen into familiar rhythm.

I started to believe nothing could rattle this quiet happiness.

Until that afternoon, when everything shifted.

It started like any other late afternoon—golden light streaming through the pines as we walked into The Battered Barrel to grab a quick drink before heading home after some shopping. The place was warm and familiar—with low lighting, worn wood floors, country music playing, and the hum of laughter in the air.

Sam nodded to a few regulars... that easy confidence radiating off him like always.

Then I saw her.

She was leaning against the bar, talking to the owner. Tall, striking, all legs, and effortless beauty. Her laugh carried. Her presence turned heads. And when her eyes landed on Sam—she lit up.

"Sam Sterling," she said, all warmth and familiarity as she pushed off the bar with a smirk.

Sam's steps slowed. "Holly?"

They hugged—casual, friendly, but my stomach twisted anyway. There was a history in the way they moved around each other. I could feel it.

"I didn't know you were back," he said, stepping back just enough to take her in.

"Just visiting my brother," she said, glancing at me briefly before returning to Sam. "And apparently, just in time to see you looking all grown-up and rugged."

She looked at him. "It's been a long time."

Sam nodded. "Yeah. It has."

The pause stretched. Too long.

"This is Emerson," he said, his hand resting lightly on the small of my back. "My girlfriend."

"Nice to meet you," she said, her voice smooth, unreadable. Then she looked at Sam again. "So... still living out here?"

"Yeah," he nodded, sliding an arm casually around my waist. "Running the marina now."

"Of course you are." Her gaze lingered on him a second too long. "You always had a thing for building something from nothing."

It was a compliment, I think. But it made my stomach turn anyway.

They chatted for another minute—catching up on mutual acquaintances, old jobs, and how long it had been. I smiled. I nodded. I laughed in the right places. But inside, I felt fourteen again—like I was standing outside a party I hadn't been invited to.

Eventually, we said goodbye. She touched his arm as she left. "Good seeing you, Sam."

He smiled. "You, too."

And just like that, she was gone.

But the knot in my stomach stayed.

We sat at the bar, ordered drinks, and made small talk. But I wasn't really present. I was stuck on the way she looked at him—like she knew a side of him I hadn't met yet.

Sam noticed. Of course he did.

"Hey," he said gently, tilting his head to meet my eyes. "You okay?"

I took a breath, bracing myself. "Did you date her?"

He paused, then nodded once. "Yeah. A long time ago."

"She's beautiful," I said, not even trying to hide it.

"She's okay," he said honestly. "But she's not you."

I looked down, my throat thick. "It's not that I think anything's going on. I just... I didn't like the way she looked at you. Like she's been somewhere with you that I haven't."

Sam's hand slid over mine. "Emmy, I've never looked at anyone the way I look at you. Ever."

I blinked, holding his gaze.

"She's history," he said. "You're the present and the future."

The words didn't solve everything. But they settled something in me. The ache quieted.

We drove in silence most of the way home. Not because we were fighting. Not because we didn't know what to say. But because the air between us was full of things we hadn't said yet.

When we got home, I lingered by the porch while Sam got the mail. I watched the sky shift behind the trees, the winter wind tugging dried leaves across the steps.

When Sam joined me, he leaned against the railing, arms crossed, gaze distant.

"I haven't seen her in years," he said quietly. "Didn't expect to."

I said nothing.

I turned slightly toward him. "So... what happened with you two?"

He exhaled slowly, like he'd been waiting for that question. "We dated for about six months. But she wanted a house and a ring and a kid on her hip, and she wanted it immediately. I wasn't in a rush. And I couldn't see a future with her."

"Why?"

He shrugged. "She was nice. But everything was surface. We didn't have real conversations. She wasn't curious about the world, and didn't ask hard questions. I felt like I had to shrink parts of myself just to keep things easy. We had fun, sure, but fun fades if there's no substance."

I nodded, processing that.

He went quiet again, watching the wind move across the lake. Then he said it.

"You ever wonder what would've happened if we'd met when you used to come here for the summers?"

I blinked, surprised. "What?"

"I was away at college and then moved to California for my first job around the time you came here."

"Yeah. I don't remember ever seeing you back then."

He glanced at me. "I think about it sometimes. If our paths had crossed. If I had been here for a visit when you were old enough. If the timing had been just right... and we had found each other."

I looked away. "Would've saved me a lot of heartache."

He was quiet for a beat. "Why did you marry him, Em?"

I hesitated, but the look in his eyes wasn't judgment. It was understanding. Maybe even grief.

"It felt like what I was supposed to do," I said quietly. "Everyone wanted it. My parents adored him. We were friends. It all fit—on paper."

"And off paper?"

I exhaled. "Brad was polished on the outside. Inside, he was immature. He drank a lot. He was an angry, bitter person inside. He snapped over small things. He wasn't abusive—not physically. But there was this tension around him. Like he was always one bad moment away from exploding."

Sam's jaw tightened.

"He wasn't a kind person," I said. "He wasn't a good person. And I never loved him. Being with him felt like being with a cousin. Familiar, but never *right*. And definitely not romantic. I was never attracted to him in that way. So, my gut always told me something was not right."

Sam looked at me for a long time, then said, "I hate that you lived like that."

I swallowed. "Me too."

He reached out, brushing his fingers lightly against mine. "You know what I think?"

"What?"

"If we'd met back then... I don't think you would've married him."

My throat tightened. "You think I would've been brave enough to walk away?"

He held my gaze. "I think one look would've been enough."

The silence between us stretched.

"Yeah. It would have." I smiled.

"I hate that we lost that time," he said. "But I'm glad I have you now."

I nodded, my voice barely a whisper. "Me too."

Later that night, as he slept with his arm curled around me and his breath warm against my shoulder, I closed my eyes and imagined a version of us that started years earlier.

And for once, I didn't grieve the past.

I just held on tighter to what we had now.

I didn't want to waste another second.

Not when I knew what it felt like to lose time.

Not when I knew now what love was supposed to feel like.

CHAPTER 38

When the World Stopped

You never know it's the last normal day—until it ends in sirens. Or silence.

It was one of those quiet, golden afternoons where everything felt easy. A new porch swing lay half-assembled at Sam's feet, a fresh bag of screws tossed beside it, his tool-belt slung low on his hips.

He was wearing a light blue thermal shirt and black joggers, cheeks flushed from the cold, humming something off-key as he measured where to bolt the chain. Frost clung to the window-panes, and his breath fogged the air each time he exhaled. His hands were bare, roughened by work, and red from the chill, but steady as ever as he adjusted the level. I watched him from the kitchen, making popcorn.

He glanced up through the window, caught me watching him, and winked. "You making coffee?"

"Of course."

His grin warmed me more than the stove. "You're a goddess."

I brought it out—two steaming mugs, the popcorn in a bowl. We sat on the back steps, bundled in blankets, our knees touching. The grass was stiff with frost, the air crisp and quiet, the sky a soft winter gray tinged with fading light. Everything felt still. We were suspended in a moment I didn't know was about to vanish.

"You're gonna love it once it's up," he said, stretching his arms over his head. "I'll play some music, we'll watch storms roll in, drink too much whiskey."

I laughed. "You say that like it hasn't already happened."

Sam leaned over and kissed my shoulder. "I love you."

"I love you, too."

He stood. "Let me finish this."

About two hours later, I was washing dishes in the kitchen. I felt him step in behind me, his hands bracketing my shoulders, kneading gently.

"You're tense," he murmured.

"I'm not."

"You are. Want me to fix it?"

"Later."

He chuckled, then he wrapped his arms around me. He kissed the side of my neck. "God, I love you."

I leaned back into him.

Then—he stilled.

"What's wrong?"

He exhaled, slow and shaky. "I feel... lightheaded."

He braced himself against the counter.

"Sam?"

He blinked and swayed slightly. I reached out to try to soften his fall as his knees buckled.

"SAM!"

I tried to guide him gently down, but he was already going. His body slumped like someone had cut his strings. One second, he was mine—warm, alive—and the next, he was just heavy and still. My arms cradled his shoulders as he collapsed to the floor, his eyes rolling back, his skin suddenly ashen.

"SAM! Look at me—SAM!"

My world detonated.

I scrambled for my phone, frantically dialing 911.

"My boyfriend—he just collapsed—he's not responding—oh my God, hurry!"

I dropped to my knees, the phone sliding from my hand as I pressed my ear to his chest.

Nothing.

No pulse.

No breath.

"NO!"

I grabbed the phone and put it on speaker. The operator gave me instructions, and I started CPR.

"One, two, three, four—" I counted out the compressions, through screaming sobs. "Please, Sam, PLEASE. Don't leave me."

Tears streamed down my face, falling into his chest. I pushed. Breathed. Pushed again. My arms burned.

"He's too young. Please, God, don't take him," I begged.

The sirens were still far. It had been minutes.

Where were they? WHERE WERE THEY?

I kept going... my body trembling. My lips on his. My palms pushing his chest. My voice a broken chant.

Then—they burst in.

A dozen people. EMTs. Police. Firemen. A blur of shouting and movement. One pulled me back, gently but firmly.

"Let us work."

I watched from the corner, on my knees, praying.

They shocked him.

Once.

Twice.

His body jerked violently on the floor, and his chest rising with force... only to fall back into stillness. The sound of the paddles slapping against his skin will haunt me forever.

The medic looked over and made eye contact with me. I couldn't even make out what she said, and then she injected him with something.

He was lifeless. And pale.

I sobbed.

They loaded him onto the gurney.

"Ma'am, you can't ride in the ambulance."

"I HAVE to—"

A firefighter stepped up. "I'll drive you. Come with me."

I barely remember the ride. I was shaking so badly I couldn't hold my phone. My teeth chattered. I couldn't breathe. I thought I was going to throw up.

Outside the ER, I was so cold, but I didn't care. I didn't want to be around all those people in the waiting room. I sat alone and waited. And prayed. And sobbed. I rocked back and forth, fingers dug into my thighs. People passed. No one looked at me. I was invisible, dissolving.

Then—the door opened, and the fireman walked to me. "Did the chaplain talk to you?"

"The CHAPLAIN?! Why would the chaplain—oh dear God."

"They revived him. He's alive. But his heart's *very* weak. He's in a coma."

The air left my lungs.

A coma.

I broke. Right there on that wooden bench, I sobbed until I couldn't sit up. My chest seized like it was cracking open. I couldn't breathe without gasping. The sounds coming out of me weren't human. They were the kind of sounds that only come when something is being ripped away. The fireman tried to console me, but I curled in on myself. I could still feel Sam's body going limp in my arms. His weight. The silence.

They let me see him a half-hour later.

He was still. Tubes everywhere. Machines breathing for him. Constant beeping. I held his hand and begged.

"Sam, come back to me. Please. I love you. I need you. I can't lose you. Not now."

Later, I sat in the ICU waiting room. The sterile lights were too bright, the sounds too quiet. They told me he was stable. To go home and rest.

But how the hell do you rest when your world is inside a hospital bed and no one will let you near him?

They were taking him for tests. They said he needed scans, more monitoring, and adjustments to his oxygen levels. What he needed was me.

I stayed until they made me leave.

The fireman who drove me to the hospital had given me his number before he left. I didn't want to call anyone, didn't want to speak—but when it was finally time to go, I did. He came back. No questions asked, just a quiet kindness. His name was Hutch.

The second I stepped into the cabin, everything unraveled.

It didn't feel like home anymore. It felt like a body without a heartbeat. Like someone had cut the wires that made this place feel alive.

The porch swing was up. A screwdriver lay forgotten beside it. The popcorn bowl sat where we'd left it. His coffee mug still on the counter, 1/4 full.

I stood where he'd hugged me—seconds before everything went black.

And I stared at the spot on the floor where he collapsed.

They left his shirt. Torn down the front.

I picked it up, pressed it to my face. It still smelled like him.

Then I dropped to my knees and screamed.

My chest cracked open, like something wild was trying to crawl out.

Silence answered.

So I screamed again. Louder.
It didn't matter.
No one could hear me.
No one could bring him back.
And that spot on the floor just stared back—like it was keeping his soul.
I screamed until my throat gave out.
Until all that remained was the shaking.
I couldn't stop it.
And then I wrote.
Because I didn't know what else to do.
If he couldn't hear me, maybe he could see my words. Maybe somehow, they'd find him.

My love,

It doesn't feel real. You were smiling and laughing six hours ago. Now I don't even know if you're coming back. I tried to catch you. I begged them to hurry. I tried to breathe for you. I told God to take me instead. I prayed for you to stay with me. I told you I loved you. That I needed you. Why did this happen? How could this happen? You were so healthy. You were the strongest person I've ever known. You were invincible to me. Please, Sam. Please come back. I can't lose you.

I love you endlessly. FBOW.

-Emmy

And I waited.
Waited.
Prayed.
Cried.

I called Ute, voice cracking, trying to explain what I didn't fully understand myself. She'd meet me at the hospital in the morning.

I curled up in our bed, clutching his blue thermal. It still smelled like him. It was scary being there without him.

And in the dark, I whispered into the silence, "Don't you dare leave me. I won't survive it."

I didn't sleep. I couldn't. I laid on his side of the bed, pressing my face into his pillow, breathing him in until the sobs wracked my body so hard I thought I'd choke on them. The silence was unbearable. The absence of his arms, his breath, his warmth—it was like being buried alive.

I stared at the ceiling until morning came.

And then it was Day Two.

The sun rose like it didn't care he was gone. Like it didn't know my life was crumbling. I hated it for that. I hated everything.

I made it back to the hospital by 6 a.m., even though visiting hours didn't start until 7. I begged them to let me in early, but they wouldn't. I paced the hallway like I was going to wear grooves in the floor. When Ute arrived, I melted into her arms. Neither of us said a word at first—we just held each other, clinging to some fragile thread of hope. I buried my face into her shoulder like a child. She rubbed slow circles on my back while I shook.

The doctor came not long after. His face was tight and professional, but his eyes gave him away. He sat us down and told us what we already knew—Sam had a heart attack. He was still unresponsive. The scans weren't showing any signs of improvement.

His tone shifted slightly—gentle, careful. He wasn't just giving us updates. He was preparing us. He said the longer the coma lasted, the lower the chance of a full recovery. That every hour mattered. That it could go either way.

I think I stopped breathing.

"Is he suffering?" I asked.

"No," he said. "He's comfortable."

Sam was on life support. Machines were breathing for him. The meds were keeping his heart working like it should. And all we could do was wait. Hope. Pray. Try not to fall apart in the meantime.

When they finally opened the doors, we walked in together. But when I saw him, I staggered. Ute caught my elbow.

He was so pale.

Wires curled like veins across his chest. The man who once towered over me, who filled every room with certain presence and energy, now lay there utterly still. His chest rose and fell in mechanical rhythm, the sound of the ventilator pressing into the silence like a loud ticking clock.

I reached for his hand.

It was warm—but not as warm as it should have been.

And when I looked at the heart monitor, all I could think was—

That heart used to shake the walls.

I wept into his chest.

And for the second time in two days, I broke.

I kissed him everywhere I could. And I held his hand.

But he didn't hold mine back.

Ute and I sat in silence, just staring at him, praying. I didn't move for hours. I was there for every single minute of visiting hours—the only time I left his side was to use the bathroom. I didn't eat. I couldn't. Ute brought homemade muffins and tried to coax me, but the nausea was too strong. Even water was a struggle.

When the nurse came in and quietly told me it was time to go, she added that they'd be running more tests in the morning—including a brain scan—and that I should come a little later. I kissed his forehead, whispered that I'd be back as soon as they let me, and let Ute lead me out. It felt like I was leaving part of my soul in that room.

The drive home felt longer than it was. Every streetlight and every shadow, reminded me that he wasn't with me. And when I stepped back into the cabin—it didn't just feel empty... it felt wrong. The air was still. The silence sharp. His scent was in the air... but no *him*.

I sank into the couch, holding his thermal, and opened my notebook.

Sam,

It's been one day, five hours, and twenty-six minutes since you collapsed. An entire day without your voice. Without your touch. I haven't eaten. I haven't slept. I wake up gasping, haunted by the image of you on the kitchen floor. I can't stop shaking. I've been throwing up. And my hair is falling out in chunks. My body doesn't know how to survive without you. You told me you loved me, and then you just fell. God, Sam. I am begging you. Every second that passes feels like I'm being peeled open. I sit beside your bed, holding your hand, but you won't squeeze it back. I kiss your face. I beg you to come back to me. I don't even know who I am without you. You held me up, made me believe I could be someone whole. You can't leave me. You can't. Please, my love. Just stay.
I love you. I love you. I love you.
-Emmy

That night, I sat on the porch swing. He was supposed to have been there with me.

My hands wouldn't stop trembling. I wrapped them in a blanket, but they still shook. I whispered his name into the wind. I listened for a sign. For *anything*.

Nothing came.

When I went in to drink something, I vomited into the kitchen sink. I still hadn't eaten. My body was in revolt.

By the time I crawled into bed, I felt faint. Like my body had shut down to survive. I tried to sleep. But every time I closed my eyes, I saw his body on the kitchen floor. Lifeless. His lips blue. The way the medics shocked him, again and again, while I screamed prayers. While I begged God to take me instead.

When I woke on the third day, my arms were tingling from clutching his pillow all night

The phone didn't ring. No updates. Just silence. A silence and stillness that felt like death.

His shoes were still right where he took them off, by the back door. I still hadn't moved anything, even his coffee cup. I wanted everything to stay exactly the way he left it.

I stood in the shower for an hour and didn't realize the water had gone cold.

I pulled one of his hoodies from the drawer and put it on. It still smelled like him.

I stared out the window, watching the lake, the trees, the swing swaying slightly in the breeze, like it knew something I didn't.

My sweet Sam,

Are you still with me? Please tell me you're still here. I need a sign. A twitch of your hand. A flutter of your eyelids. A shift in the air when I speak your name. Just let me know you haven't let go. If you're already gone, I'll carry you in every breath. Every step. Every morning I shouldn't have to face without you. But God, I don't want to write you into memory.

I want you here. I want your arms around me. Your laugh in this house. Your coffee mug next to mine in the morning. You waited your whole life for something real. And now that we finally have it... you can't leave. Please, Sam. Don't let this be it.

I sat in your chair tonight, reading your notes. There was a scribble in the corner, "FBOW. Even if the unthinkable happens." But please please fight. I don't care how you come back to me. I'll take anything. A whisper, a breath. I don't need perfect. I just need you. This isn't how it was supposed to go. You waited so long to find the right person, and now I'm here. I'm right here, Sam. Please don't let the unthinkable happen. Just come back. I'll wait as long as it takes. I'll be right here.

Forever yours,

-Emmy

The panic was gone—but not because I was calm. Because I was cracked open and emptied out. I walked into that hospital room like a ghost, like some other woman wearing my skin. I sat beside him, and the moment I took his hand, my eyes burned, but no tears came. I had cried everything out.

Ute came again. She held my hand, but her grip was different now—gentler, like she was already grieving. "This is exactly how it was with his father," she whispered. And then she turned away and cried, shoulders trembling. I couldn't comfort her. I couldn't even comfort myself.

When she left, I pulled my chair closer to his bed and rested my forehead against our joined hands. I told him I still believed in him. That our life was still here—unfinished, waiting. I whispered every detail. The smell of sawdust on his clothes. The way the old porch swing creaked when he shifted his weight. How the light hit his hair when he worked. I told him I'd trade anything just to hear his voice again. I'd burn this whole world down if it meant he'd come back to me.

But there was nothing. No response. No sign.

Just me again—gutted, hollow, and empty. I wasn't crying anymore. I wasn't even breathing right. Just existing. Just air in my lungs that no longer knew what to do.

I couldn't bring myself to leave the hospital, but the nurse gently said it was time. So I did what I always did now—I walked out without him.

I walked into the cabin like it wasn't mine anymore—like I was trespassing in a life that had already ended. It was too quiet, too still, like it knew.

I didn't shower. I didn't eat.

I went to our room, laid his thermal on the bed, and crawled in wearing his hoodie again.

Then I picked up my phone and played his last voicemail—

"Hey, just heading home now. Thought about you the whole

damn day. I don't say that enough, do I? Also... I miss your face. That's all."

His voice filled the room like a ghost. Like a goodbye I wasn't ready for.

I clutched the phone to my chest and pressed my face into his pillow, aching to hear it again.

And again.

And again.

I don't remember falling asleep.

I only remember waking to the sound of my phone buzzing.

I answered, my voice cracked.

"Hello?"

A nurse.

Her voice was calm. Too calm.

"Miss Sinclair, I need you to come in right away. There's... been a change."

And then—

Nothing.

Just silence.

Just that one word.

Change.

I froze... like my body knew what my mind refused to hear.

And I couldn't tell if it was hope—or the end.

I didn't know if "change" meant a miracle—or goodbye.

CHAPTER 39

When the World Breathed Again

The world was still dark when I drove, headlights cutting through the fog, and windshield wipers brushing away the dampness that clung to the world around me. I didn't remember the drive… just white-knuckling the wheel.

I repeated the nurse's words in my head until they didn't mean anything anymore. "There's… been a change."

I parked crookedly. Slammed the door. Ran.

The elevator wouldn't come fast enough. I took the stairs two at a time, my heart choking in my throat. By the time I reached the ICU floor, I was shaking again. Sweat down my spine. My legs numb.

The nurse met me at the doors.

"Miss Sinclair?"

I nodded, but couldn't speak.

"He's awake."

Everything inside me stilled. Froze. Then cracked wide open.

My knees felt weak.

She put her arm around me.

"He's groggy and confused, but stable. We extubated him thirty minutes ago. He asked for you."

. . .

I was already moving.

The hallway felt like a tunnel. I passed people in scrubs. Voices. Machines. Everything was blurred. I pushed through the door—and then I saw him.

Sam.

His eyes were open. Bleary, red-rimmed, and unfocused.

But *open*.

He turned his head—slow, wincing. His gaze landed on me like a question. Like he didn't trust what he was seeing.

And then—

"Emmy?" His voice cracked, thin and hoarse.

I didn't answer.

I just ran to him.

My knees hit the tile beside his bed as I reached for his hand. Warm. Weak. But there.

I brought it to my lips. I sobbed into it.

He blinked slowly, the fog in his eyes gradually clearing. "I remember," he said, voice rough, barely audible. "I was in the kitchen. I felt lightheaded... like the floor had tilted under me."

I froze, my breath catching. "You remember that?"

Sam nodded slowly. "Everything went heavy."

His fingers twitched in mine.

"I could hear you," he said, barely above a whisper. "Talking to me. I wanted to answer you. I just... couldn't."

My throat burned, tears rushing forward again.

"I wasn't gone, Emmy," he rasped, voice raw and broken.

His throat sounded like it hurt to speak. He reached for the cup beside the bed. I helped him take a slow sip of water, then he tried again.

"My body quit, but I was still there..."

He paused, breath catching.

"I heard you crying. I felt you there. I just... couldn't get back to you."

I laid my head gently on his chest to hear the beat of his heart. "I thought I lost you."

He exhaled slowly. "I followed your voice all the way back."

Ute slipped into the room an hour later. She cried so hard she couldn't speak. Just touched his hair and kissed his forehead, saying, "Praise, God."

Later, I helped him sip some juice. The nurses checked his vitals. The doctor explained that he was cautiously optimistic. Sam's heart would need time—and help. Medication, cardiac rehab, and close monitoring would be essential. His memory might be foggy. He'd be tired. But he was here.

Awake.

Alive.

We stayed as long as we could. He drifted off—exhausted, but breathing. I stood at the glass, watching his chest rise and fall. This time, it wasn't mechanical. It was *his*.

And mine.

Back at the cabin, everything looked the same.

The swing. The coffee mug. The screwdriver. They were all still on the porch.

But this time, it felt different.

Because he was coming home.

I walked into the kitchen. Stood in the spot where he fell. Pressed my hand to the floor. Whispered a quiet thank you.

Then I turned off the lights, sat on the porch swing, and let the night wrap around me.

The stars were everywhere.

And at last—I breathed.

We didn't talk much on the drive home the next afternoon.

Sam's hand stayed in mine, weak but warm. I stole glances at him every few miles just to make sure he was still breathing.

The hospital had discharged him with instructions, warnings, and a bag full of medications I couldn't pronounce. The doctor said it was okay to take him home—as long as we followed every instruction to the letter.

He was alive.

That was all I could cling to.

When I pulled into the gravel drive, the cabin stood there waiting for us—still and quiet, like it had been holding its breath.

Sam let out a low exhale. "God," he whispered. "I'm happy to be home."

I helped him out slowly, carefully, like one wrong move might undo the miracle we'd been given.

He paused before going inside, his eyes tracing the porch swing. The popcorn bowl. The screwdriver.

It was still there, waiting.

We walked inside, and he went straight to the kitchen.

I'd imagined this a hundred times—what it would feel like to bring him home. But I hadn't prepared for the fear.

Sam blinked fast. His hand tightened on mine. "I was standing right here," he said, voice rough. "When it happened…"

"I know." My throat burned. "I remember every second."

He took it all in—slowly, as if he were seeing it replay in his mind. "It's like time stopped."

"It did," I said.

And then I broke. Just quietly. A tear slid down my cheek before I could stop it. Then another. I tried to wipe them away, but Sam caught my hand.

"It's okay," he whispered. "We're fine."

I shook my head, sobbing now. "I just—I didn't know if you'd ever come home."

He wrapped his arms around me. "I'm here," he said, voice breaking.

I buried my face in his chest. He smelled like antiseptic and soap and something else now—something more fragile. But he was *here*. My hands clutched his shirt like I still couldn't believe he was real.

"I thought I lost you," I choked.

We stood there like that, pressed together in the middle of the kitchen, surrounded by the life we almost lost.

Eventually, I helped him to the couch. He moved slow and cautious. I tucked a blanket around him, kissed his forehead.

"Don't leave."

"I'm not going anywhere," I said.

I curled into him as carefully as I could, with my head on his shoulder, my hand over his heart. I just needed to feel it beat.

"I'll take the pills," he whispered. "Do the rehab. Whatever they say. I'll do all of it."

"Good," I whispered. "Because I need forever."

"I'll give you forever," he said.

And for the first time in days, I closed my eyes.

And smiled.

CHAPTER 40

The Way We Love

I woke up and sat on the porch swing, which was even more special now. The lake was serene, and the quiet wrapped around me like a scarf.

Inside, Sam was sleeping. Healing.

It had been a few quiet months since his heart attack. He rested. I wrote. Everything felt louder now—sharper. Music. Laughter. The way he looked at me across a table. You don't walk through that kind of fear and stay the same.

I saw it every time he looked at me like I was still here—still his—after nearly losing it all. Life had shown its sharpest edge. We met it with everything we had.

Thankfully, there was always something to warm up in the fridge—Ute's quiet way of making sure we didn't forget to eat.

I used to think freedom would feel like running. Like flight.

But it didn't.

It felt like coming home to yourself after years of being lost in someone else's life.

I thought about who I used to be—the girl who tried so hard to be chosen, to be perfect... to be safe.

And then I thought about now.

This moment wasn't about loss.

It was about return.

Because what I had now wasn't a curated life or a perfect image.

It was CPR on a kitchen floor. It was porch swings and popcorn. It was the kind of man who begged the universe for one more chance to love you right.

And now—

I was finally in a life that felt like mine.

That morning on the porch, I felt the quiet shift inside me. The ache was still there, but softer now. We had survived the storm. And somehow, we were still standing.

And in that stillness, I started to notice the quiet things—the ones I used to overlook. The small efforts. The unexpected grace.

That night, Sam took me to The Oasis. The ride was quiet. The hum of the truck beneath us, the road stretching ahead, but all I could focus on was him.

When we arrived, he took my hand, lacing his fingers through mine, and led me through the restaurant, past the bar, and out to the terrace.

It was breathtaking.

The entire patio was ours. Hanging lanterns glowed above us, casting a soft golden light over the intimate setup. Twinkling fairy lights were strung between the beams and wound around the railings, illuminating the private view perched over the lake. A crisp chill lingered in the air, just enough to make the warmth of the lights feel like a quiet kind of luxury. The water below shimmered with the fading light, streaks of molten gold bleeding into violet and deepening blue as the sun slipped beyond the horizon. A single table sat in the center, dressed in crisp white linen, a bottle of champagne chilling in a silver bucket.

From up here, the marina flickered with lights, the water mirroring them like scattered stars. Even after seeing it countless times, it still felt magical.

More than that, The Oasis had grown into something even bigger than before. The gardens weren't in full bloom yet—still waking from winter's grip—but the design was already striking. Stone walls curved through the landscape, lantern-lit pathways wound between tidy hedges and early spring buds, hints of color just beginning to peek through. Peony shoots were pushing up, their promise not far off. Even without the flowers, it felt magical. The expansion hadn't just changed the space—it had transformed it into something timeless.

"I still can't get over how this place looks." I ran my fingers over the delicate lace tablecloth. "It's heavenly."

Sam leaned back slightly, his gaze sweeping across the marina and garden below—the kind of look a man wears when he sees a dream made real, brick by brick, breath by breath.

His eyes lingered on the lawn. "First wedding's in a few weeks."

I nodded, smiling. "Chris and Michelle's big day."

"Yeah," Sam said, a flicker of satisfaction crossing his face. "Those two were meant for each other. The whole town's coming. Sunset ceremony, dancing under the stars. It's going to be special."

Sam reached across the table, his fingers finding mine, his grip strong and sure—just like every other promise he had ever made. "It's exactly what I hoped it would be," he murmured, thumb grazing over my skin. "A place that feels timeless, where people come for the happiest moments of their lives."

He popped the champagne, pouring us each a glass before lifting his in a silent toast. I clinked mine against his, watching him over the rim as I took a sip.

The rest of the dinner passed in a blur of laughter, teasing, and shared glances that lingered too long. His hand brushed mine more than once, his eyes holding mine just a little too long, and I let myself sink into it.

By the time we finished, the sky was a deep, star-speckled blue. The fairy lights around us flickering like fireflies.

And when he stood and offered his hand, I took it without hesitation.

Not because I needed saving.

But because I was finally steady enough to walk beside him.

Into a life we weren't chasing anymore—

One we were already living.

Fully, freely, and ours.

CHAPTER 41

Where We Belong

A few days later, the world was quiet, and wrapped in stillness. Just the water kissing the hull and the breeze skimming my skin as Sam cut the engine, letting the boat drift into the quiet breath of the day.

Even the boat reflected us—sapphire blue and shimmering white, like our birthstones. Sapphire and diamond. Strong, brilliant, and unmistakably us.

It had been a quiet winter. More healing. More writing. A season of stillness—but also of rebuilding. Not just between Sam and me, but in other places I never expected.

My mom and I began to mend the broken pieces between us. She called more often. Sent flowers when Sam was in the hospital. One day, a photo arrived—it was of me and Gram, long ago, with the biggest smiles on our faces. "Thought you should have this," she wrote. She listened—really listened—when I talked about my book, about Sam. Things were warmer now. Not healed, not whole. But something had shifted. A quiet effort. A start. One I was willing to honor.

Maybe one day, I'd find a way to talk to my dad again, too.

. . .

The wind off the lake still carried winter's bite, but we didn't care.

Sam leaned back against the captain's chair, easy, confident. One arm slung over the wheel, the other resting on my thigh.

I watched him—sunlight in his hair, strength in his hands. Completely at ease.

"You ever driven a boat before?" he asked, breaking the silence.

I shook my head. "Never."

A smile unfolded as he shifted toward me, reaching for my hand. "Then it's time."

I hesitated, looking at the controls. "Really?"

His fingers curved around mine. "Absolutely."

He guided my hand over the throttle. The boat surged forward, smooth and powerful. I laughed. He grinned. That was all it took—us moving ahead.

Then Sam reached past me, easing the throttle back. The boat slowed, the engine quieting to a soft hum before shutting off completely, leaving us drifting in peace.

The silence held everything—what we'd fought for, what we'd lost, and what was still waiting.

He leaned back against the seat, tugging me into his lap. With my face resting against his shoulder, I ran my fingers through his hair.

Then, finally, Sam's voice broke the quiet, low and thoughtful. "So, my love, what's next?"

I took a breath. "I want to publish my book."

Sam's fingers tightened around mine, warmth rising with the certainty of his belief in me.

"I want to tell the story—not just of love, but of becoming. What it means to finally choose your own happiness in a world that demands everything else. To push through the pain, the judgment, the ordinary hard days—and still believe in something more. Yes, it's a love story. A soul-deep, once-in-a-lifetime kind of love. But more than that—it's about a woman who fought to become herself. And the man who helped her believe she was worth it."

"You've written it beautifully. You *have* to share it with the world," he said softly.

I glanced over the water, then back to him, my voice softer. "But the most important thing I wish for? A family."

His expression didn't change, but something in his eyes shifted—something deep, something certain, like he'd been waiting to hear those words.

He brushed my hair behind my ear, his fingers lingering against my cheek. "Yeah?"

I nodded, my throat tightening. "With you. I want little hands grabbing onto ours. I want bedtime stories and tiny footprints in the sand. I want a life with simple, joyful moments. And I want to spend forever showing you how much I adore you."

Then he swallowed, his voice rough. "You have no idea how much I want that, too."

I smiled, letting the words settle between us—soft, sacred.

And in that quiet, I pictured it. What it might feel like to build a family with him.

He exhaled slowly. "You're going to be an incredible mother, my love."

Then, his lips curved, slow and knowing. "If our babies inherit your fire, the world doesn't stand a chance."

Laughter bubbled up, breaking the weight of the moment and turning it into something lighter, brighter.

Sam dragged a hand over his chin, then nodded toward the console. "Alright, Captain. Time to name the new boat. What should it be?"

The answer came without hesitation. "F.B.O.W."

I swallowed as my fingers brushed the edge of my pendant. "It's us. It's what you said on our first date. It's what changed everything. Other people might not get it, but that's the point. It's *ours*."

Then, in one smooth motion, he pulled me against him, his

lips claiming mine in a kiss that felt like a destiny woven through every touch. Everything we'd been through, everything we were, and everything ahead.

When he finally pulled back, he rested his forehead against mine, his breath warm against my skin, his voice nothing but a whisper.

"F.B.O.W."

"I can't believe how far you've come. Sometimes I think... if you hadn't been so brave, if you hadn't taken a stand in your life, we wouldn't be here now."

He dragged a hand down my back. "And I'd still be waiting... for you."

I turned to look up at him.

And I knew—whatever life brought us next, I was already home.

CHAPTER 42

The Answer Was Always You

The fire crackled softly, its golden light pulsing like a heartbeat, casting flickering shadows across the freshly painted walls. The evening air was brisk, but it carried a sense of peace, wrapping itself around us like a comfortable embrace. Sam had insisted on building a fire tonight. I didn't question him. He was always thoughtful like that, an expert at making the ordinary feel extraordinary.

We sat on the rug in front of the hearth, my legs curled beneath me, a glass of wine in my hand. Sam, leaning back on one arm, seemed unusually quiet. His eyes were fixed on the dancing flames.

He looked at me then, his deep brown eyes locking onto mine with an intensity that grabbed me. He didn't speak right away. Instead, he leaned forward, set his glass aside, and took my hand in his.

The tension between us was different tonight. It wasn't laced with playful teasing or the lazy heat of a Sunday morning in bed. This was something richer.

I shifted slightly, brushing against him, and his fingers tightened. Just a fraction. Just enough.

"What are you thinking about?" I asked softly.

His head turned toward me, eyes locking onto mine.

"Emmy," he began, his voice low, almost hesitant. "There's something I've been meaning to say... something I've wanted to say for a long time. But I needed to be sure the timing was right."

I swallowed, my pulse quickening. His words hung in the air, heavy with promise. "What is it?" I whispered.

He stared into my eyes, his thumb gently brushing over the back of my hand. "Do you know what you mean to me? What you've brought into my life?"

I shook my head, speechless.

"I've always thought of myself as a man who could handle anything," he said, his voice quiet but thick with feeling. "Losing my brother, my father, rebuilding my life after the pain... I thought I'd learned how to live without needing anyone. And then you came along."

He squeezed my hand, never breaking eye contact. "You turned everything I thought I knew upside down. You walked into my world, broken and battered by people who should have protected you... and yet, you were still so loving and kind. You didn't even see it, but I did. Every single day, I saw your grace."

I watched as he exhaled sharply, dragging his free hand through his hair, his fingers lingering at the back of his neck like he was holding himself together. Then he looked at me—really looked at me—and I saw it.

His chest rose too fast, his breath unsteady, fingers curling around mine like he was afraid to let go. Like the words might wreck him before he got them out.

Tears blurred my vision, my breath catching, my whole world narrowing to him. "Sam..."

He held up a hand, gently silencing me, his lips forming the faintest smile. "You're the bravest person I've ever met. Not because you stood up to your family or walked away from a life that was suffocating you, though those things were incredible. But because you still believed in love. Despite everything, you didn't let the world make you hard or cynical. You opened your heart to me, to this cabin, to this life we're building together."

"I never thought I'd find someone who truly understood me," he continued, his voice breaking now. "Someone who saw me—not just the man I was, or the man I could be, but the man I am. And... you see me. You get me. And you love me. That's the greatest gift I'll ever have."

His throat worked as he tried to steady his voice. "When I collapsed in the kitchen... and everything went black—I didn't see my life flash before my eyes. I saw you. Your face. I heard your voice. The pain in it. And I felt your soul aching in the letters you wrote."

He shook his head, eyes shining. "And the only thought I had —my last thought, if it came to that—was that I wanted you to be my wife. I hadn't even asked you yet, and all I could think was, *God, don't let me leave her before I get to call her mine.*"

He reached into his pocket then, and pulling out a small, weathered box that looked older than both of us combined.

My heart stopped.

I *knew* that box.

Small, with black worn velvet, frayed at the edges. Its weight heavy with decades of love stories. I could almost feel the warmth of Gram's hands lingering on its surface, hear the soft creak of the hinges as she'd once opened it, whispering about forever.

And now—

Now Sam was holding it, and it felt like stepping into a dream.

"Sam," I choked, my hand flying to my mouth. "Is that...?"

He nodded, his eyes shining with unshed tears. "It is."

My hands trembled as he placed the box in my lap. I traced the outline of the lid, breath shuddering, afraid to open it, to break the moment, to believe it was real. Slowly, I opened the lid, revealing the delicate, breathtaking antique engagement ring I'd adored as a child.

The ring carried a thousand stories. The platinum band, worn smooth by years of love, its filigree still as intricate as the day it was made. Tiny diamonds glittered like constellations, their light cradled by sapphires deep as twilight. At its center sat a brilliant, round diamond—large, mesmerizing, a star in its own right.

Gram had worn this ring. Her love, her legacy, was etched into every engraving, every carefully placed stone.

A sharp breath hitched in my throat as my fingers ghosted over the sapphires... over the diamonds that glowed like captured starlight.

And then—it hit me.

Sapphires. Diamonds.

Our birthstones.

This ring—this exact ring—had been my favorite piece of jewelry as a child. I had slipped it onto my finger with innocent adoration, spinning fairytales in my mind about a love that stood the test of time.

And now?

Sam held it in his hands, waiting for me.

It wasn't a coincidence.

It was never coincidence.

Somehow, long before either of us even knew, this ring was always meant to be mine.

"Where... how did you... ?" I stammered, my voice breaking.

"My mom," he said simply. "Bernice gave it to her years ago. She asked her to keep it safe. When I told her I was going to propose... she gave it to me. Said this ring was always meant for you."

My vision blurred as I lifted the ring from its velvet bed, but the dam truly broke when I saw the folded note tucked gently inside the lid. I carefully unfolded the paper, my grandmother's familiar handwriting jumping off the page like a whisper from the past.

Precious Emmy,

I wish I was there with you. I wish I could have seen you fall in love. I wish I could have seen you with your soul mate, finally. But I am always with you. Because you are part of me, and I am part of you. I hope you finally see what I always saw in you. Now, you have everything you will ever need.

I love you always,

Gram

I clutched the note to my chest, my sobs breaking free as Sam pulled me into his arms.

When I finally pulled back, he cradled my head in his hands, brushing away my tears with his thumbs. "Emmy," he said, his voice low, certain, like a promise sealed in stone. "I love you more than life itself. You are my heart, my home, my everything. Be mine, for the rest of my life. Will you marry me?"

A sob wrenched from my chest, my hands shaking as I clutched his face like I could hold this moment still. "Yes!"

He slipped the ring onto my finger.

And then—

His hands caught my face—strong, sure, a little shaken—his fingers threading into my hair as if he couldn't hold me close enough. And then his mouth crashed into mine.

The world disappeared.

I gasped, and he swallowed the sound, tilting his head, deepening the kiss, stealing the breath from my lungs as he dragged me under.

No hesitation, no restraint, nothing between us.

I felt the weight of the ring now resting on my finger, pressing against him as I held him. Like proof. Like fate.

I knew without a shadow of a doubt that I was exactly where I was meant to be.

In Sam's arms.

I pulled back slightly, enough to look up at him.

"You say I gave you strength, but you gave me something I didn't even know I needed. You gave me... me. You loved me before I knew how to love myself. And every day since, you've made me feel like I matter." I said, as I looked into his eyes.

Sam's fingers combed through my hair, his touch reverent as he leaned in, his forehead resting against mine. For a moment, we just sat there, breathing each other in, letting the world fall away.

A tear rolled down his cheek, and I wiped it away with my thumb before pulling him into a kiss that was as much a declaration as it was an answer. His lips met mine with a tenderness that made my knees weak, his hands holding me as if he couldn't bear to let me fall.

When we finally broke apart, Sam reached into his pocket and pulled out a small folded piece of paper.

"I didn't just plan to ask you to marry me tonight," he said, his lips curving into a soft smile. "I also wanted to show you something."

He unfolded the paper and spread it out on the rug in front of us. A rough sketch—but instantly recognizable. It was the cabin, fully renovated and expanded—with a wrap-around porch, a sprawling garden out front, and a large dock extending into the lake.

"This is us," he said, pointing to the little figures he'd drawn standing on the porch. "This is the life I want to build with you. Not just a house, but a home. A place where we can grow together, make memories, and dream bigger than we ever thought we could."

I stared at the drawing. It was such a simple thing. But that was Sam—always showing me, in ways large and small, that I was his world. That I was his, just as surely as he was mine.

"I want to plant peonies with you in our new garden... the one we'll build together. Teach you how to build things with your own hands, to create a life that's ours in every way. Wake up to your sleepy smile, bring you coffee, and cook for you just because I love the way you light up when I do. I want to read every single word you write. And dream alongside you." His fingers weaved into mine, his voice softer now, "And more than anything, I want every day to begin and end with you. Until my last breath."

"And," he murmured, "I can't wait to see little feet running around this place. I want to watch you rock a baby to sleep on that porch swing. And I'll tell them how their mom is the toughest woman I've ever met."

A sob ripped through me before I could stop it. I threw my arms around his neck, holding him so tightly I could feel the steady beat of his heart against my own.

"Yes," I whispered against his ear, my voice trembling with the weight of everything I felt. "Yes to all of it. To you. To us. To forever."

And right there, nestled in his arms, I knew—

This wasn't just a moment.

This was every moment that ever mattered.

CHAPTER 43

Where Loyalty Lives

I watched Sam as he moved through the kitchen, barefoot and half-dressed, humming some old song under his breath as he poured our coffee. I curled into the couch, fingertips gliding over the ridges of the ring—the weight still new, still strange, but shimmering with something that felt like magic.

He turned, catching the movement, and a deep smile took over his lips.

"Still getting used to it?"

My gaze shifted from him to the ring. "It doesn't feel real."

Maybe because it's not the only thing that finally feels complete. I'd sent my manuscript to my editor last night—the story that had poured from me in pieces was finally whole. Just like I was.

He walked over, reached for my hand, and kissed it. His touch, as familiar as my own heartbeat, brought a sense of comfort that no words could ever convey. Especially now. Especially after almost losing it all.

We stepped onto the back porch and stood there, side by side, our breaths visible in the cold dawn air, watching the sky shift and bloom with color.

"This view never gets old," he said, his voice rough with that deep, morning rasp that always sent a shiver down my spine.

"It's breathtaking," I replied, leaning into him.

The words felt inadequate, but then, how could I describe this moment—this feeling?

It wasn't just the beauty of the sunrise or the serenity of the lake.

It was everything.

The life we'd fought for. The love we'd built. The freedom we'd claimed.

Sam wrapped an arm around my shoulders, pulling me closer.

When I opened my eyes again, the sun was cresting the horizon, casting soft light across the water. I turned to him, noticing the way the light soothed the rugged lines of his face.

"You know what I've realized?" I asked.

He tilted his head, his eyes curious. "What's that?"

"This," I said, gesturing to the lake, the cabin, the sunrise. "This is all I ever wanted. It's simple. A cabin, a lake, just us. Nothing glamorous. But it was all I had ever needed."

I swallowed hard. "I didn't just find you here, I found myself. And you saw her before I did."

He shook his head. "You fought for it." He trailed his fingers down my arms, lacing them into mine. His grip was warm, secure, everlasting.

"I just got to stand by you and watch you become who you were always meant to be," he said, his voice quiet but sure.

Then, as if sealing a promise, he reached for the delicate pendant resting against my collarbone—the one he had designed just for me. He adjusted it gently, his fingers lingering at my neck, his touch tender and deliberate.

"And I love our life. I wouldn't change it for the world."

I drew a breath.

"I never really knew what loyalty looked like," I said quietly.

The truth settled—not sharp, just honest.

I placed my hand over his heart. "You are where loyalty lives," I whispered.

A breath caught in my throat, but I didn't look away. "And everything I left behind... that's where loyalty lied."

Sam took my hands in his. He exhaled sharply, his gaze locking onto mine.

"No matter what happens, I will stand by you. I will fight for you. And I will protect you. For the rest of my life. And beyond."

"It's you and me against the world." His thumb brushed over my cheek.

We stayed there for a long time, wrapped up in each other as the sun climbed higher in the sky. A quiet wind stirred the bare branches, sending a few stubborn leaves drifting down like ghosts of autumn. The lake stretched before us, still and glass-like, reflecting the amber hues of morning. In the distance, a pair of deer stepped cautiously from the tree line, their movements unhurried, as if they too, could sense the stillness of this moment.

"Dance with me, future Mrs. Sterling." Sam stood, holding out his hand.

I smiled. as I reached for him, my fingers sliding into his palm, fitting there like they were always meant to. With ease, he pulled me to my feet, his arms wrapping around me as we swayed on the porch. The world faded, leaving only us, our breaths mingling in the crisp morning air.

I rested my head against his shoulder, sinking into the warmth that had always been home.

Then, his voice—soft at first, almost hesitant. Then deeper. Richer. Resonant.

He started to sing, his words barely a whisper.

The moment *For the First Time* left his lips, goosebumps raced across my arms.

A quiet sob lodged in my throat, but I didn't stop him. I couldn't.

I clung to him, feeling every note settle into my bones... into my heart.

The song. The words. And the man who had loved me through it all.

It was us. Every lyric, every breath, every slow, swaying step we took on that porch.

I swallowed hard, pressing closer as his voice dipped lower, a quiet, reverent murmur against my temple. He wasn't just singing. He was telling me, in the only way that mattered, that this was real—that he'd been waiting his whole life for this.

I felt like every missing piece of me had quietly fallen into place... like I had finally become whole.

His hands slid up my back, holding me firm against him, grounding me in a way only he ever could.

When he pulled back just enough to meet my eyes, his voice was raw, on the edge of emotion.

"You are the love of my life."

I smiled through the tears slipping down my cheeks. "And you're my one and only."

We danced until the sun climbed high. We danced until nothing else existed—just the quiet rhythm of our hearts and the unwavering certainty that this was ours.

And now, standing in his arms, swaying to the song that had already been written for us, I was sure—this was our destiny. Tested, scarred, and fought for with all that we had.

This wasn't just the end of one chapter. It was the beginning of everything.

Not written in pages, but in the spaces between them. In every promise, unspoken but kept. In the way his arms would always pull me close. In the way I would always, always belong to him.

And as the winter wind whispered across the lake, as his heartbeat echoed beneath my palm, sure and true, as his breath warmed my skin—

I knew.

No matter where life took us, I would always know where loyalty lived.

Forever wasn't something we found. It was something we became.

Epilogue

It had been almost a year and a half since everything changed. Since Sam collapsed on our kitchen floor and came back.

We got married that November at The Oasis—just as the trees surrendered to fire. The entire garden had turned to gold. Crimson maples arched overhead like cathedral beams, and the winding stone path was lined with copper beech leaves and flickering lanterns.

Every bloom was at its boldest. Deep burgundy dahlias. Burnt orange ranunculus. Golden marigolds. Ivory roses edged in rust. Ornamental grasses swayed like silk, catching the last of the sun. Clusters of heirloom pumpkins and flickering candles sat at the base of the arbor.

It felt enchanted. Like the earth had bloomed one final time— just for us.

Sam waited beneath the arbor, suit tailored but his boots dusty. He didn't speak when I reached him. He just took my hand and pressed it to his heart, right over the place where everything had started. Where everything had come back.

It wasn't a spectacle. It was sacred. A vow in the place that built us.

Now, nearly two summers later, we were out on our dock, where quiet moments lived and futures unfolded.

The evening air was warm and thick with the hum of August —the kind of heat that softened everything, that made time slow down for a beat. The lake was still, mirror-like beneath the fading sky. The sun had dipped low, brushing the clouds in soft coral and rose gold.

Sam stood barefoot at the edge of the dock, tan and relaxed. His white T-shirt hugged his body in the breeze, cargo shorts loose on his hips, his hair wind-tossed. He looked like every dream I'd ever had—all grown up and somehow still mine.

He grinned as I walked toward him, hands in his pockets, eyes instantly softening when they found me. "You've got that look. The one that usually means I'm about to be emotionally destroyed."

I laughed. "Maybe."

He arched a brow, stepping closer. "Is this a trick? A test?"

I shook my head and brought out a slim white envelope. "Just open it. And don't drop it."

He took it slowly, still suspicious, but I saw the shift the second he pulled the photo free.

Stillness.

Silence.

Then his eyes flew to mine, wide and wet. "Emmy…"

He looked back down. His breath caught. "Wait—are there—"

"Two," I said, voice trembling. "There are two."

His mouth opened, but no sound came out. Just a laugh. Then a sob. Then both.

He clutched the ultrasound photo like it was a miracle, then clutched me harder.

"I don't even know what to do," he said, burying his face in my neck. "I feel like my heart's about to explode."

Tears spilled before I could answer.

He grabbed me, lifting me right off my feet as he turned us both in a circle.

"Twins?" he breathed. "We're having twins?"

I nodded against his shoulder, gripping his shirt with both hands.

"We are so blessed!" I said through tears.

He stepped back just enough to cup my face, his own wet with tears now, his breath shaky. "I don't even—" His voice broke. "You've already given me everything. But this…"

He kissed me, with every ounce of love I'd ever known, every breath we almost lost, every quiet day we'd earned.

Then, he looked down at the photo again, smiling through tears. "Two babies. God help us."

I laughed, wiping my cheeks. "Better sleep while we can."

"Guess we're gonna need two of everything," he muttered, already counting cribs and car seats in his head.

He smiled and pulled me close again, the photo cradled between us like a secret, a miracle. I closed my eyes and whispered a quiet thank you—to the God who had carried us, to the second chances that didn't have to come, to the love that showed up when I least deserved it.

The cabin was finished now—new walls, new floors, and a whole new life. Every room held a piece of us. It wasn't just mine anymore. It was ours. Built for more. Built for what was coming.

Outside, the garden we planted together had finally taken hold. Peonies bloomed in thick, fragrant waves beside the porch, wildflowers scattered like confetti along the stone path. And the porch swing—our swing—was still there, steady beneath the beam Sam had reinforced himself.

We'd already chosen the room that would one day become the nursery. It sat at the end of the hall, bathed in morning light, still empty—but waiting. A room made ready for the kind of love that hadn't yet arrived.

Behind us, the cabin lights glowed warm. The lake stretched wide and still.

My second book was due to release in two weeks.

The manuscript was done—the title was set.

But this? Right here?

This was the *real* story.

And I couldn't wait to tell it...

Holding his hand.

Carrying our future.

Behind the Book

Where Loyalty Lies is more than my debut novel. It was born in the quiet ache of heartbreak, during the hardest season of my life. After losing my husband, I began writing letters to him. Raw, unfiltered words just to make it through the day. I was a mother of five, piecing myself back together one line at a time. Somewhere along the way, those letters became this story.

Emerson's journey is personal because much of it is rooted in truth—my truth. And if this book has found its way to you, I believe it was meant to. Maybe you're here for love. Maybe you're here to feel something real. Maybe, like me, you're still learning how to keep going. Whatever brought you here, I'm deeply grateful you stayed.

Thank you for holding this story in your hands. It holds so much of my heart.

Acknowledgments

First and foremost, to God—thank You for carrying me through the darkest valley and lighting the path I never saw coming. This book was born in grief, but You gave me the courage to turn heartbreak into hope. Every word on these pages lives because You sustained me. I pray it honors the love You've placed in my life.

To the love of my life—this story wouldn't exist without you. Losing you left an ache no words could fix, but writing became the way I kept loving you. These pages are my heart, still beating for you. Still trying to make you proud and keep our love story alive.

To Lauren—my incredible girl. You didn't just cheer me on. You *built* this with me. You read every chapter with love, found every Easter egg, and reminded me what this story means. This book will always be part yours.

To my Little Women—Mia, Nicole, and Allison—your joy lifts me, your belief fuels me, and your love is the wind beneath my wings. Every day, you cheer me on, give me room to chase this dream, and remind me what matters most. This story is for you. Proof that even from the hardest places, something beautiful can grow.

To Alex—thank you for loving me in your own quiet way. Even if you weren't part of the writing itself, you're part of everything that matters.

To my mom—thank you for supporting this dream. I'm grateful for this new chapter between us.

To my Beloved Early Reader Team—Heidi, Noelle, Ashley, Michelle, Ari, Ariadne, Katey, Rebecca J., Rebecca C., Brandi,

Baylee, Alisha, Julie, Erika, Breezy, Kelsey, Crystal, Chassidy, and Kelly—thank you for reading early drafts, offering insight, and pouring into this story with your time and belief. Some of you cheered loudly and often. Some quietly. But all of you helped shape this story, and I'm so grateful.

To my editor, Brandy—thank you for lending your editorial eye and generous time. Your insightful feedback helped sharpen this book in meaningful ways.

And finally, to every person who read, posted, reviewed, messaged, or whispered "I believe in you"—you're part of this book's journey now. You helped bring it to life. Thank you, from the rawest corners of my heart.

A Note from the Author

If this story moved you, I'd truly love to know. A quick review on Goodreads and Amazon means the world. It helps other readers discover the book—and supports indie authors more than you know. Thank you.
http://bit.ly/WLLGoodreads
http://bit.ly/WLLAmazon

Want more? Join my newsletter for behind-the-scenes peeks, exclusive giveaways, and early looks at what's coming next. You can also support me as an indie author and shop signed books, book swag, and more in my Book Store.
www.ellechristopher.com

Scan the QR code on the About the Author page for links to my website, socials, etc.

1. At the beginning of the novel, Emerson leaves behind a life built on expectation and appearances. What do you think finally pushed her to walk away and do you think it was enough?

2. Emerson's relationship with her family is strained by judgment, expectations, and conditional love. How does the novel explore the difference between being loved for who you are versus who you're expected to be?

3. How did Emerson's relationship with her family impact her ability to trust or be vulnerable?

4. Emerson struggles with feeling like a disappointment. How did that inner conflict shape her decisions and how did she eventually overcome it?

5. The theme of "loyalty" is woven throughout the book. What do you think real loyalty looks like in a relationship, and how did Emerson and Sam demonstrate it?

6. How did your perception of Sam evolve throughout the story? What made him different from the men in Emerson's past and why was that difference important?

7. Which emotionally intense scene hit you the hardest, and why? How did the rawness of these moments deepen your connection to the characters and their journey?

8. Sam's heart attack was a turning point—not just for Emerson, but for him. How did that experience shift Sam's perspective on life and love? In what ways did it influence his decision to propose, and how did it deepen their connection?

9. Emerson's grandmother plays a significant role in shaping who she becomes, even after death. How does Gram's legacy influence the choices Emerson makes?

10. The setting—the cabin, the lake, The Oasis—feels like its own character. What role did the environment play in Emerson's transformation and healing?

11. Some locations in the book were inspired by real places. Did the vivid descriptions make you want to visit any of them? Which places felt the most alive to you? (Spoiler: a few of them actually exist!)

12. What moment in the book stayed with you the longest and why?

13. If you could ask either Emerson or Sam one question at the end of the book, what would it be?

14. The romance in this novel is slow-burning, emotionally intense, and deeply grounded in real-life stakes. How does that compare to other romances you've read? Did it feel more powerful to you?

15. Throughout the story, Emerson grapples with the pressure to maintain appearances—choosing image over happiness for much of her life. How does *Where Loyalty Lies* challenge the idea of perfection or superficial success? Do you think this struggle is common today, especially for women?

16. What role did writing play in Emerson's journey back to herself? Have you ever used writing, art, or creativity to process something personal?

17. This novel was written through the lens of profound personal grief. In what ways do you think real loss can deepen a love story? How do you think that shaped the emotional tone of this book?

18. Knowing that much of Sam and Emerson's love story was inspired by the author's real-life love story, how did that affect your experience as a reader? Did it make their connection feel more powerful, more intimate? How did it feel to witness a fictional story rooted in real, once-lived love?

19. Were there moments that felt so raw or specific they almost didn't seem fictional? What lines or scenes felt like they came from real life?

20. This book explores both romantic and familial love—sometimes in tension. How do those competing loves affect Emerson's choices throughout the book?

21. Sam survives his heart attack, but the author's real-life husband did not. How does knowing that affect the way you experienced the story? Did it change how you interpreted the ending, or how deeply you felt certain moments?

22. How can writing be a way to process pain, preserve love, or find peace? Did this book shift how you see storytelling as a form of healing?

23. Emerson's journey is one of personal growth, self-discovery, and reclaiming her life. What moments stood out to you as turning points in her transformation?

24. In what ways did Emerson's bravery inspire you, and how did her evolution shape the love story at the heart of the novel?

25. Did this book shift your thinking about what it means to be loyal to yourself? What does choosing your own happiness look like in your life and how hard is it to do?

Also by Elle Christopher

Sneak Peek

Turn the page for an excerpt from Elle Christopher's new novel

UNTIL YOU FOUND US

Book Two in the Tunbridge Series
AVAILABLE FALL 2025

Until You Found Us

Jack punched a kid today.

Not a hard punch. Not the kind that breaks skin or gets you expelled. But hard enough that his teacher called me, her voice tight and hesitant, unsure how to explain the words she overheard.

"Another boy said... something. About his father."

I didn't need details. I could already see my son's little fists curling in defense of a man he's never met. A man who walked out the moment I told him I was pregnant.

I said I'd talk to him. My voice was even. Practiced. The kind of calm you learn when you've got no one to fall apart with.

There's an ache I've stopped trying to name. It settles behind my ribs the moment the house goes quiet—after the rush of breakfast, the hunt for socks, the chase to school drop-off—and it stays until bedtime, when I finally exhale and let it wrap around me like an old, familiar coat.

Now I'm sitting in my shop, staring at a half-made bouquet that won't arrange itself. The marigolds are wilted. The sunflowers droop, heads bowed like they know something I don't.

I want to cry, but I don't.

Jack is four. So is Lucy. They're all softness and storm, still learning what to do with big feelings. And today, Jack used his hands instead of words.

I told him that wasn't okay. And then I held him until his shaking stopped.

"I just didn't like what he said, Mama," he whispered into my shirt.

"I know, baby." I kissed the crown of his head. "But we don't fight with our hands. We fight with truth. And you already know yours."

But do I?

Some days, I feel strong. Other days, I feel like I'm holding up an entire world with arms that were never built to carry this much.

A bell jingles at the front of the store. I glance up, heart tightening, but it's just Mrs. Gibbs from the church down the street. She wants three centerpieces for the ladies' luncheon, all in fall colors.

"Nothing too sad," she says, eyeing the drooping sunflowers.

I nod, forcing a smile.

After she leaves, I sink into the stool behind the counter, tea gone cold beside me. It's October, but Georgia hasn't gotten the memo. The air is thick and humid, clinging to everything like regret.

I check the time. In two hours, I'll pick up the twins and pretend I'm not worn thin. I'll make dinner, read *Goodnight Moon* for the thousandth time, and tuck them in with the same prayer I whisper every night.

"Let them feel loved. Let me be enough."

I don't know if I believe God is listening. But I say it anyway.

Every night.

Because maybe someday... someone will hear it.

The bell above the door jangles again.

I don't move.

If it's another customer, I'll smile. I'll help. I'll string together soft words and floral filler like I always do. But for just one more minute, I stay still. Because when I move, I have to pretend everything is fine again.

There's a half-eaten granola bar in my purse. The kind Lucy likes with the yogurt coating that melts into sticky fingerprints. I pull it out and nibble the edge, thinking about the centerpieces I still need to finish and the bills I haven't paid. My thumb traces the worn edge of a photo stuck in my wallet—Jack and Lucy, both covered in frosting, grinning with gap-toothed pride on their fourth birthday. Just the three of us that day. A store-bought cake, a few balloons from the dollar store, and the world's loudest bubble machine I now regret ever purchasing.

But they were happy.

And I held it together.

"Mama, look at my teeth!" Lucy had squealed, shoving cake in her mouth and grinning wide.

"Beautiful, baby."

It was a good day. But even the good ones are laced with this thread of missing. Of what-ifs. I never wanted perfect. I just wanted someone in the trench with me. Someone to high-five at bedtime when all five books were read, and both kids were finally asleep.

Someone who'd look at me and say, "You did good today."

I twist the Always Ring on my thumb. Not from a marriage —just a promise I made to myself, eight months pregnant and panicking, desperate for something solid. I found it at a pawn shop. A plain band no one else would look twice at.

But to me, it meant: keep going.

I wear it when I need to remember I still belong to something.

The bell rings again, followed by a voice I know.

"Alice?"

I blink, then stand. It's Emily—my younger sister. Just twenty-eight, and already ten steps ahead of where I was at that age. No kids. No dead-end relationship. A corporate job she pretends to love, and a boyfriend with a five-year plan.

"Hey," I say.

"You okay?" Her eyes scan me. She's always reading too much.

"Yeah. Just tired."

She raises an eyebrow. "Jack's teacher told me."

I freeze. "You talked to Jack's teacher?"

"Well, she didn't actually tell *me*. She's friends with Maryanne, who's friends with Tiff, whose kid is in Jack's class."

Of course.

Small towns are efficient like that.

Emily's expression softens. "You're doing your best. He's a good kid."

I nod, swallowing the lump in my throat. "He just... he's already getting labeled. And he doesn't even know why."

"You can't control what people say."

"No, but I wish I could protect him from hearing it."

Emily sits on the counter like she did in high school, kicking one heel softly against the cabinets. "You ever think about letting them ask?"

"About him?"

"Yeah."

"I don't even know what I'd say."

Emily's quiet. Then she says the thing I hate admitting. "Maybe they don't need a story. Maybe they just need a dad."

I don't respond.

Because she's not wrong.

After she leaves, I finish two of the centerpieces and start the third, losing myself in the rhythm of stem-snipping and color pairing. Maroon chrysanthemums, deep orange lilies, accents of silver dollar eucalyptus. I forget my exhaustion for a minute. Flowers don't lie. They're quiet, honest things. They just bloom and fade on their own time.

I check the clock again. Pickup is soon.

I lock the shop and get in the car, buckling the empty back seats before I remember I'm alone. I do that sometimes. Out of habit. Out of hope.

The school is a ten-minute drive. I pull into the car line just as the kids spill out in their haphazard row of backpacks and jelly-stained shirts.

Lucy sees me first. She waves like I've been gone for days. Jack is more reserved, walking slowly, his face serious.

He climbs in, silent.

"Hey, buddy," I say gently.

"Hi."

Lucy chatters the whole way home about leaf rubbings and story time and how she wants to be a pumpkin for Halloween but a fairy at the same time.

When we pull into the driveway, Jack lingers in his seat.

"Jack?" I say.

He looks up. "I don't care what that boy said. I'm not sad about not having a dad. I have you."

The ache behind my ribs blooms, sharp and beautiful.

"I'm not sad either," I whisper.

But it's not true.

Some nights, I still dream of someone knocking on the door. Someone who didn't leave. Someone who kneels down and says, "I'm here now. Let me carry some of this."

But Jack is watching me, and I don't say it out loud.

Because what I have is real. Messy. Half-broken. But real.

And then the doorbell rings.

I'm not expecting anyone.

About the Author

Elle Christopher writes romance that cuts deep and heals slowly. Her stories are raw, immersive, and character-driven—crafted for readers who want to feel everything and fall hard. She writes about growth, grit, and the kind of love that changes you forever.

Elle is a mom of five, including two sets of twins. After the sudden loss of her husband, writing became her lifeline. What began as love letters to him in the depths of grief became a story of healing, hope, and self-reclamation. Her daughters are her biggest cheerleaders, brainstormers, and the wind beneath her author wings.

She lives just outside Atlanta, in Georgia's horse country, surrounded by books, cats, and the beautiful chaos of a full house. When she's not writing, she's exploring with her kids or soaking in the quiet, everyday joys—always rebuilding a world rooted in love and beautiful words.